09\17

KT-104-468

KᴀᴀA

PRAISE FOR *THE OTHER TWIN*

'Sharp, confident writing, as dark and twisty as the Brighton Lanes' Peter James

'If your sister died under suspicious circumstances, how far would you go to uncover the truth? *The Other Twin* crackles with tension as Poppy's search for answers leads only to more questions, her grief palpable and real as she learns her sister India's deepest secrets. Hay's impressive debut is a complex, twisty, disorienting tale that truly keeps readers guessing until the very end' Karen Dionne

'Superb, up-to-the-minute thriller and an amazing crime debut. Prepare to be seriously disturbed' Paul Finch

'The writing shines from every page of this twisted tale ... debuts don't come sharper than this' Ruth Dugdall

'This chilling, claustrophobic tale set in Brighton introduces an original, fresh new voice in crime fiction' Cal Moriarty

'Slick and compulsive. A welcome new voice in the genre, Lucy V. Hay's writing is fluid and to the point, sometimes frantic, and often chilling. *The Other Twin* is unique and compelling. Deliciously tense, and clever' Random Things through My Letterbox

'Delightfully disorientating, chilling in its deception, *The Other Twin* burrowed its way into my brain ... a heartfelt and emotional exploration of identity, acceptance and what it is like to be "different" even in a community where difference is the norm. If you like your psychological thrillers dark, compelling, twisted, thought provoking and emotional with a real sense of the here and now then you are going to LOVE this!' Chapter in My Life

B000 000 021 5355

ABERDEEN LIBRARIES

'I am gobsmacked. This book, these characters and this story will stay with me forever. Never have I read a book where I had NO idea what was going to happen. I couldn't guess where the plot was going, but I didn't want to, either. I wanted to enjoy the ride. This is how to write a debut novel. This is how you write your twentieth novel. This is how you write ANY novel. Pure perfection' Emma the Little Bookworm

'A psychological thriller meets sensuous mystery combined with important social constructs of our era. *The Other Twin* is a whirlwind of secrets and emotional turmoil. Hay takes the reader on a "Through the Keyhole" tour of picture-perfect families and a lifetime of lies … An invigorating read and one with plenty of surprises lurking in the shadows' Cheryl M-M's Book Reviews

'Whoa. Where did this book come from? This is more than simply a story about the effects of prejudice and suicide. There is a dark and twisted mystery at the heart, one that runs through it from first page to last. It is also a story of family, of separation and of loss. But most of all, it is an exploration of the devastating impact that lies, anger, control and deception can have on a family. The ending is poignant and moving, the sense of acceptance and overall freedom which emanates from the page is a truly beautiful thing' Jen Med's Book Reviews

'*The Other Twin* took my breath away. The final part had me holding my breath and I couldn't turn the pages quickly enough. I lost count of the times I thought I knew what happened only to be proven wrong a few pages later. A fascinating read' Steph's Book Blog

'*The Other Twin* grabs from page one and doesn't let go. A propulsive, inventive and purely addictive psychological thriller for the social media age' Crime by the Book

'Lucy V. Hay's writing is fantastic. Clever and insightful, the narrative rolls along at a heart-pounding pace, beautifully describing the online world and the affluent families of Brighton. I haven't read anything like this before. From the very current social media element to the shocking and utterly brilliant ending, everything is stupendous! *The Other Twin* is set to be seismic! From the narrative, to the characterisation, the myriad aspects of this novel conspire to create a masterpiece! I can't wait to see what Lucy writes next' Ronnie Turner – Astra

'Beautifully written and hugely layered, this storyline slowly peels back like an onion until the core of the story is revealed and the tears can finally be shed. Dealing with relevant, contemporary issues and highlighting the way in which social media can be used both to reach out and to accuse and blame, Lucy Hay has created a contemporary thriller with a heart of darkness. A terrific read – go buy it now!' Live and Deadly

'Lucy V. Hay's cleverness lies in how she immerses her story into a pool of emotions, capturing every event and painting it with feelings, leaving hints and hiding them in a blanket of lies, allowing the tension to creep closer to you with every page, until the curtain is drawn and everything comes to light … blinding, surprising and extraordinarily painful … magnificent' Chocolate 'n' Waffles

'A gripping and very timely read with more than enough twists to keep you guessing. I really love this, the crisp writing and sharp shocks … an author to watch' The Booktrail

'Filled with highly descriptive prose, an amazing sense of place and authentic dialogue. The characters are strong, believable, diverse and suitably flawed. The multi-layered plot kept me engrossed all the way through. Each layer was gradually peeled away to reveal yet another surprise. I devoured it in one sitting' Off-the-Shelf Books

THE OTHER TWIN

ABOUT THE AUTHOR

Lucy V. Hay is a novelist, script editor and blogger who helps writers via her Bang2write consultancy. She is the associate producer of Brit Thrillers *Deviation* (2012) and *Assassin* (2015), both starring Danny Dyer. Lucy is also head reader for the London Screenwriters' Festival and has written two non-fiction books: *Writing & Selling Thriller Screenplays,* plus its follow-up, *Drama Screenplays.* She lives in Devon with her husband, three children, five cats and five African land snails.

Follow Lucy on Twitter *@LucyVHayAuthor*, on Facebook: *facebook.com/LucyHayB2W* and her website: *lucyvhayauthor.com*

The Other Twin

L. V. HAY

**ORENDA
BOOKS**

Orenda Books
16 Carson Road
West Dulwich
London SE21 8HU
www.orendabooks.co.uk

First published by Orenda Books 2017
Copyright © L. V. Hay 2017

L. V. Hay has asserted her moral right to be identified as the author of this
work in accordance with the Copyright, Designs and Patents Act, 1988.

All Rights Reserved. No part of this publication may be reproduced in any
form or by any means without the written permission of the publishers.

A catalogue record for this book is available from the British Library.

ISBN 978-1-910633-78-6
eISBN 978-1-910633-79-3

Typeset in Garamond by MacGuru Ltd
Printed and bound by CPI Group (UK) Ltd, Croydon CRO 4YY

*This is a work of fiction. Names, characters, places and incidents are either
products of the author's imagination or are used fictitiously. Any resemblance to
actual events, locales or persons, living or dead, is entirely coincidental.*

SALES & DISTRIBUTION

In the UK and elsewhere in Europe:
Turnaround Publisher Services
Unit 3, Olympia Trading Estate
Coburg Road
Wood Green
London
N22 6TZ
www.turnaround-uk.com

In the USA and Canada:
Trafalgar Square Publishing
Independent Publishers Group
814 North Franklin Street
Chicago, IL 60610
USA
www.ipgbook.com

In Australia and New Zealand:
Affirm Press
28 Thistlethwaite Street
South Melbourne VIC 3205
Australia
www.affirmpress.com.au

For details of other territories, please contact *info@orendabooks.co.uk*

'An abuser can seem emotionally needy. You can get caught in a trap of catering to him, trying to fill a bottomless pit. But he's not so much needy as entitled, so no matter how much you give him, it will never be enough. He will just keep coming up with more demands because he believes his needs are your responsibility, until you feel drained down to nothing.'

—Lundy Bancroft, *Why Does He Do That?*
Inside The Minds of Angry and Controlling Men

To Mr C

You always got it, which is why I love you.

L xx

PART ONE

Past Simple

/ed/

One

'I'm not doing this anymore,' he says. 'She won't say anything.'

'We all know that's not true.'

He flinches from the silence that follows. Her expression gives nothing away. But that's her all over: she can mask the anger deep inside her. It's what makes her dangerous. *She Who Must Be Obeyed.*

'And what do you propose we do, instead?' she says at last, folding her thin arms.

He grasps for an alternative, but it's futile: he can come up with nothing. His body sags in defeat, his eyes cast downwards at the stone floor.

'I thought so.' A shark-like smile crosses her face.

Resentment blooms in his gut. Heat travels up his gullet and cloys in his throat. He can't breathe. He doesn't trust himself to speak. He clenches his fists, keeping them by his sides, digging his fingernails into his palms.

'We've been through all this.' She puts one of her cool, papery palms to his face. From afar anyone would think it an affectionate gesture. It's not.

'I don't care,' he whispers.

'You know you do,' she chastises. 'Think of the others. We all agreed. Remember?'

White-hot anger blazes through him now. He'd never agreed, not really. Her gaze flickers to the clock on the wall. Already she is planning her next move, so sure of her victory over him. He proves her right; still he says nothing. *Such a coward.*

'Just play the game.'

Those words: a mantra, a verbal talisman. Designed to get them all to fall into line. She'd drilled them until the words would come unbidden to their own lips. She'd told him he was the protector, the big man. He had to look out for everyone, present their best side to the world. No one must know the truth.

It could spoil everything.

He breathes in the sickly vanilla scent of her perfume. He speaks through gritted teeth. 'Maybe I don't want to play the game anymore?'

She blinks, momentary surprise in her eyes. He hasn't talked back to her in years. But then she recovers her nerve and stands her ground, all swagger and bravado. 'You're being ridiculous.'

Despite her rictus grin, he sees her realising she no longer has the upper hand. He meets her shining eyes and enjoys sensing her apprehension; she thinks he might hit her. He knows he won't, but her anxiety pleases him. He is nearly a foot taller, broader across the chest and shoulder, all muscle. He could grab her by her slim neck with just one of his hands and strangle her, dangling her above the floor … *If* he wanted to. And she knows it.

But his boldness does not last. Like a soap bubble, his defiance bursts, leaving nothing concrete between them. She knows how much he fears her wrath; how he will attempt to scrabble to safety. But his grip is always too weak: he will fall backwards, hopeless, into her suffocating embrace.

'You're supposed to look after them.' She enunciates each word, so each one drops like a rock. 'Remember?'

He feels his courage slide back down into his boots, into the floor beneath them. His head dips in shame. He swallows as the gloating steel edge returns to her voice. The familiar ball of pain in his throat stops him from speaking. The icy fingers of anxiety tear inside his ribcage, like a tiny creature clawing its way out of his chest.

He nods, acquiescing at last.

'You've done the right thing.'

He can feel the triumph radiating from her. Her bony hand pats his shoulder, her long nails like a bird's talons.

She turns, her high heels clacking on the red kitchen tiles, her long skirt sashaying around her ankles. The kitchen door swings behind her as she leaves.

A sudden howl escapes him. He sweeps one arm across the kitchen worktop. Saucepans, ladles, plates and Pyrex dishes go crashing to the floor, smashing. Pieces skitter across the tiles and disappear under the stainless-steel cabinets.

It's not enough. He grabs more items from the sideboards and sends them flying. Cutlery and tins crash against ceramic; squash bottles bounce onto the kitchen floor; drums of coffee and sugar spill their contents. Granules pour onto the hob and countertops. Their subtle aromas fill the air.

He digs in the back pocket of his jeans and pulls out his phone. Desperation clamours through him as he scrolls through his contacts. He could call her, warn her. He should warn her.

But his thumb hovers above the call button. What would he say? Would she even believe him? He's not even sure he believes the threat himself.

As the swell of emotion recedes, he feels lost. He tells himself he's being ridiculous. He must pull himself together. Tamp down his rage, as always.

He puts his phone back in his pocket.

Two

Jenny, Jenny, Jenny…

…I like it. Your shining name rolls around my mouth, smooth like chocolate melting on my tongue. Vanilla and cocoa, sweet and soft, just like you. It makes sense.

But the truth is hard and ugly, like a fifty-pence piece forced in between my teeth. I bite hard, try to force it down my throat. It catches in my gullet. Their lies are too big to swallow.

It was never meant to be like this. You should soar, but instead you are a bird in a gilded cage. They celebrate the false shell, denying the real you inside. They say it is for your own good! But their language of care is one of control.

Well, no more. We see them for what they really are. We trudge onwards, holding onto each other, supporting the other when one of us threatens to fall. We can do this. You are and will always be my twin soul. Real girls.

Soon you will be free. As I am, now.

I love you.

India xxx

POSTED BY **@1NDIAsummer**, 22 December 2016
41,567 insights ⏎ **SHARE THIS**
  ⏎ ***Blithefancy*** added: *I can't even #heartbroken*
  ⏎ ***writerchic88*** likes this

↩ **keel3y666** says: *Suicide is selfish!!!*

   ↩ **Ariel_jewel** replies to **keel3y666:** *OMG check your privilege*
   #mentalhealthmatters

      ↩ **keel3y666** replies to **Ariel_jewel:** *Bet its not real*
      #attentionseeker

         ↩ **Ariel_jewel** replies to **keel3y666:** *'it's'*

↩ **heartsanddiamantes** likes this

↩ **bushwhacker** likes this

↩ **warriorwasp** reblogged this from **1NDIAsummer** and added: *SO SAD*

Three

I awake, ravenous, in the early evening. Winter darkness forms at the window. Head banging, I sit up. I'm in a tangle of sheets on the floor; I've rolled off my grubby futon. As I reach for my phone, a sharp pain shoots down my neck and through my shoulders. *Getting too old for this shit.*

I wear just a vest and knickers. I'm lying on a selection of condom wrappers, crisps packets, empty pizza boxes and junk-food cartons. My hair is in a gluey mass at the back of my head. I don't even want to think about what caused that.

Predictably, my mobile is dead, the battery long since drained. I stagger to my feet and feel blindly for a charger. I find one already plugged into the wall next to the toaster, amid a shower of crumbs and globules of jam. I plug it in. I grab a glass, filling it at the sink and gulping the water down gratefully, as if I've walked across the Sahara the previous evening.

What the hell happened last night?

On the countertop, a hastily scribbled note with a phone number: 'CHEERS, D XX'. A flash of an image comes to me: just a body, no face. Pressed jeans, best shirt, a mop of curly hair with boy-band white teeth. *Where did I find him?* I can't recall. I become aware of this stranger's hands and lips on me: a red mark on my breast; sensitivity between my legs. I am unconcerned.

I put the rest of my dirty laundry in the basket, pulling off my clothes as I do so. Naked, I pad through to the bathroom, my nostrils flaring at the rank smell. I clamber into the shower anyway and let the water trickle over my head. I'd hoped for a power shower, but in this area the water system is ancient, the pressure nil. I wet my hands and lather myself with liberal amounts of shower gel, washing his touch, his taste away. I watch water swirl down the plughole and imagine D, or whatever his name is, falling into its dark depths, forever trapped in the pipes.

Never. Again.

I turn the shower off and dry my body and hair roughly, before letting the towel fall onto the bathroom floor. Still nude, I walk through to the living space and open a drawer. Virtually all my clothes are dirty. I dress hurriedly in mismatched items – the only ones I have left. So, that's my Saturday night sorted: I'm off to the all-night launderette near the station. *Yay.*

I remember my phone, still plugged in by the toaster. I see its red light flashing from across the room. As I pick it up, I note the SILENT icon; I forgot to change it back after work yesterday. Expecting a few texts, maybe a couple of missed calls and my usual email spam, I swipe a finger across the screen.

29 MISSED CALLS.

17 TEXTS.

3 VOICEMAILS.

All from the same number, listed as MUM.

Raw fear courses through me before I open any of them. My mother is the laconic type; she's not the kind of parent who goes chasing. I read the texts:

—'PHONE ME NOW'

—'POPPY FOR GOD'S SAKE ANSWER'

—'CALL ME'

—'CALL ME'

—'CALL ME'

The same, plaintive message, over and over.

I hesitate. There's a part of me that doesn't want to know what could have happened at home while I was pissed out my skull.

It has to be Tim.

A litany of causes of death crashes through my mind. Heart attack, one of the biggest killers of middle-aged men. Or perhaps a stroke, or a brain embolism. Tim has high blood pressure. He's been overweight since I met him twenty-five years ago, when I was just five. He'd pick me up as a little girl and crush me to his barrel chest. He called the spare tyre around his middle his 'love handles' and for the past quarter of a century has resisted all attempts to make him slim down for the good of his health. He'd sing The Beatles' 'When I'm Sixty-Four' every time Mum so much as tried to broach the subject.

He's sixty-three now, could he not have made it to that celebrated age?

You hear of it all the time. But you always think it will happen to someone else; someone else's family. Death is just a concept, not real. Could my stepfather really be lying dead and cold on a slab, while I was doing something as banal as cleaning my flat and sorting my washing?

I don't hit the RECALL button; I don't need to. Mum's name flashes again silently on screen, her smiling face appearing on my smartphone a curious contrast to the dread piercing my chest. I let it ring twice, then press the green button and place the phone to my ear.

I brace myself for impact. 'Mum…?'

Mum does not launch into accusations or reproaches for being off the grid. She attempts to say my name, but instead just emits this pained, low moan, like a trapped animal. It sets my teeth on edge and threatens to open the primeval floodgates in me, too.

Insight hits me. My life is split in two: *Before* and *After*. My brain bucks against the weight of what's coming and strains to make sense of the fear deluging through my veins. In years to come, every time I hear tears in someone's voice, I will see the wall of this studio flat, the crack that leads from the television on its bracket towards the dented fridge.

But still I don't want to believe something terrible has happened. I don't ask the question – 'Is it Tim?' – because I don't want to hear the answer. I try to speak, attempt to say something stupid like 'Happy Christmas!' and make it all go away. I know it can't, but I'm desperate to hold onto my *Before* life, the one that had seemed so shit when I woke up, surrounded by the detritus of my reckless existence.

Anything other than this.

Then Mum speaks, her words clear, almost deadpan. It's not Tim, after all.

'It's your sister.'

Four

I blink. I find myself on a train, heading towards Liverpool Street station. I'm vaguely aware of cheery, anticipatory faces around me. It's Saturday night, so people in their twenties are everywhere, hands thrust in pockets, leaning against one another, the carriage a hive of excited activity.

The doors of the train swish open.

'She's dead. India's dead.' Mum's voice on the end of the phone seemed alien. It still feels like a bad joke.

'H-how? What? Why?' I stammered.

Bewilderment cascaded through me, followed by an ice-like certainty: Mum wouldn't have said something like this for no reason. Then, even stranger, another thought occurred: *But it's Christmas.* As if Death takes time off during the holiday season.

'Come home,' Mum whispered.

I could discern it was taking every bit of strength she had to form the words. She was threatening to unravel.

'See you in a few hours.' I sounded more in control than I was.

I drift through the middle of all of the crowds, making my way through the labyrinthine tunnels of the Tube. I walk up steps, on autopilot. I am untouchable: shoals of people divide and reconnect around me. I wander through bright-white hallways. The floor starts to move, travellators and elevators beneath my boots.

A blast of outside air makes its way down into another station – Victoria this time. I shiver; I have no coat. I have no luggage. Just the clothes I stand up in, my handbag. As I queue for yet another ticket, I catch sight of my reflection in the plate-glass window of a late-night burger joint. I look a sight. I'm wearing thin leggings, a pyjama t-shirt. I button up my cardigan, absent-minded. All my dirty laundry languishes back at the apartment, with the rest of my *Before* life. My hair, still wet, hangs in ratty knots around my shoulders.

At last I make it to the head of the queue. Behind the glass, a woman taps at a computer. She has neon-coloured threads woven into her cornrows, contrasting with her dull, grey uniform. Weary irritation forces her limbs into squared-off angles, the sign of the perennial night-shift worker. She says nothing, waiting instead for my instruction, one manicured hand poised over the keyboard.

'Single to Brighton,' I say.

My ticket issued, I make my way towards the boards. I've got twenty-five minutes until the next train. That's the difficult part of travelling, isn't it? The waiting. In side rooms, on benches, in hallways. Waiting in the vehicles you're travelling in, connecting you from A to B. The destination is all that matters.

Everywhere I look there are newspapers. Carried under arms, lying on seats, fallen into stairwells. I grab one up, hungry for information, yet unable to shake the bizarre sensation that none of this is real.

I discover my younger sister is not front-page news. India is relegated to a side column, her humanity stripped away:

YOUNG WOMAN, 24, FALLS ONTO RAILWAY TRACKS

Trains were halted for several hours between Brighton and London on Friday night after a young woman fell from a bridge onto rail tracks. India Rutledge, 24, was sighted running away from Brighton Station between 18:00 and 19:00. It is thought, about an hour later, she made her way to the notorious bridge located further down the track.

People on board the 20:12 to London Victoria report hearing 'a loud bang', though no one saw the young woman fall. The train driver is being treated for shock. British Transport Police are appealing for witnesses.

I read and re-read the report, my brain refusing to take the details in at first. I look at my watch and note the date again: 23rd December.

India's birthday.

Earlier this week – in my *Before* life – I'd posted a card. I'd chosen it without care, grabbing it from a newsagent's near the school where I was working. I'd not wanted to give India any more ammunition. I wanted to show her – and my parents – I can be the 'good' sister. *For once.*

It's India's birthday, yet she's dead.

I'm six, nearly seven. The Christmas holidays are forgotten this year, because my sister is born two weeks early. There is no Christmas tree, no presents under it. My mother has been completely caught out by the new arrival.

The baby comes home from the hospital trussed up in a car seat. My sister is wearing a pink knitted bonnet and a baby-gro with embroidered strawberries on. I am dressed nicely too: my hair is plaited, my puppy fat forced into a dress a little on the small side. It pinches under the arms.

I am sidelined as relatives, friends and random associates take turns to look at my replacement. Still in that car seat, my new sister is placed on the polished coffee table. The best china, cups and saucers and shining silver teaspoons, are placed next to her. Adults coo, exclaiming how good, how tiny or how cute this baby is, bringing cards and presents with them.

None are for me. I grow bored waiting for the adults to say how nice I look, or ask how I am getting on at big school.

So I drift closer to them. But their attention is still solely on the new kid, the one who only yesterday was still in *my* mum's belly. Just twenty-four hours ago I heard only bad things about this baby: how she gave Mum indigestion, or heartburn or an aching back. *My* mum had put her bloated ankles up on the pouf in the living room. She'd eaten chocolate spread straight out of the jar. She'd complained about being pregnant and how it lasted forever. But today, all is different: the baby is here and all is forgiven. India is only good.

I join two women on the floor. They sit on their heels next to the coffee table. One is the tall, thin woman from across the road who's always in a rush and pushing a pram, her face set in a grim line. But not today; she is all smiles.

The other is the classroom assistant at my school: Miss Macey. She has big hands and a big gap between her two front teeth. She reads storybooks in silly voices, but not today.

Both are enchanted by my sister. I want them to look up, smile at me.

I lean on the coffee table. My weight makes it rear up. Two of its stubby legs leave the floor. There's a clash of china as cups and saucers slide. The car seat rocks perilously backwards. Multiple female cries of alarm fill the air, as if sound alone can cushion the baby's fall.

But the baby does not fall.

Miss Macey grabs the car seat handle with her big hands. A collective sigh resounds from the adults, like the hiss of air brakes on a double-decker bus. My mother stares at me with shiny eyes, as if she hates me.

'What have you done?!'

I stand there, my six-year-old brain unable to process my mum's anger. Delayed embarrassment lands its black butterfly wings on my face, bringing with it red cheeks. I take in the adults' wide eyes, frozen where they stand or sit between my mother and me.

The moment melts just as rapidly. I'm able to move. I flee to the stairwell, too-jolly adult voices behind me, covering up their own anxiety.

An hour or so later, I see the grown-ups leave at last, shuffling through the hall. All of them pretend not to see me, morose on the bottom step.

Most people go without fuss, without bother. But not India. She goes out with a bang. Literally. And this time, I'm not there.

Sister. What have you done?

Five

My train finally arrives at Brighton station.

I look up and see the large clock suspended from the criss-cross slats of the station roof. The stars in the dark sky above contrast with the neon lamps that light the station with their sickly glow. The closest coffee shop is closed, its doors locked. The ticket barriers are open.

A young couple with a sleeping child follow me off our train, the father effortlessly hoisting the little girl over his shoulder. He links his other arm with his partner's; she stares up at him with starry eyes. She is younger than me. *India's age.*

I watch them as they disappear through the ticket barrier into the brightly lit concourse and onto the street. I shift my handbag on my shoulder, shivering now with the cold. The mild December weather has transformed abruptly. Beyond the ticket barriers, the doors of the station stand open. As I draw closer, I can see a night bus and the taxi rank, a light dusting of snow on the pavement and on the closed food carts. Dirty-grey grit on the ground. Slushy footprints amble downhill, into the town beyond.

Outside the station, I catch sight of the Transport Police poster mounted on a stand labelled 'INCIDENT'. I know what will be under that word, along with an appeal for witnesses and information.
Suicide.

Did you know, suicide on the railways kills nearly three hundred people a year? That's 4.5 percent of suicides every single year. It says so – right there on the Network Rail posters and on Samaritans banners on buses, so it must be true.

(**Suicide**, *noun.* 1. The act of killing oneself
intentionally. 2. An efficient and simple way of dealing

with life's shit. 3. The very last item on your 'to do' list.

Related words: kill, die, stupid, selfish.)

These aren't just my words, but the words of hundreds of thousands of others left to pick up the pieces (another cliché). Except we're not picking the pieces up. We're shovelling them, our arms heavy with the weight of dirt and rocks, as well as a side helping of that other related word, 'guilt'. We have to live every day with the label of being the one whose mother, father or sibling killed themselves. We're left with endless questions, which are branded forever on our skin: *Could I have stopped it? Did I miss the signs? How can this have happened? Why wasn't I enough?*

But I've barely spoken to India in four years. The last proper conversation we had, she stood on the front doorstep of the house I am returning to now. She was dressed in another of her hoodies, thrown on over a pair of pyjama trousers. She was watching me leave home again, her bare feet pale pink on the concrete step.

'Running away,' she'd sneered that morning, blocking my bedroom doorway as I shoved clothes and toiletries into my case.

'Hardly,' I'd retorted, her words making me prickle. 'London's an hour away; if that.'

India folded her arms. 'So stay.'

I faltered. It was the closest to an apology I would get from my sister. But then I remembered why I was going. 'You know I can't.'

India's top lip curled. 'You won't, you mean.'

What do you care? I wanted to scream at her, back then. My leaving had nothing to do with her, not really. But my younger sister had to get involved, had to meddle … as usual. I didn't want to argue with her, but she'd picked a side and it wasn't mine. She'd drawn a line between us.

I turned as I reached the corner. From the doorstep, India gave me a sarcastic little wave, her lip pulled back in that perpetual sneer of hers. I almost returned it with The Finger, but didn't.

If I'd known that was the last time I would see my sister breathing, would I have done things differently? Perhaps I would have raced back, thrown my arms around her. But after all that had happened between us, I know she'd have flinched away. A simple hug would have been misconstrued, examined for ulterior motives.

I wander the way the young family went moments before. My breath comes out in trails. I can no longer feel the soles of my feet. I slip through the ticket barriers and towards the taxi rank, though I have no money left. I could get in one of those vehicles, direct it to my parents' house and get them to pay the bill, but I don't want to arrive to more rolled eyes, just like when I left. Not now. Not *After.*

So I set off along the pavement, moving down the hill from the station, cutting through to the red-brick labyrinth that is The Lanes. It won't take me long to walk, perhaps forty minutes. Maybe I can even wake up my frozen limbs along the way.

Bare branches reach up into the inky sky in Whitehawk as I turn onto the grimy street I left four years ago. Our old Coach House looks exactly like I left it. No one has painted it in the time I've been away, so its white render is a dingy grey. Someone has tagged a cryptic message with spray paint on the garage door.

I can see the doorstep, but no India stands there now. It is empty but for a small, ginger cat sitting patiently on the frosty handkerchief of a front lawn, washing its paws. It looks young, barely out of kitten-hood. Is it ours? I have no idea. In the past four years, I've only met my parents in London when they have come up for dinner and a show. I realise, too late, that I've avoided India, just as she's avoided me.

My freezing finger presses the doorbell. I have no key. It's only as the porch light goes on and Tim's worried face swims into view through the frosted glass that it hits me how late it is, how a caller would ordinarily worry my parents at this hour. But the worst has already happened. No other bad news can match it.

'Poppy!'

There is a rattle of the security chain and my stepfather opens the door. Shorter than me by a full half a foot, Tim still wafts that musky smell of secret cigarettes he thinks my mother does not know about. His widow's peak creates a 'w' on the top of his round, broad head.

I attempt an incongruous smile, as if this is a normal reunion. Then I'm suddenly hot and I disconnect from reality, like someone has turned off a switch.

I lurch towards him. I feel Tim's meaty hands under my armpits, holding me up. He yells something I don't understand. Perhaps my mother's name, because she comes running down the stairs from the living room above, her bare feet thwacking on the tiles. Her hair is unbrushed and she has her dressing gown on over her rumpled clothes.

'Poppy, Poppy...' she coos, smoothing a hand over her hair, helping my stepfather hold me up.

It takes both of them to manhandle me through the doorway. I am not overweight, but like Tim, Mum is much smaller than I am.

Like an automaton I move forwards and without knowing how I got there, I am in my old bedroom: I know it from the smell, rather than its décor, because it has all changed. The once-green walls are now yellow. It is bare, devoid of personal touches, not even a vase of flowers on the nightstand. New, starched curtains are open, a chasm of black night yawns beyond.

I don't care. I collapse, face first onto the bed. I just lie there, breathing in the scent of fabric conditioner: jojoba. India reappears in my mind, twisting her mouth with a smile, correcting Tim's pronunciation – 'No, Dad. *Ho-hoba*!' – before dissolving into a fit of giggles.

I am only just aware of my parents' hushed voices, muttering between themselves. One of them places another duvet over the top of me, followed by a thick fleece blanket. I want to say something, even if it's only 'thanks', but I cannot. I am immobile.

When the overhead light turns off, I pass out.

Six

He grips the handlebars of the exercise bike. He feels the burn in his thighs, knees and core. An involuntary grunt escapes the back of his throat. Not that anyone can hear it: dance music pounds through the speakers, in time with a set of three-coloured disco lights that flash sporadically in his eyes. *Fuck's sake.*

The dungeon-like spin studio is dark, no mirrors. It's the only one in use in daylight hours: the yummy mummies and night-shift girls don't like seeing their flabby arses hanging off the bike seats, or their cellulite shaking as they pedal. He averts his eyes from flesh bulging out the backs of too-tight leggings and the armpits of sagging sports bras.

He could pick any of the women in the room and know their story. *So. Predictable.* On young, chubby left hands, there are shiny new rocks: they're trying to slim down for a wedding dress. On older female hands: a mark where a band has been, as women past their prime attempt to slim back down after the comfort blanket of marriage. Women are so obvious in their crusades to find a man, mould him and call it 'true love'.

The spin instructor calls out encouragement in his reedy voice during breaks in the music. He's a white guy, friendship bracelets on his girlish wrists, another on each one of his ankles. Another shirt-lifter, no doubt: they're bloody everywhere, especially in Brighton. The instructor's sternum peeks out of his vest, he is all knees and elbows, his skinny legs powering down on the pedals. But he's probably stronger than he looks; lean and wiry, like his own father.

Dad was a bare-knuckle fighter in his youth. He liked to boast that he won the stake money for the family business by knocking Frankie 'The Beast' Harding out in an illegal, unlicensed fight in the backroom of Joe's Gym on Carnivale Street. That money enabled him to buy his own van and tools, setting up as self-employed and saying goodbye to casual labouring forever.

Not long after that he'd met the love of his life. She'd been a salon girl over at her aunt's. She hadn't cared much for hair cutting, but she did have a head for business. A few months later, she was ensconced by the phone in a shiny new office, a ring on her finger. The origins of the family empire. *The rest, as they say, is history.*

He turns the bike's resistance up to the top. He can feel the start of a stitch in his side, raw pain stabs the backs of his calves, making him feel light-headed. But it's a relief to feel something pure – something he doesn't need to hide. Exercise is his only true release.

Heat flushes up his neck and face. He can feel sweat shaking from his flesh, like a dog just out of a pond, as he speeds the pedals round and round, teeth clenched.

He's almost disappointed when he recognises the opening bars of the warm-down song. The women in the room seem to breathe out a collective sigh of relief as they grab for the resistance handle, taking it down just one or two notches to the beginning, their faces red with exertion.

He grudgingly follows suit, taking his down from eight, resolving to come in the evening when more men would be there. Maybe then he might have some real competition. Of course, he never airs these opinions. The world's gone mad for supposed equality, but in real terms it's special treatment women desire. They want to be in charge, but they want to play the victim, too. None of them can be trusted. As far as women are concerned men are as good as children. If one ever dares to step out of line, he's a beast.

He laces his fingers together and stretches out his arms. He can feel himself reconnecting, rebooting. This is state zero, the kickoff, the most at peace he will ever be. He savours the momentary quiet in his head; it won't be long before the endless cycle of crap rushes at him again. Drip by drip by drip, it will deplete his reserves of patience and fill him up with what feels like poisonous gas, straining at his skin, no way out.

Seven

The next few days pass in a fog. I remember only fragments. I do not cry. Instead I am agitated, moving from room to room, restless yet trapped. I am reminded of a school trip to a farm, seeing ewes and cows doing the same, crashing against the metal barriers that confine them, their eyes wild with fear.

Christmas has been cancelled again, twenty-five years on from my sister's birth. India's gone. *Dead*. I just can't reconcile the word with the reality, when she'd been such a vital presence. It seems unthinkable.

I sit in my sister's room, hunched on her chair, staring at the things she's left: sheaves of her beautiful drawings on the desk; notebooks full of her neat, looped handwriting; photos she's taken on the pinboard – extreme close-ups of flowers; landscapes; sunsets. India had been so artistic, so gifted. I see her everywhere: lying on the bed, her legs propped up on the headboard, painted toenails in the air.

What a waste.

Though I'd been jealous of India when she was born, I fell into the role of big sister with ease. Being six years older, I discovered it was fun to have a younger sibling, especially as India sought to emulate me every chance she got. By the time I hit my late teens, it had been up to me to drop her at school on the way to college, or make her tea. Mum and Tim worked long hours running the arcade down on the pier, so India wanted me to read to her, or to help her with her homework. A deep ache opens up inside my chest; tears threaten, but I blink them back, determined to be *doing* something. For India.

I search the desk. There are piles of papers, magazines and letters, some still sealed and discarded. I open the official-looking ones in a bid to gain some insight into my younger sister's life. A doctor's letter, inviting India in for a smear test; a fine for an overdue library book; a referral letter to a psychiatrist.

India was depressed?

I root through her desk drawers, then her bedside cabinet. Inside, a packet of antidepressants, the blister-pack full. India has not taken any of them.

I am filled with rage, both at my sister for not taking the pills, then my parents, for not making her. But India was an adult. What could Mum and Tim have done – grounded her? I fold up the psychiatry appointment letter and shove it in my pocket. I don't know why. All I know is I won't rest until I discover what really happened to my beautiful, talented little sister.

A doctor arrives at the Coach House to see me. I don't remember his name. I recognise him as an old friend of Tim's. He is a tall, pale man in his late sixties with a perfectly bald, dome-shaped skull. He leans on a cane. Neither has come to him with age; he's had both since he was a young man.

The doctor has the studied, yet genuine air of an educated man who's pulled himself up by his bootstraps without forgetting his roots. I was at school with his daughter – a thin, meek girl with eczema who sat alone and looked no one in the eye.

The doctor mutters theories about emotional trauma and 'the next few days being crucial'. I ignore both him and my parents. The weight of India's loss hangs over all of us, acknowledged yet somehow still inconceivable. Is this shock? I suppose so. Yet again, words are simply not enough to describe the reality of the situation.

But my extreme confusion and distress are short-lived. I feel myself reconnecting. I return from wherever I've been, to some semblance of 'normality'. Now, I am dressed appropriately, borrowing underwear and leggings from my sister's wardrobe and a plain top from my mother's. My long, mousey-brown hair is washed, pulled into a side ponytail.

I borrow Tim's iPad without asking and call up my sister's Facebook profile.

I scroll through India's photos first: a couple of pictures of her at a birthday party, tagged from someone else's album, plus a few more at someone else's wedding. In each one she looks separate from the other people in the frame, standing apart from everyone else. India doesn't look sad, or even bothered. She looks independent, at ease with herself, the way I remember her.

But the camera must lie.

There is a photo of my sister alone. She's used it as her profile picture. She's at a festival, a flower garland in her hair. India looks about nineteen or twenty, as I remember her. Her stance is very different in this pic. She's laughing, wearing a crop top and a hippy skirt with bells around the waist. In one hand, she holds a half-full plastic pint glass.

Scrolling down her profile page, I note my sister has written statuses more and more frequently. She was doing so five or six times a day in the weeks running up to her death. Most of the statuses are *vaguebooks*. (**Vaguebook,** *noun*. A purposefully vague, often one-word status update, designed to invite a response.)

Clicking through, some of them now seem suicidal: 'whatever'; 'frustrated'; 'done'.

That familiar anger rises to the surface again. *Why didn't anyone see what was going on?* Then, more guilt: *I should have been here*. Besides, such statuses are only illuminating with hindsight. *Before*, they could have meant anything.

Underneath each of India's statuses, there's a handful of 'likes' and replies. A couple of Goodreads notifications come next, more auto updates. India was reading *Frankenstein* at the time of her death, though she was stuck at twenty-nine-percent finished for months. There are a few memes, mostly positive-thinking guff, complete with cute animals, rainbows, fairies and unicorns. I don't recall India ever being into stuff like this.

There's a selection of links posted to her Facebook profile: all to www.1NDIAsummer.com. A personal blog.

The police have already told us about this site, but it has taken me until now to gird myself to read it. There aren't many entries; they span a six-week period leading up to India's death. Each one refers to a codename; India's logic isn't hard to follow – they're all from classic fairy tales: *Frog King, Wicked Witch, The Wolf, Sleeping Beauty … Ugly Sister.*

I'm stung when I see the last one: could 'Ugly Sister' mean me? But reading it, I see nothing in the entry I recognise. But would I? Could this be my sister's last thoughts about me? *Please, no.*

The final post is different. This one is addressed to 'Jenny'. The police have called this entry – India's final post – a suicide note. But it's not. A note, anyway. Something about the blog post seems to jar. Like that stand-out detail in the newspaper coverage about India running away from the railway station, only to mysteriously appear at the bridge, an hour later.

You will be free … As I am now.

India might be free, but she has condemned the rest of us. I can't fathom how she could do this to us. Surely it can't have got so bad for her? But how would I know? Maybe India did it *because* of me; because of our fractured relationship. Even if that wasn't the answer, our feud cannot have helped her feel any better. Could I have tried harder to heal the rift between us? Yes. I was her older sister after all.

We'd been so close until I left. And when I did, I was still angry with her – for picking a side that wasn't mine. Now, in hindsight, I realise that what irritated me most was that I knew, deep down, that she was right.

But something else niggles at me. Even faced with such compelling evidence, I can't believe India could have killed herself. Before our dispute, we'd shared a strong bond. So, as fanciful as it seems, I feel certain I would have 'felt' my sister's distress had she been in extreme spiritual pain.

I will find out.

Eight

Bodies crush against one another. Vintage neon posters glint in the black light, advertising long-defunct nineties' DJs. The décor looks like it was last updated back then: lime green and bright orange, strips of paintwork coming away as condensation pours down the walls in the ill-ventilated, dungeon-like venue.

He wanders, aimless, a half-full beer bottle dangling from his hand; he makes his way through writhing limbs. Ravers and pillheads who should have grown up two decades ago dance in jagged shapes, tongues out, piercings and pot bellies on display. Heat buzzes through his solar plexus as sweat trickles down into the small of his back. Music pounds from unseen speakers on every side of the room, yet he hears none of it; only the jarring, endless white noise in his head.

The crowd parts, tide-like, as a woman appears in front of him, blocking his way. At first glance, she reminds him of India – pasty with panda eyes – and momentarily, she's right there, in front of him. Hands on hips, blame on her lips as ever:

'It's up to you now,' she'd said; 'you can stop this.'

But then the woman presses against him, a lazy smile on her face. India would never have done that, for obvious reasons. The vision bursts, like a bubble.

Up close, he knows the woman is older than she looks in the half-light. But she's OK-looking in an aged, slutty, Taylor Swift knock-off kind of way: mussed-up blonde hair, replete with a damsel smile and fuck-me eyes. He allows her to toy with him. A woman like her would wear dental-floss underwear – if she wears any at all. She's probably got a Brazilian under there; he always was a sucker for that.

She rubs her breasts against his chest in a way that would be comical, had it not been for the dull ache of the hard-on pressing itself against his jeans. He considers grabbing her hand, taking her outside. He envisages twisting her arm behind her back and pressing her face against the brickwork as he pushes his hands up her skirt and inside her. She would whimper and cry out, but she would like it. He can tell: she has 'tramp' shot right through her bones like a stick of rock.

But his thoughts are interrupted by the tell-tale vibration inside his jeans pocket. He knows without looking what it is: yet another text message. He's been doing his best to ignore her all evening. He knows that if he leaves it any longer, she will send one of the others after him, to 'help'. But of course, it will only make things worse. He flexes his free hand into a fist, feels the tendons strain in his wrist. He can't stay.

He trudges up the steep, concrete steps from the bar like a condemned man and emerges into the night, ears ringing. A shiver works its way across his shoulders; he's just in his shirt sleeves. A harsh breeze skitters through the January air, stirring rubbish in its wake. He pulls his phone from his pocket and presses a finger against the screen. In capital letters, her demand: 'I'M WAITING!!!'

He throws the beer bottle down, relishing the tinkle of smashed glass as it hits the piss-stained doorway. This place is a dump, not like some of the classier joints in town (*mentioning no names*). He eyeballs the lone doorman, waiting in the shadows. The bouncer is a squat, short guy with the face of a rugby player, crowned with a squashed nose that looks like it's been broken multiple times. The guy's earpiece is looped around a cauliflower lobe, leading down his bull neck. He considers rushing at him; he might be able to work out some of his frustrations before any of the other bouncers make it outside to help. But the doorman stares ahead, features blank. He's wasting his time. His antagonism will not be returned.

He wanders on. He's stalling and knows it. He needs to get a move on and locate who *She Who Must Be Obeyed* has sent him after. But he feels reckless tonight; there's no longer the same urgency, now India is gone. Guilt prickles through him as he thinks this, but he squashes it down. He never asked her to get involved. He told her to back off. It's not his problem.

But perhaps it is. Perhaps he should never have told *She Who Must Be Obeyed* that India had found out. He shakes himself. What difference would *that* have made?

He pulls a cigarette from behind his ear, where he left it. He tastes the tang of his sweat on the filter as he brings his zippo to the tip. He clicks the lighter shut with a flourish of his hand, replacing it in his back pocket. He breathes in deep, savouring the mix of the fresh, winter air and the flavour of tobacco. His lungs flood with warmth and abruptly a woozy sensation works its way through his chest and head. When was the last time he ate? He can't remember. He's spent most of the past few days lurking in his room, drinking and watching mindless violence on TV. Ever since he heard *she* was back.

He stops as a gaggle of queers totter into view from a nearby alleyway, arms linked. They're giggling like schoolgirls, already drunk at only ten o'clock at night. They're three men in extravagant evening wear, OTT suits in bright colours and sequins. As one with a neon-pink bowtie turns, he spies a touch of rouge on both of the guy's cheeks, glitter eyeshadow on both lids. *Weirdos.*

Another man in just a wife-beater appears from the opposite direction. He seems untroubled by the cold night air, his thumbs hooked into the belt loops of his jeans. He's well built, crop-haired, *normal.* A guy like him. He feels his heart lift. He can exchange a look with this guy, gauge his disgust. Feel a sense of belonging, if only fleetingly.

But the other man smiles broadly at the one in the bowtie, links arms with him. He acts like wearing glitter and make-up is the most natural thing in the world. He turns back and looks over at him, white teeth gleaming. The guy's accent is Italian, or Spanish; it lacks the *schwa* sound, the 'uh' sound that comes naturally to native speakers. His pronunciation comes out as 'oh' as he says:

'Coming?'

Before he can answer, there's a splutter of juvenile laughter at the double-entendre.

'*Later* darling! Later!'

A set-up. They can sense his animosity, after all. Like dogs. His cheeks burn. With woman-like cackles at his expense, they turn their backs on him and mince off together. He swallows his raw fury, pushing it down deep within the pit of his belly. He's suddenly sick of it all. Let *She Who Must Obeyed* come after him, harangue him. He doesn't have time for this never-ending river of shit.

As he stalks back down The Lanes in the direction of the seafront, something catches his attention. A number of bored-looking patrons line the steps of yet another bar, this time a converted church. They huddle together as they struggle to light matches against the wind, exiled out onto the red paving slabs of The Lanes to smoke. Others talk with plastic glasses of beer in their hands, seemingly impervious to the cold, breath pouring out in white plumes.

He's unsure what's drawn his eye, but then he sees it again. Sudden movement behind a woman in slashed denims, with a proud, green Mohawk. Her steam-punk friend notices his gaze and scowls at him, giving him The Finger. He takes no notice.

Just as he thinks he imagined it, another movement in his peripheral vision betrays what he's searching for: a flash of red under the white fairy lights, as someone up ahead ducks out of view. He knows what it is, instantly.

A long, red wig; spun nylon, like doll's hair.

'Oi! Get back here!'

The volume and aggression in his own voice surprise him. He drives himself into the small crowd around the converted church. Wide-eyed civilians turn in his direction and jostle against him, thinking he's trying to get into the club. A couple of women tut loudly, but he has no time for their disapproval. He needs to get through the small throng, but despite its diminutive size, the other people push back against him. Their strength is buoyed by the walls on either side of the narrow lane: a bottleneck.

There's a surge forward now, forcing him to reverse. He feels the hard touch of multiple palms on his chest, accompanied by a chorus of 'Wanker!' and 'Arsehole!' He's propelled backwards. For a second, he thinks he might trip and fall flat on his back. His arms sail outwards, either side, steadying himself. He's attracting the gaze of nearly everyone outside the converted church now, but he is looking over their heads.

Beyond the bottleneck, someone stops and turns back, looks at him.

The silhouette of a girl.

Her face is in the shadows, but he knows what she looks like: skin painted porcelain white; black stain on her lips, bell sleeves falling around her small hands. From her left, she trails her ridiculously high heels; her feet are bare.

She steps under the orange light of a streetlamp; her face is illuminated. She wears a sardonic grin, buoyed by the space and people between them. She raises her other hand and points it at him: a single finger with a black-glitter, talon-like nail. She wags it at him, side to side, like he were a dog at obedience class. He feels anger bloom in his belly all over again. *That little shit!*

'Jenny!'

She turns. On the other side of the bottleneck, a young man appears from a doorway. The bright-green, luminous FIRE EXIT sign over the top casts its sickly glow over his chiselled features. He's tall, thin and blonde with catalogue-model good looks and intricate tattoos around both his forearms. The building is brightly coloured; designer, neon graffiti dances its way across the brickwork. The blonde nods, as if to say, *In here.*

He groans inwardly. He knows this place; he should have gone here first, instead of trying to get wasted. Frustration builds in him again as he observes the girl pick her way across the lane towards the blonde.

But she can't resist one last glance back at him, all the other bozos still in his way. Impotent and angry, he is forced to watch as she stops and tilts her head, bird-like. She smiles and offers him a mocking little wave, before running after the blonde.

The fire exit slams shut after her.

Nine

'Who's Jenny?'

It's the loose time after breakfast. Mum is repairing one of India's hoodies. It's the red one, her favourite. I remember my sister chewing at the sleeve, rubbing it across her lips as she stared at her laptop screen.

The laptop is with the police right now; I feel a niggle of disloyalty work through me. India would hate that. She guarded that machine jealously, barely letting anyone so much as glimpse the screen. 'Technohead', my stepfather called her. India would roll her eyes and laugh, as if the very word belonged in a museum.

'No one.' Mum's attention is on her stitching.

'Surely it has to be *someone*?'

'No. She didn't know anyone called Jenny.' Pins are perched on Mum's lips.

I persist. 'India was twenty-four. You can't have known all her friends.'

Mum looks up at last. 'She didn't have any friends.'

I stop short. 'That doesn't sound like India.'

'Yes, well, you hadn't seen her for a long time.' Mum's tone is even, almost bored. But I know my mother too well. This is the pitch she affects when she is trying not to be drawn into something.

I'm galled by what she's said – by the simple truth. Over the last four years, India and I only interacted briefly: texting, or sending birthday and Christmas cards.

I pursue my question. 'It just doesn't feel right.'

Mum purses her lips.

'I mean, why write to this Jenny and not one of us?'

'Why does anyone do what they do?' It's not a question, but a declaration. She is not looking at me, apparently absorbed in her task; doing what she has to, in order not to unravel.

'Have you read this?' I press on the link for India's blog and enlarge it on the iPad. I turn the screen towards my mother.

'I can't, not yet.'

I concede immediately, but she still moves her face very deliberately away from the tablet. In her eyes I see fear, as if catching a glimpse of the screen might pull her down, free-falling into it. She is holding onto her composure by her fingernails; it's excruciating to watch in a woman who is normally so pragmatic.

I tap 'Jenny' into the Facebook search bar. A dozen pop up, a series of smiles and pouts for the camera. I scroll through them, checking each one that's noted as a mutual friend with my sister.

There are three.

The first is Jenny Wilson, a matronly-looking woman in her early seventies. I recognise her as an old piano teacher of ours. The other two I don't know. They both seem to be around India's age. The first, Jenny Emmett, is blonde, with a round, moon-like face and a huge smile. She's holding a book in one hand and a pencil to her mouth with the other. Behind her, there is an extreme close-up of coffee beans in black and white. She's in a chain café.

The other is listed as 'Jenny Moriarty (was Cho)'. Hers is a more arty shot, probably taken by a boyfriend or husband. She's on a beach, wearing sunglasses, a sheer sarong wrapped around her slim frame. Jenny looks over her shoulder, a hand raised to her forehead. I can see only one half of her features, her face is obscured.

I turn back to Mum. 'Maybe Jenny was someone she worked with?'

'India lost her job. About eighteen months ago. Redundant.'

This is news to me. When I left, India had a good job working in the accounts division of a graphic-design firm.

'She did a few shifts down at Elemental, but that's all she could get.'

'Elemental?'

'A café bar, down on the seafront,' Mum looks up, not quite managing to hide the exasperation in her voice. 'I told you all this ages ago.'

I open my mouth, but then there's another flash. D's disembodied hands up my skirt, my wreck of a flat. I'd been drinking far too much lately, perhaps Mum *had* told me? Shame blooms in my gut. *If only I had been paying more attention.*

Tim appears from the living room, a newspaper under one arm and a fixed, humourless smile on his face. Tim is old school. 'Keep on keeping on' his motto. No. Matter. What. 'Coffee?' he asks.

In answer, Mum throws her mending down on the table, upending her sewing box. Hundreds of pins scatter across the kitchen tiles, lightly musical as metal hits ceramic. A sob attempts to erupt from my mother, but she clamps a hand over her mouth as she rushes from the room. Stupefied, I gape at Tim.

'It's alright love, I'll get these.' Tim indicates the pins, now dotted all over the floor. He still has that ridiculous grin painted on his round face.

Blinking back tears, I set the iPad down on the table, India's note to Jenny still on the screen. I grab my coat from the back of the kitchen door and shrug it on as I walk out.

Ten

I falter as soon as I make it outside. *Where the hell am I going?*

The frost is still a hard shell on the ground, my boots crunch on the back-garden path. Dew sparkles on the trimmed topiary next to the decking. The barbecue pit is scrubbed clean, though the grill is orange with rust.

Another flash of memory: India and me one summer. We're drinking wine and playing Twister on the back lawn. Mum, an exasperated look on her face, rushes out onto the patio to see what we're cackling about. Within five minutes India has persuaded our normally reserved matriarch to join us, entwining her limbs with ours in increasingly bizarre poses.

The garden gate's hinges squeal in protest as I open it. I let it crash back on the latch.

I make my way downhill, towards the seafront. I see the burnt-out shell of West Pier first, then the neon lights of Palace Pier, still visible against the pale sky. When we were growing up, we'd spent so many summers there, at Mum and Tim's arcade. I'd watched tourists and locals alike sending good money after bad through the penny-falls machines or the grabbers. We were not allowed to play. Tim would survey his kingdom and remind India and me: 'House always wins.'

I pass various posters boasting of attractions 'coming soon', springing up mushroom-like amid the forest of hotel signs. Some of the buildings' fronts are bedecked with scaffolding as they update during the quieter winter months. Tired and bedraggled bunting runs the length of the seafront, attempting to compete with the chain restaurants' brightly coloured signage. Overhead, the December sky is so grey I can't make out where it ends and the churning sea begins.

The pebbles and shale of Brighton beach have been left dry by the retreating tide.

I make my way past the Doughnut Groyne and The Kissing Wall sculpture, towards the steep concrete steps leading down to the beach. Most of the old boathouses have their aluminium shutters down; only a single café stands open, serving coffees to hardy off-season beach-goers.

I drift onto the beach, kicking stones beneath my boots. The shellfish and artists' kiosks stand idle, padlocks across their flimsy, multi-coloured doors. Joggers push wordlessly on past me, plugged into headphones. Women steer buggies, their eyes dull and bored, their kids wrapped up against the cold in fleeces and blankets that don't permit them to move.

I look behind me, in the direction of Western Esplanade. Beyond the Odeon and the Conference Centre is a large, new building: a massive, marble monolith. Locals called it a monstrosity when it was erected twenty years ago, but in the decades that have followed opposition has thawed. This is largely due to the amount of work and extra tourism it has brought into our city.

The Obelisk resort.

Light reflects off its tall windowpanes. Purpose-built by the (in)famous Spence Family, The Obelisk is perhaps twenty storeys high, matching the tall, black column outside. Even out of season, I can see the hotel is busy. There is a steady stream of patrons and staff snaking out of the front doors like ants, carrying bags and moving cars around the back. The Obelisk is the epitome of high-end luxury, catering to its residents' every whim … or so the rumours go.

As I squint, I notice that a limo stops out front. The chauffeur gets out the driver's side and races around to open the back door on the side facing the hotel. I can't see who the occupants are, but I can guess: Gordon Spence and his wife, Olivia. Gordon is a sixty-plus suburban Popeye with loose jowls and a rotund belly. He always undoes his cufflinks and rolls his shirtsleeves up, showing off his faded-green builder's tattoos. He likes to remind everyone he's not forgotten where he came from. In contrast, Olivia has modelled herself on the traditional aged trophy wife. Her hair still the brassy bottle blonde of her twenties, her too-tight facelifts making her look like she's been badly burnt.

I've never met either of them, but I've seen them plenty in the local papers. The whole family are publicity hogs, getting involved in every initiative in the city. Any excuse to remind Brighton The Obelisk is one of the biggest employers in the area. Every school kid in Brighton knows their story: how Gordon and Olivia started with nothing. The Obelisk had been their dream as they clawed their way out of poverty, building their empire brick by brick. That dream has paid off, big style. Good luck to them, I say.

I turn away, looking now for the café bar where India did the odd shift. *What was it called?*

Elemental.

I make my way towards the line of bars on the seafront, and soon find the right one. It leads just off the beach, its sign aluminium, punched-out letters, blue neon shining through. I remember the venue was an American diner when I left. Must be under new ownership.

Through its large front window, I see a couple of mothers drinking coffee, seated in a booth as their toddlers play nearby. At the bar sits a man in a suit, his back to me, hunched over. His posture cries despair; the whisky tumbler in his hand, right now, before midday, even more so.

I cross the threshold and a bell tinkles, making the two mums look up before returning to their conversation. The man at the bar does not move. The décor feels futuristic, high-tech. I can see the aluminium theme is continued throughout, lining the tables and bar tops, more blue neon piping around the optics. On the wall, the food and drinks menu is a mock periodic table. To the left of the bar, a small stage, a poster beside it advertising an open-mic night. It's a cool place, somewhere I might like to go, day or night. I can see why India might have enjoyed working here.

The man at the bar stands, and as he turns, I note he looks a lot younger and more cheerful than I presumed. He gives a brief grin as he clocks me beside him, and chucks a note down on the bar, calling out as he does so.

'Customer out here. Cheers!'

'Alright Steve, see ya later!'

I recognise the other voice as it filters through and stiffen as a man appears from the back. He's wiping his wet hands on a tea towel, offering up an automatic smile.

'What can I get you…?'

The smile freezes on his face as our eyes lock. He takes me in. Even four (*nearly five*) years on, I still feel prickles down my back just looking at him. He's not changed much, just some subtle differences: his head is still shaved but now he has a short goatee. There are flecks of white in it, contrasting with his dark skin. He's immaculately turned out, although not wearing the kind of designer shirt he used to, but a faded, grungey-looking t-shirt and jeans. He's bigger than he used to be, too, especially in the chest and arms: 'hench', as the kids would say (*adjective*, British informal. Fit, with well-developed muscles (male only)).

I find my voice at last. 'Matthew.'

Eleven

'Poppy.'

Too late, it hits me: Matthew is not pleased to see me. I'm irritated momentarily that Mum didn't mention that Elemental is his, then remind myself she's not thinking straight at the moment. *None of us are.*

I'm unsure what to say. 'This place is … nice.'

Matthew does not accept the compliment. Instead he tilts his head, assessing me, like he thinks I'm about to trick him. His hands flex at his sides.

'It's good to see you,' I say softly, unable to stop myself.

Matthew's body is rigid, his stare jumping from me to the rest of the bar. It's empty now, the two mums gone. It's just him and me.

'I'm sorry about India.'

But I know Matthew too well. Even behind his attempt at a studied neutrality, I see his panicked thoughts roil.

'That's what I wanted to talk to you about.' I try to sound impersonal as well. 'Mum says India was working here?'

Matthew's posture slumps. I watch a myriad of emotions pass across his face: hurt, anger, *relief*. He settles on nonchalance. 'That's right. Drink?'

Before I can tell him what I want, Matthew reaches under the counter and sets a glass and a bottle of Coke in front of me. Red label of course, I hate Diet. *He remembers.*

'Thanks.' I ignore the glass and pluck a straw out of the holder by the till. I shove it into the neck of the bottle.

Matthew leans both hands on the bar. 'I didn't have enough work for her out of season.' It's as if he feels compelled to fill the silence between us. 'She did weekends, the occasional event. I would have used her more in the summer had she…'

Had she not died. Had she lived. Delete as appropriate.

We both take a deep breath and recover our bearings.

'When did you see her last?'

Matthew's eyes flit upwards. 'I guess a couple of weeks before, well, you know. There was an office Christmas party here. She worked that one, I think.'

'How did she seem, to you?'

'Fine.'

My gaze drops to his large hands, the angle of his wrists. On his left I note he's wearing a different watch, not the one I bought for his birthday, four (*nearly five*) years ago. We celebrated that one on our own, hiding from everyone all day. His parents and siblings had made so many calls, we unplugged the landline and turned off our mobiles. We hid, giggling, with hands clamped over each other's mouths as various family members banged on the door downstairs.

'Today is our day,' Matthew said.

Our old flat was above an old-school tobacconist in a dodgy area of Hove. It smelt of pipe smoke, but we grew used to it quickly. There was a grubby kitchenette, a shared bathroom across the hall. Pigeons nested in the corners of the roof, making a racket day and night. There was always a door slamming somewhere. But it was ours and we were happy there.

Until *The Ultimatum*.

'Not suicidal?' I drain the last of my Coke.

Matthew gives an uncharacteristically nervous blink. 'No. Guess I was wrong.'

'I guess.'

This new Matthew is spiky and awkward, all sharp edges. His old, warm fuzziness is gone: he no longer seems safe. But what is *safe?* Why are Safe Guys always equated with boredom? A Safe Guy is someone you can count on, who will do anything for you. He means what he says, there is no second guessing. Sometimes Safe Guys are called 'real men' or 'gentlemen', although those words can suggest other, less favourable, connotations: player, womaniser, pimp. But

Matthew was none of these things. Any consideration he afforded me back then was not because he wanted anything specific in return. It was because he loved me. Simple as that.

But that was *Before*. Now he feels different.

I did that.

I look up and find his gaze on me. He hesitates, then takes the plunge.

'What do you think is going to happen – when you've found out why India killed herself?'

I wince at his choice of words. I look away, tears stinging my eyes, that familiar pain in my throat. 'I don't know.'

'Let her go,' he murmurs.

'I can't.' I hop down from the barstool and away from the bar, creating more distance between us. 'Thank you for your help.'

Matthew mimics me, backing away behind the counter. 'Don't mention it.'

I waver a moment then turn on my heel, calling over my shoulder as I go, 'Well, see you later maybe.'

'Goodbye, Poppy.' Matthew's voice is flat.

The doorbell tinkles as I let myself out.

Twelve

I arrive back at the Coach House. I feel off-kilter, disturbed by how seeing Matthew has affected me. An unwanted montage of images slides through my memory, blurring like scenery through a train window: we lie together on our broken-down old bed; we watch a movie, my head resting on Matthew's shoulder; water cascades over his toned, dark skin in the shower, then he gives me a cheeky smile and pulls me in with him, even though I'm fully clothed.

When I enter the Coach House living room, these memories dissolve. I find a strange, pale man sitting there. He's not that old, perhaps mid-forties, but he's already got a comb-over. He wears a cheap suit that smells like it hasn't been laundered in a while, which is made more obvious rather than masked by the liberal dousing of aftershave he has given himself. I struggle to stop my nose wrinkling up.

He jumps up from the threadbare old armchair, strides across the room in what seems like two steps and grasps my right hand in both of his, which feel limp and cold.

'Miss Rutledge…' he begins, oozing smarm.

'It's Wade.'

I say the words softly, almost embarrassed as I claim my no-good natural father's name as my own. He and Mum had married when still in university, only to regret it mere months later, but not before I was in Mum's belly. I can barely remember my father, now. All I can fashion in my mind is a grey goatee; weathered hands; the smell of a woody aftershave, like rain on wet bark. I haven't seen him since before Tim and Mum were married. Yet I've kept the name, a teenage rebellion that feels disloyal now.

The man corrects himself. 'Miss *Wade*. Peter Thackeray, from

Thackeray and Son,' he says, 'though truth be told, it's just me now … I'm the son,' he adds, in case I am unable to follow. He smiles. His gums are receding; each tooth protrudes like a yellow tombstone, decay etched around every edge. A lifelong smoker.

'Good to … erm … meet you.' I extricate my hand and try to take a step away from him. But he follows me. We end up doing a curious dance towards my mother's sideboard.

'Peter's from the funeral director's.'

I turn to see Mum struggling in with a tray, a teapot, milk jug and the best china wobbling on it. On a plate, the biscuits she keeps for VIPs.

Peter Thackeray finally moves away and sits down opposite Mum, who is pouring the tea. He keeps his oily, insincere stare on me.

'We're just picking … y'know.' Mum attempts breezy, but finds herself unable to say the words needed: casket; flowers; order of service.

Mr Thackeray opens a briefcase and brings out a selection of glossy leaflets and catalogues, all tastefully designed in low-key colours, with photos of dignified flower arrangements inviting us to forget their context. But how can we?

I turn, finding Tim behind me. *Do they want me to help?* I send him the unspoken question. He offers me a strained smile then an almost indiscernible shake of his head. Relieved, I push past him into the hall. I race up the stairs to the bathroom, slamming the door behind me, heat enveloping me as a sudden nausea hits.

Afterwards, not wanting to risk being drawn back into the conversation, I go into India's room. Her belongings sit in a plastic bag on her desk. Retrieved from 'the incident', the policewoman said when she brought them back to us. From *her body*, is what she meant. At least she also brought back India's laptop.

I answered the door to her, so had to sign for my dead sister's things. I didn't show them to Mum. I held them at arms' length, went straight to India's room where I dumped them.

Looking around now, I acknowledge small changes in my peripheral vision. The bed is made, the sheets straightened. Mum has placed my sister's washing and ironing in a neat pile, as if she will put it in the drawers herself. On top of the pile, the red hoody.

I pick it up, smelling the fabric, wondering if I can sense my sister still inside the fibres. But I can smell only fabric conditioner. I yank the hoody over my head, determined to feel closer to India, somehow. Then I grab the plastic bag from the desk and sit down on the bed.

I crack the seal, letting the items fall out onto the duvet.

First, a policeman's business card: 'Detective Sergeant Kamil Rahman, Family Liaison Officer'. I put it in my pocket.

Next: India's house keys; a half-pack of tissues; a roll of mints, unopened.

Then the last item: India's mobile. The screen is cracked and there are scratches all down the back of the handset. *Being hit by a train can do that.* I press the power button and am surprised when the LED screen flickers and the start-up animation begins.

When the phone is fully live, I scroll through it. I click on the photo gallery first. There's a selection of selfies. I smile despite myself, as I see India pouting; she always did love the camera.

There are more pictures, mostly landscapes: sunsets and flowers. A couple of memes and cute animal pics saved from the Internet. The email inbox is full of spam and social-media notifications. India has received no personal messages.

The voicemail icon flashes.

I put the phone to my ear and steel myself, hearing my sister's dulcet tones for the first time in years: 'Hi, this is India. Leave a message after the beep and I might get back to you ... IF I feel like it!' Pain lances through me as my sister's bell-like laugh is cut off and the recordings start up.

The first voicemail is an automated message from a bank; then there's a bored-sounding Indian man trying to sell a fraud protection service. The next few are just static, before the caller hangs up. It's the fifth that grabs my attention.

'Oh, God. India…' The voice is whispery, hoarse. I can't tell if it's a woman or a man. I can hear the raw grief choking in his or her throat. My own tears well up inside me in sympathetic response, but I force them down again. '…You shouldn't have waited for me.'

Then the caller hangs up.

I press the LED screen to display caller ID, but am dismayed to see the caller has withheld his or her number. When the voicemail asks if I want to listen again, I press the button for YES. I listen to the short message over and over, my certainty growing with every successive listening.

I'm sure the voice belongs to a woman. It was left on 22nd December. The night India died.

It has to be the mysterious Jenny.

Thirteen

⏎@Wolfman404: *WTAF was that all about today?? Don't pull that shit on me again. My life's complicated enough as it is. Don't wanna hear it.*

⏎@1NDIAsummer: *OK, I'll stay away. But I'm not the one pressurising you. You know it's true. You CAN stop this*

⏎@Wolfman404: *U think it's as easy as that??*

⏎@1NDIAsummer: *Never said it was easy*

⏎@Wolfman404: *Wot is it U want?? Attention? Ur like a kid*

⏎@1NDIAsummer: *No. Just think about what I'm saying*

⏎@Wolfman404: *Go fuck urself India*

⏎@1NDIAsummer: *Look, I get it. I know it's hard. But if not now, when? This can't go on forever.*

⏎@Wolfman404: *U don't get it. AT ALL*

⏎@1NDIAsummer: *You can stop all of this.*

⏎@Wolfman404: *U actually readin what U typin?? Look, if you don't back off this is gonna get bad for you*

⏎@1NDIAsummer: *It's in your hands*

↩@Wolfman404: *OK u've swallowed some self-help book or some shit. Done*

↩@1NDIAsummer: *PLEASE! Look, I'll beg if you want me to. Just do the right thing. You OWE her.*

@Wolfman404 leaves the conversation.

@1NDIAsummer leaves the conversation.

PART TWO

Present Continuous

/ing/

Fourteen

Tossing and turning, he dreams of her: the feel of her skin, the curves of her body. Darkness surrounds them, he can only see her up close; only she exists. He doesn't know where they are. *It doesn't matter.*

'I love you so much,' he mutters.

She says nothing, but she kisses him like she used to. The pull towards her is magnetic, as if he's powerless to stop himself. Waking, his naked skin is sheened in sweat, his muscles twisted in frustrated desire.

Body and spirit aching, he drags himself into the shower, letting the hot water sluice away his sins. Skin tingling, he wraps a towel around his waist and pads through to his bedroom. He jumps in surprise as a shadowed figure passes in front of the window, dark against the open Venetian blind.

She Who Must Be Obeyed.

'That key was for emergencies only.'

She gives no indication she has heard, nor does she turn in his direction. She stands at the window, her back to him. She's dressed in black. She has her hands on her hips, one heeled foot out in front of her as she regards the view of Brighton stretching beyond the glass. She stifles a yawn behind her hand. He opens the wardrobe, grabbing clothes off the hanger.

He waits. She doesn't take the hint.

'I need to get dressed?'

She tuts, irritated, as if he's being ridiculous, or falsely modest. In the small room, he towers over her. In two or three steps, he could grab and choke her if he wanted to. But he knows her unannounced appearance is a test. It's one he can't afford to fail.

Not today.

He goes into the small bathroom. His bulk barely fits in the narrow space as he shrugs on his clothes, but at least the door has a lock. He fastens the buttons on his shirt haphazardly, taking a quick look in the small shaving mirror as he does so. Haunted eyes stare back.

She is waiting on the threshold as he pulls open the bathroom door. He stops himself from flinching at her proximity. He won't betray his weakness. Not again.

She gives him a tight-lipped smile and straightens his tie for him. 'That's better.'

He doesn't thank her. It didn't need straightening. It's a tiny act of defiance, but one he savours. She doesn't seem to notice.

Without warning, she grabs his tie. Yanks his face closer to hers.

'Don't think I don't know.' Her gaze is icy, furious.

He affects a blank stare back. 'Know what?'

'That *she's* back!' She lets him go, placing her hands on her hips again.

His stomach lurches; his mouth fills up with sour saliva. 'It won't make any difference.'

'It better not.' She pokes him in the chest with another one of her meticulously painted nails. 'Remember what she did, OK?'

'Fine.' He murmurs. He forces anger to the surface, an antidote to the fear of her that swells in his chest. *Always: women telling him what to do.*

But this time, she is unconcerned; it's as if she can feel the anxiety radiating from him in waves. She sighs and shakes her head slightly, as if he were a child. She turns on her heel and disappears through the bedroom door into the hallway, without looking back.

For a microsecond, he thinks about closing the door after her. Pulling the deadbolt across, staying in his flat as she beats on the door, impotent, demanding he come out again. A smile twitches his lip as he considers this pointless, yet badly needed, act of rebellion.

'Hurry up, then!' Her voice, thin and demanding, travels back down the corridor towards him.

His treacherous feet follow her.

Fifteen

Finally, it is time.

The cars arrive. The hearse waits outside the house, a man in a long black overcoat and stick in front of it, ready to walk ahead of the procession. In the back, the casket. It is all but obscured by a massive flower tribute, spelling out my sister's name. It's the kind of pale yellow you buy a pregnant woman when you're not sure if she's having a boy or a girl.

Another flash enters my head now: running up the hospital corridor with Tim to see my new baby sister, carrying a present wrapped carelessly in Christmas paper. I peered into the crib, expecting to see a baby like I'd seen on television: rosy-cheeked and smiling, much bigger. Instead I saw this wizened, tiny thing, her features crumpled up, her tiny hands thrown back either side of her head.

'What do you think, Poppy?' My mother looked exhausted, her face white, dark circles under her eyes. She and Tim waited for my verdict, eyes wide.

I shrugged. 'She's alright.'

They laughed.

The long-lost relatives are directed to one car. I'm directed to the other, with Mum and Tim. Mum gets in and slides right across to the window opposite, as if her plan is to open the door and get straight out the other side, and only Tim's hand, clasping hers, prevents her. Mum does not look at him, her sights fixed ahead. He stares at her ear, the side of her head, his chin almost resting on her shoulder.

I lean forward and place a hand on Mum's knee. Her gaze alights on my face. I'm shocked by how lost she seems. I try and say something, but nothing comes out. Mum's focus swims away again. I sit back in my seat, looking out the back window as the cars set off, the hearse in front of us.

We arrive at the church. It's the one where Tim and Mum got married, before India was born. I was a flower girl then, carrying a wicker basket full of rose petals, but now my hands are empty. *Should I have brought something?* I don't know what the protocol is. I realise that at nearly thirty, this is the first funeral I have been to. I guess I have been lucky, but that word sticks in my craw now.

More guilt presses down on me as I see the wreaths and flower sprays, propped up next to the open plot meant for my sister. I am surprised to see so many people waiting outside the church, chatting in reverent tones about everyday things: their kids' schooling; troubles at work. *Proof that life does indeed go on.*

The idle chit-chat ceases as people see my mother. Tim's arm is clamped around her, holding her up. A ripple of sympathy works its way through the small crowd. Tim nods in acknowledgement, then gestures to me to take Mum's elbow. I do so, expecting her weight to transfer to me, but she does not lean on me like she did Tim. I feel oddly rejected, though I don't know why.

My stepfather makes his way to the hearse with three other men. One is a Canadian relative of my mother's, a man with a face almost as circular as his rotund belly. Another is the adult son of our family doctor, whose name I don't recall. He is about India's age and tall, ruddy-cheeked, with slightly buck teeth. He's handsome in a horsey kind of way. I speculate about whether he could have been my sister's boyfriend. *But wouldn't Mum have mentioned that India was seeing someone?*

Then I notice the last pallbearer. He is a slight man, balding now, though his pallid face is puckered with old, red acne scars. His suit, though undoubtedly carefully pressed that morning by his wife – *I know she is fastidious* – already looks crumpled, like he's been wearing it for days. The man takes a few puffs of his cigarette, then grinds it under his £2000 shoes and scuttles after the others. I watch him go, unable to compute.

It is Alan Temple, Matthew's father.

My mind reels. *When did Mum and Tim start speaking to the Temples again?* But I don't have time to puzzle this now, as the rest of the Temple family arrives.

Maggie, Alan's wife is the first to reach us. She looks pristine, as if she's walked straight out of a Laura Ashley catalogue (*if the models in it were ever black*). Though Maggie's face is a little more lined, she looks more or less the same as when I saw her last. She clutches her bag to her stomach and wears her tightly coiled hair smoothed up into the same bun style I remember. She has an expression of studied sorrow, but surely she can't have known India well? She plucks at my sleeve, so I offer her a thin-lipped smile.

'Kirsten, darling,' Maggie says to Mum. 'I just don't know what to say.' Her gaze flickers, steely, towards mine. She acknowledges me with a slight curl of her upper lip. '…Poppy.'

Ana, the Temples' eldest child by just three minutes, hovers behind her mother. I see her take a deep breath, bracing herself to speak with me. Ana is as stylish as her mother, though in a vintage way, all tassels and scarves.

'Kirsten, Poppy. So sorry.' Ana regards me with pursed lips, like she's trying not to let accusations spill out. Tension rolls off her in waves. It's clear she is only here under sufferance. I perceive rather than see there's something different about Ana. It rankles. I'm not sure what it is.

'Thank you,' I say, automatic. Mum nods.

'Poppy.' Matthew meanders up behind his sister, giving me a cursory acknowledgement. The familial resemblance between him and his sister is unmistakable: the long faces, high cheekbones, heart-shaped chins. He's clean-shaven, the beard he was sporting at Elemental the other day gone, his face as smooth as his cue-ball head. That's when I realise what is different about Ana.

'I like your hair like that.'

The words are out before I can figure out whether they're appropriate or not. Ana reaches a hand to her halo of mid-length corkscrews as I say this. Standing next to Matthew, I note they look like opposites; his yin to her yang. I've never seen Ana's natural hair; she always relaxed it, like Maggie. Her mother insisted on it when we were younger, saying Ana looked 'even prettier' with straightened hair. Ana confessed to me she hated the acrid smell of the chemicals; the way they could burn her scalp if left on too long. There was a time when she was off school for weeks, and I didn't see her. Afterwards she told me it was a hair thing – she was allergic to a new product, and Maggie had let her stay at home rather than be seen in public with 'bad hair'. To this day that story has never rung true.

What is true is that Ana always acquiesced to Maggie. Well, no more it seems. And I even think I see a flash of irritation pass across Maggie's face, obviously judging it the wrong thing to talk about at a funeral. But India was *my* family, not theirs.

The five of us make more small talk to stop another silence from swallowing us whole. Our families were close once; the three of us children inseparable. Now, Ana's hand clasps her twin's elbow in a proprietorial gesture, a warning in her eyes telling me to *stay away*. Matthew doesn't appear to notice.

A thought occurs. 'Where's James?'

Maggie appears to start, as if she hasn't expected me to remember her third child. But why wouldn't I? Maggie called her youngest a 'happy accident', pleased that what she'd thought was an early menopause turned out to be a final baby. Matthew and Ana were fifteen when Maggie and Alan brought the placid little infant home. I was about thirteen. India was six or seven, bringing James one of her old teddies. I recall the twins' slight disgust at the thought of their parents still 'doing it', but both doted on their baby brother, treating him like he was made of china. At least, Matthew did.

'He's away at school,' Maggie cuts in before either of the twins can answer. I don't think I'm imagining the slightly smug, or at least proud tone, especially when she continues, 'He's *very* gifted.'

'Oh yeah, he's special alright,' Matthew mutters.

Maggie's nostrils flare at her son's sarcasm, but she doesn't allow herself to turn towards Matthew.

'How old is James now, he must be, what, fifteen?'

'Nearly eighteen.' Maggie flashes me a pearly-white smile as she sees the shock on my face. *Time really does fly.*

I'm distracted as Mum breaks away from our little huddle and wanders off towards the threshold of the church. Maggie smiles, gestures for me to go after her. I throw the Temples an apologetic glance and follow my mother into the building.

Stopping at the back of the pews, I glance towards the altar: Mum sits down there now, alone, head bowed as if praying. I look around the church, not taking anything in. As I make my way down the aisle, I can see the priest waiting in his robes near the lectern, hands clasped behind his back. It all seems surreal.

Then I find myself drawn to another figure, sitting perhaps two pews ahead of me. Her body language is apologetic, turned a few inches away, so she's facing the wall rather than the altar. I can see the bumps of her spine in her neck, through her sheer blouse. She is wearing purple, like Ana Temple. In her straight, dyed-auburn hair, there is a large, purple, satin flower. She does not look up as we all file in past her, but I don't need her to. I am sure I know who it is.

Jenny.

Sixteen

I take my place on the pew at the front, next to my mother and Tim. Everyone present, the priest launches into a low-key and informal remembrance. He's about Tim's age, though he has an incongruous amount of hair and small, round John Lennon-type spectacles. I look around and see other people dab their eyes with handkerchiefs, though no one appears to be sobbing openly.

During the service, I am distracted. I find myself glancing behind me, at the young woman in purple with clashing red hair, sitting at the back. I'd wanted to pay close attention, listen to what others would say about my beloved sister, say goodbye. Though I'd never been to a funeral, as India's approached, I began to realise their significance for those left behind, how they help with the healing process. But now, faced with the prospect that Jenny is here, in the same room, endless questions are burning on my tongue; I'm desperate to voice them.

My impatience alerts the young woman. When she catches my glance for the third time, she hoists her handbag over her shoulder, in readiness to stand. Feeling a surge of panic at the thought of losing her, I wheel round to watch her shift out of her seat, walking, slow and purposeful, towards the church's exit.

'Tim,' I murmur, seeking his permission to leave.

My stepfather looks up, away from his hand clasped in my mother's. Her head is dipped, her eyes closed, lost inside herself. He gives me that nod again.

Grateful, I stand and hurry down the aisle, holding a tissue to my face as if overcome. A few guests look up in my direction, but with sympathy, not accusation.

I move from the dimness of the church back into the bright

sunshine of the graveyard beyond, frost still sparkling on the ground. I struggle to focus on where the young woman could have gone.

I see her up ahead, cutting across the cemetery. I know where she is going: the bus stop on the road opposite. I race across the grass after her, dodging tombstones as I go, a macabre slalom race.

'Jenny!' I call.

She does not turn around. I catch her up with ease and put my hand on Jenny's bony shoulder. She stiffens under my touch. Her head swings around.

She is neither of the two Jennys from Facebook. But that doesn't mean she isn't the one India's suicide 'note' was addressed to.

'I'm sorry, I shouldn't have come.' Jenny averts her eyes from mine.

I try and catch my breath, adrenaline coursing through me. 'I just want to talk to you.'

'There's nothing to say!' The girl's voice is desperate.

'Please, I just want to ask you some questions...'

'Stay away from me!' She jabs a finger at me, it connects with my sternum. The sudden, sharp touch shocks me. I let go of her.

Rooted to the spot, I just stand and watch her go, my chest rising and falling with my small gasps. *What now?*

'Poppy?'

I wheel around. Matthew stands behind me, his face a picture of concern. The distance between us the last time we met seems to evaporate. I choke back a sob and lean against him, like my mother had against Tim; he lets me, folding his big arms around me.

Something snaps deep within me.

Raw grief hits me in the solar plexus, folding me over. Matthew tries to keep me upright, then gives up. He lets me squat down on my heels as I attempt to pour the grief out of myself with a low, animalistic moan, my whole body shaking. As light glints on the sparkling grass, a thought surfaces in my brain: *How can the sun be shining when my only sister is dead?*

*

Reality returns with the sound of the organ in the church. Muffled voices sing a hymn for India. I sit on a bench under a willow arch, next to an angel with no head, my own resting on Matthew's shoulder.

I look down and see my tights are laddered. Absent-mindedly, I pick at the hole, making it larger, drawing his attention. Matthew gives me a wan smile. He removes his arm from around my shoulders. I miss his touch, his warm body against mine.

'I thought she was Jenny – the girl India wrote her last blog post to.'

Jenny, I want Matthew to say. *Your mother is wrong. Jenny exists.*

But he doesn't. 'That was JoJo,' he says.

I am incredulous, but as I repeat the name, my brain makes the connection. JoJo – India's best friend from school: *bestie, BFF, fat friend.*

'*Jabba* JoJo?'

Matthew shrugs. 'People change.'

I realise why I didn't recognise her. JoJo Musgrave was five or six stone heavier the last time I saw her. What's more, it was her hair that was purple, rather than her clothes. But one thing still puzzles me: If JoJo is *not* Jenny, then why did she flinch when she saw me?

Could JoJo Musgrave be hiding something?

I lean forwards, trying to re-establish the connection we had earlier. I brush my lips against his. Matthew stays where he is on the bench. His body faces outwards, away from me.

But he doesn't dodge me. He lets me push my body up against his side, press my mouth against his. His lips part. I kiss him properly.

But as I move a hand onto his right thigh, he jerks away. He raises the back of his hand to his mouth, like he's wiping away a bad taste.

Me.

'I'm sorry.' My apology blurts out of me now, four *(nearly five)* years too late. It is as sudden as my visceral grief, minutes earlier.

Matthew's face is impassive. 'Just words.'

Over his shoulder, I see the priest emerge from the church. The pallbearers shuffle behind him, shouldering India's casket. The procession moves towards the open grave. In my peripheral vision, I see two men in cheap black suits waiting just beyond a large stone memorial in the shape of a Canterbury cross. They both wear sunglasses, like the Blues Brothers. Later they will replace them with dirty overalls and shovel earth onto my sister.

As I look away, I catch sight of another man, this time standing some way back from the church. He's a white guy with broad shoulders, in a dark suit and tie. He has an unruly mop of curly hair, though he's far enough away that I can't make out his features in much detail. He's not carrying any flowers; nor does he appear to be visiting any particular grave. He sucks on the filter of a cigarette, his body language ragged, anxious. Each exhalation forms a smoky cloud around his head.

Even so, I sense him looking straight at me.

More people file out of the church. Maggie and Alan take their place at the graveside, opposite my parents. Only Ana hangs back, glaring at me sitting next to her brother. I look for the man who'd been standing towards the back of the cemetery. I can no longer see him.

'She really hates me.' Though she cannot possibly have seen the kiss from inside the church – *none of them could have* – I feel that somehow Ana knows.

Matthew turns his head towards me at last. I want him to say she doesn't hate me; that he doesn't either. But instead he regards me with a single raised eyebrow. As if to say, *Can you blame her?*

The ceremony draws to a close and people begin to drift away, the Temples included. Mum and Tim move back towards the cars, waylaid every few steps by this or that person offering their condolences.

Now everyone has moved away, I take the opportunity to look into the grave. My sister's coffin nestles within the cold earth, the fuzzy, fake-green grass lining its top. India is inside that pine box, her pale skin mottled, veins black with dead blood.

They say your hair and nails grow for a year after a death. *Can that be true?* I wonder if someone in the future might dig my sister up again, pore over her bones. Or perhaps the graveyard will be assimilated back into municipal city ground. It might be fought over and sold, bought by businessmen like Alan Temple. Maybe luxury flats will be built on top of her, interring my poor sister's remains under concrete forever.

I can't stop any of that happening, but I can still do one thing for India.

'I will find out what happened to you,' I tell her.

Seventeen

The wake takes place at the Coach House; the Temples do not come. The long-lost relatives gather in the kitchen, muttering in hushed voices around plates of untouched food, rapidly going stale. I stay as long as is considered proper, then retreat to my room.

I look again at that final blog post of India's on the iPad. Suddenly, it seems important that I read it on India's own laptop. Perhaps I could even access the blog itself, see if she'd written any more drafts? I realise the police will have looked already, but I have to see it with my own eyes.

I boot up my sister's machine for the first time since its return from the police station. Guilt prickles through me. For a meddler (or perhaps *because* of it?), India was fiercely protective of her privacy.

But I don't get far. Straight away I'm asked for a password. I make various attempts to guess it, to no avail. After five tries, some kind of security measure kicks in. I discover I can no longer type on the laptop at all; the keyboard is disabled. Locked out! I am beaten at the first hurdle. *Damn it.*

I've never taken much interest in the online world. I can use Microsoft Office, email and Internet Explorer, but that's about it. Blogs have always seemed utterly pointless to me. Who'd want to read someone's online diary? Nosy people, I guess: blackmailers or angsty teens.

Regarding the locked screen, I feel the same surge of panic as when I saw Jenny/JoJo leave the cemetery. I choke it down. I may be clueless, but there are others who aren't. *Time to call in the cavalry.*

I call up an online business directory on the iPad, searching for computer-repair shops. I call all the chain stores first. But they're all fully occupied with giving demos and troubleshooting for people who've received shiny new systems for Christmas. I then work my way through a list of indie shops, but get only answerphone messages telling me they're still closed, to re-open after New Year's Day the following week.

Something occurs to me. I reach inside my bag for India's phone. I don't have Matthew's phone number anymore, but my sister must have it, so Matthew could notify her of any bar shifts he had for her.

Sure enough, I find it filed, not under 'T' for Temple, but 'M' for 'Matt'. I smirk when I see it. *Matthew has never been a Matt!* He answers within two rings.

'Calling me from India's phone – seriously?' Matthew's already guessed it must be me.

I sigh. 'Sorry. It was the only way.'

I imagine him on the other end: the muscles in his jaw taut, gripping the handset to his ear, his eyes closed. In my mind's eye, he is in the Hove flat, standing next to that old bay window we couldn't open. I know he can't live there anymore. I realise with a pang I don't know *where* Matthew lives. Above Elemental, perhaps? Or worse, he might live with another woman by now. My stomach lurches at the thought.

'What do you want?' Matthew's voice is still curt, but there's something else there too. It takes me a second to place it: uncertainty. He's conflicted.

I seize my chance. 'You know how computers work?'

We both know he does.

'I have to get inside India's blog. I need your help. Please?'

There's a pause as Matthew seems to think this over. I can hear music in the background. There's the unmistakable low roar of voices out on the lash. He must be in Elemental. Just as I feel certain he's about to ask me to come round with the laptop, his mental shutters come down.

'I'm busy.'

He hangs up. I gape at the handset, unable to believe it, my anger boiling up. *Twat.*

I cast my eye down the lists of indie computer shops on the iPad again. There are another two or three listed over the page. Going through the motions, with no other option, I stab another number into my phone. It rings … and rings.

Just as I'm about to hang up, a bored voice answers. 'Mike's Repairs.'

I stand outside Mike's manky shop, my arms weighed down by India's laptop. There's a grille on the dusty window, a variety of electronics arranged artlessly behind it. The lights are off and there's a CLOSED sign on the door. I attempt to open it, but it's locked.

The guy on the phone – Mike, presumably – wasn't keen on me coming today. He attempted to talk me through a basic jailbreak procedure, but everything he said made no sense to me. However, he soon changed his tune when I offered him an extra one hundred quid – in cash – for his trouble.

I ball up a fist and bash on the glass, making the rickety door shake. A light comes on inside. The door wrenches open. A tall, spindly man stands there, a look of unbridled irritation on his face. His age is impossible to tell: he could be as young as twenty-five, or as old as forty. He's wearing a checked lumberjack shirt that does not suit him at all. He'd look more at home in a neatly pressed jacket and tie, shined shoes.

'Mike?' I enquire.

'If you like.' He looks me up and down, then at the laptop in my hands. Something appears to click. 'Oh, it's you. From the phone.'

I smile, uncertain. 'That's me.'

He steps aside and waves me into his workshop. There's a large digital clock over the till; it reads 19:16 pm. I put the laptop on a workbench that's littered with circuit boards, wires and screwdrivers. Mike does not speak or even look at me. He sniffs loudly and gathers a selection of gadgets and gizmos. He plugs one of them into the USB socket of my sister's laptop.

I'm uncharacteristically nervous. 'What's that?'

Mike stares at the screen. A light comes on. His fingers fly across the keys. 'You wouldn't understand.'

I let his condescension go. 'It's important this laptop doesn't get fried…'

Mike gives me a look that could wither an oak tree to dust. He continues to tap on the keys for what feels like an age. The silence is a chasm between us. I crane my neck and look sideways to sneak a peak, but can glimpse only countless reams of code. It's not green and moving, like in *The Matrix* film, but it might as well be.

Then, the tell-tale, bell-like tone of the Intel processor; the machine starts up. I breathe a sigh of relief. *So I haven't completely broken the laptop, after all.*

Mike sniffs again. 'Do you need anything specific off this machine? Photos, music…?'

'A blog.'

'URL?'

I stand there, caught out.

He sighs at my ignorance. 'The website address?'

Why didn't you just say that in the first place?? I scream inside, but I keep my cool. '1NDIAsummer – one word – then, dot com. Oh yeah: The first 'i' is a number one and N, D, I, A in capitals.'

Mike goes back to tapping the keys. 'You want the email address and all the social-media profiles associated with the blog?'

'Yes please, everything you can.'

I look around the workshop as I wait. There is a bucket of broken games consoles; another full of old computer towers. Old-style ana-logue radios line a shelf near the window, even some old clock radios. I haven't seen one of those in years. I stop myself from reaching out and touching it, for fear of Mike throwing me out. All these things are probably his friends, his babies. I suddenly have an odd vision of him plugging in at night with all of them, his eyes black pools of streaming data, his mouth open in a perpetual hiss of white noise.

'OK … done.' Mike turns the laptop around, so I can see. If he's triumphant, it's on the inside only: his face is deadpan. 'So that's a hundred for the work, a hundred for me to open up; so two hundred, plus VAT. As agreed on the phone.'

I dig in my purse, pulling out the selection of notes I promised. As I do so, I look up at the clock over the till. It now reads 19:27 pm. *Just eleven minutes' work.*

I hand the wad of cash over without comment. He takes it and smooths out the notes, placing them in the cash register with an almost reverent air. Then he looks back at me, the intruder. His eyes narrow.

'Click the Yale back, on your way out, yeah?' He wanders out the back again, leaving me standing, alone, in the workshop.

Eighteen

Sleeping Beauty

Remember the dolls' house?

Homemade, like all the best things. Cardboard and wood. Two up, two down. Upstairs, a bathroom and a bedroom. A bath, a toilet with a lifting lid, harvested from an old Barbie set. A matchbox bed, with a carefully stitched duvet. A lamp and bedside cabinet made from lolly sticks. No stairs, the dolls jump from storey to storey. Like magic.

In the kitchen, a French dresser, curved and dainty, found at a tabletop sale for 25p. It was too big for the room, but we didn't care. A plastic sink, curtains, just scraps of material; a kitchen table made of another matchbox. Little plates, tiny knives and forks. A small sofa and matching armchair, real upholstery. A magazine rack, painted periodicals on display.

Everything was perfect. How we loved it! You said you were too old and only played with it for my sake. But I saw you, playing with it when you thought you were alone. I never said anything.

All kinds of things lived in that dolls' house, not just dolls. A pink dog with a small blue jumper. A green bird that had a little microphone and would sing back anything you told it. Then one year, a plastic frog from a Halloween party bag. Do you remember it? Red eyes, a squeaker in its belly. A rubber tube led to a bulb we'd hold in our hands: make froggy jump.

It's still here. In our perfect house. It's been here all along.

Can you see it?

India xxx

POSTED BY @**1NDIAsummer**, 15 December 2016
24,783 insights ⏎ **SHARE THIS**

> ⏎ ***Blithefancy*** added: *Indie, it will be OK xxx*
>
> ⏎ ***writerchic88*** likes this
>
> ⏎ ***heartsanddiamantes*** likes this
>
> ⏎ ***warriorwasp*** reblogged this from ***1NDIAsummer*** and added: *I need to send this out, you know who you are xx*
>
> ⏎ ***bushwhacker*** likes this
>
> ⏎ ***keel3y666*** says: *YAWN*
>
> > ⏎ ***Ariel_jewel*** replies to ***keel3y666:*** *do fuck off, troll*

Nineteen

'Wake up, Sleeping Beauty!'

It comes to me as I boil water for some microwave noodles. I want to try and tempt Mum to eat. She's been sitting in front of the television for hours – since coming down from the bedroom this morning. She didn't even react when I switched it off from across the room with the remote. She stared at her own reflection in the shine of the screen, her gaze directed at something only she can see.

As steam erupts from the kettle spout, like magic, India's with me again. She's about twelve and I'm a grumpy eighteen. My little sister, in those stripy green-and-black leggings she loved, jumping up and down on my bed. I'm still in it, groaning; my stomach lurches like the deck of a ship in choppy seas. I'm hungover; my head pounds and my mouth tastes sour and fuzzy – moisture has leached from my tongue as I slept, snoring open-mouthed.

'Go away!'

I throw the pillow at her. The night before, I was so drunk I fell into bed with my clothes and even my shoes still on. Eyeliner makes black smudges around my eyes and my hair is a bird's nest. I'm an utter sight. India cackles with glee as she torments me.

Ugly Sister is not about me!

Relief courses through my body. I snatch up the iPad from the kitchen table and re-read the Sleeping Beauty entry, reminding myself of its contents. I recognise the homemade dolls' house instantly. As children, we spent hours constructing it; collecting pieces for it from charity shops; making other bits ourselves from matchboxes and strips of corrugated cardboard. We saved scraps of material from Mum's sewing projects, shiny bits of foil from sweet wrappers and sandwiches. It was a work in progress for at least two years. What could have happened to it?

I take the stairs two at a time and appear on the landing. Up above, a hatch for the small crawl space that leads into the roof. I reach up for it, placing hooked fingers into the sides. It's difficult to get a purchase, especially as it has not been opened in ages. It gives with a sudden puff of dust and stale air. I shriek involuntarily as something long, skinny and black falls onto my shoulders – giant spider's legs. Then my brain catches up and I realise it's only a trail of tangled Christmas lights.

There's no ladder. Feeling reckless and impatient, I climb up on the banister. It's a precarious position. If I slip, I could windmill backwards and end up landing on my head. At best I could break a leg. But I don't let myself rake over the possibilities. I reach forward for the hatch, and, with an ungainly leap, I clamber up, into the small roofspace.

My legs still dangling down from the hatch, I allow my eyes to adjust to the gloom inside the tiny loft. I would not be able to stand in here. It's not big enough, plus there is no real floor. Boxes and bric-a-brac are balanced on the roof joists, yellow rolls of fibreglass cladding between each one. It smells damp, and the scent of old paper permeates everything. A box to the side of me is filled with old receipts and ring binders. Tim and Mum's accounts for the arcade.

Would Mum and Tim have kept the old dolls' house? I can see a box to the right of me, two joists away. Unlike the others, it is not marked BUSINESS. I can see some toys sticking out the top: an old rag doll, her face eaten by moths, slumbers on top of a bear with a fading red love-heart on its belly. As good a place to start as any.

Gingerly, I crawl across the joists. I don't know how well built these coach houses are; I'm afraid I might stick an arm straight through the ceiling of the room below. Reaching the box of toys, I pull out more teddies and dolls; a troll doll with rainbow hair; half a dozen coloured ponies with neon-coloured manes. A couple of action figures: Batman and the Joker, locked forever in an embrace.

A plastic house in the shape of a mushroom. A giant teapot, with round figurines inside. An old bath toy, with a swimmer who would dive out again if you filled it full of water.

I reach the bottom of the box. Thwarted, I sit back on my haunches. I squint in the gloom. Having shifted my vantage point, I note something directly in front of me. Balanced on a rafter, held together by a good amount of Sellotape, is the house my sister references in her Sleeping Beauty blog post.

In my excitement, I crawl towards it. The joist beneath me groans in an ominous fashion. I stop, but nothing happens. I cross the rest of the distance with caution and take the house down as if it were made of delicate china. It's not survived the test of time well. Much of our carefully chosen felt-tip, sweet-wrapper and foil décor has faded. But more than that, the house has been resurrected at least once: it looks like it has been crushed.

I don't know how I know this, but I can *feel* it: India was the last person to touch the dolls' house. She was the one who'd retrieved it from the toy box. She had placed it, out of harm's way, on the rafter. I open the front, sure the plastic frog India references in the post will be in there. My heart lifts in anticipation: *A message for me, from my sister beyond the grave.*

But there's nothing inside. My heart plummets again. Even our carefully made furniture is gone. I turn it upside down, just in case the plastic frog is caught inside it somewhere. Nothing falls, or even rattles.

I'm confused. Why would India write about the frog in this dolls' house? What did it matter? It's obvious there is some connection to the Frog King she references, too, in another post. But what? She must have felt it was as obvious to me as it was to her, but I am no closer to understanding what my sister is trying to tell me.

My eyes blur. I wipe away the tears with dusty fingers. I've let India down, all over again.

Twenty

At a loss, I return to the blog. Thanks to Mike, I'm no longer locked out of India's laptop, and all her passwords have been retrieved. He's even stored them for me. His technogeekery Kung Fu is strong. Guilt prickles at me again, but I tamp it down. Having access to my sister's own machine will help my search. It has to.

I click on an icon at the top of India's blog. I'm taken into the workings of the site, which calls itself 'the dashboard', like it's a car. I feel like I've moved inside my sister's mind.

I discover there are no more posts in the queue, waiting to be published, and no drafts. There are, however, comments pending, so I click on the comments icon. A dialogue box comes up right away. Again, mostly spam, entreating India to buy gold, watches or Viagra.

My eye drifts towards another comments column: 'approved'. Here there is a large variety of usernames. I've already noted that India's blog is popular. Its insights – likes, shares, comments and so on – regularly hit the thousands.

Who are these people? Where would I even start?

As I cast my eye down the list, I realise one name appears at the bottom of every single post, sometimes several times: Blithefancy.

I click on the user profile and am transported to a web page: www.blithefancy.com. There is no blog or writing. Instead there is a picture of a 'sugar skull' as made popular by the Mexican public holiday, the Day of The Dead, our All Saints' Day.

In the skull's mouth: a contact button. I click on it. Another pop-up appears so I rattle a short message off: 'How did you know my sister, India?'

Before I can back out, I press 'send'. I hope for a reply straight away, but I don't get one. I decide to wait.

Not sure what else to do, I gravitate back towards India's Facebook page, but there have been no auto-updates; it looks exactly the same.

Matthew's Facebook profile is just a click away, and I can't resist looking. His account is neglected; the last status dates back six months. If the Internet had tumbleweed, Matthew's digital space would be full of it.

I scroll backwards through his page anyway. He has been tagged in a few photos of nights out, an arm around one of his boys. Matthew always did like a party. I recognise the blue-neon décor of Elemental in a couple of them.

Ana is a different matter: Facebook and Twitter are her platforms of choice. Every event in her life, major and minor, is catalogued and commentated on in real time, with added hashtags and likes. I wonder where she gets the time.

I pause on a picture of Ana in a birthing pool, bright-eyed and triumphant. A grizzly newborn rests on her cleavage. So, my old friend is a mother now. I look at the date of the picture: about eighteen months ago. To the side, Maggie Temple kisses the side of Ana's head, eyes closed, a beatific smile on her face.

There follows a stream of proud-parent pictures: baby's first smile; first steps; first taste of ice cream. The child is a little girl with a strong resemblance to the Temple twins. I note her skin tone is much lighter than her mother's.

Ana's relationship status is noted as 'complicated'. I tap on it. I am taken to a picture of Ana about six months pregnant, with a white guy. *Figures.* Ana always idolised Alan, so it stands to reason she would try and find a man just like him.

Ana has a huge, ready smile for the camera and is pointing to her swollen belly with both index fingers, as if to say, *'OMG!'* Her joy seems at odds with the Ana I saw just days earlier, but then it *was* my sister's funeral.

My attention turns to Ana's beau. He has a mop of curly hair and a fuzzy beard, and he is tagged as 'Jayden Spence'. In the Facebook picture, Jayden has an arm draped around Ana's shoulders. His head is turned away from her. He's staring to the side of the picture, towards something just out of frame, a look of unbridled irritation on his face.

I recognise him, of course. Jayden is the only son and heir of Gordon Spence, owner of The Obelisk resort. He's a playboy and Z-List celebrity, even appearing in the nationals from time to time, falling drunk out of clubs where he was attending various passé stars' birthdays. There was even a rumour Jayden would be appearing on some game show where they bury sleb wannabes and has-beens up to their necks in ants and cockroaches. For a price, of course. Jayden loves money just like the rest of the Spence family.

But it's more than that. Taking in his unruly mop of hair, his broad shoulders and slim waist, I feel even more certain it was Jayden at the cemetery on the day of India's funeral. Though he was in the distance and wearing shades, Jayden was tall, striking. He dug one hand in his trouser pocket, held a cigarette with the long, tapered fingers of the other. *But why would Jayden have been there?*

I sit back in my sister's chair as I consider this revelation. Alan Temple is a property magnate in Brighton, making his fortune buying up social housing and even building new developments. Alan has every reason to want to see his firm, Temple Construction, strongly linked to The Obelisk's first family. Could Alan have engineered this romantic partnership between his daughter and Spence?

I look through the rest of Ana's photo albums, but there are no more pictures of her and Jayden. Jayden is well known in the city; it would take a lot to make him settle down. And Ana's relationship status – 'complicated' – perhaps indicates that a child has not prompted him to do so. Maybe this has made Alan's life difficult, too?

It seems the baby is not Ana's only photographic obsession on Facebook. She's taken photo after photo of her twin brother, too. There are portraits of Matthew at Christmas; plus Matthew on their birthday, the fourth of April. Here's a picture of both of them as kids, arms around each other, like one person. There's Matthew laughing and putting his hand up, attempting to block the lens as if his sister is paparazzi.

I stop on one. In this, he is somehow diminished in comparison to the other photos. His skin waxy, Matthew sits on a hospital bed, next to Maggie. His eyes are closed, his shoulders slumped. His body language screams despair. Matthew leans his head towards his mother and she attempts to wrap her arms around him as if he is a little child, even though he is twice her size.

Maggie Temple is the type of mother I always wished *I* had. Warm, caring, dependable, she seemed so different to our reserved, yet mercurial mother. Though the twins would sometimes complain of Maggie's interference, they always knew there was nothing she would not do for her family. She left them in no doubt of that.

That day baby India came home from the hospital, when everyone had eyes only for my sister, it was *me* Maggie had sought out. She found me slumped on the stairs. She sat next to me on the second to last step, her face a picture of commiseration. Maggie Temple seemed to be the only person in the universe who understood – *or cared!* – how I felt on that first day.

Underneath the Facebook photo, Ana has added, 'You can do it little bro xxx'. Ana never lets Matthew forget she is three minutes older than him. Underneath the photo, there are over two hundred likes and probably half as many comments, echoing her. I click away from the album hurriedly, turning my attention back to my search.

I scroll through the statuses and comments on India's Facebook profile again, looking for JoJo's name, but she is conspicuous by her absence, both in the threads and in India's photo albums. I attempt to call up JoJo's name, to no avail, so I Google her full name and 'Facebook'. Her profile pops up immediately.

That's when it dawns on me: *India is blocked!* But why?

I close the laptop, grab India's phone and scroll through the contacts. As I suspected, JoJo is not listed.

So they must have fallen out. Perhaps that's all JoJo meant when she said she shouldn't have come to the funeral.

I have to ask JoJo herself.

Twenty-one

The Musgrave family home is a low-rise flat in Whitehawk, only two or three streets away from the Coach House. People are back at work, though the anticipation of New Year's Eve celebrations and tomorrow's holiday hangs in the air. The sun retreats behind a low band of grey cloud. It gives the green outside the flats an ominous look.

JoJo's mother, Cerise, stands at the fence by the bus stop outside the block. A rotund woman with a short, apple-shaped body and freakishly skinny legs, Cerise Musgrave is a Rottweiler of a woman: primed and ready to go, any time of the day or night. Behind her, three of her younger kids play on the green. They hang off graffitied play equipment, dressed in coats and scarves. Underneath, a mangy-looking dog barks happily at them.

I make my way towards Cerise. I am apprehensive. Cerise grabs the label 'chav' and wears it as a badge of honour. She considers attack the best form of defence. And her potential for violence is matched only by her fierce cunning. I can recall a time Cerise turned up at the the Coach House to 'talk' to my mother when India and JoJo were about eight. The two girls had had a falling-out about something at school. My sister and JoJo made up within minutes, yet Tim still had to drag Cerise off my mother. Ever since, Mum has always sent Tim to the door first.

Cerise's round, pasty face is more wrinkled than when I last saw her. For the first time, I realise with a thud that she is closer to my age than my mother's. I can smell she is smoking a joint, right out there in the open, but downwind from her kids. Whatever I might think of her, Cerise prides herself on being a good mother.

She doesn't even look up at me. 'You can jog right on.'

'I want to see JoJo.'

'Well, she don't wanna see you.'

Cerise does not move. The cherry on the end of her joint glowers at me. The dog seems to sense the hostility emanating from his mistress and he barrels across the frosty green to her side, ears pricked up, awaiting instruction.

I choose my words with care. 'I just want to ask her something.'

Cerise throws her finished joint down. She whistles. I think it's some sort of bizarre tactic to unnerve me, but seconds later, her kids come running. Two boys and another girl. They glare at me, arms folded, picking up on the vibe straight away.

It takes me a moment to place them. I'm shocked to see Kelly-Anne, JoJo's younger sister. She's about eleven or twelve now, with the underdeveloped, lithe form of a gymnast. Her two younger brothers, Robbie and Mickey, were just babies when I left, born in quick succession in the same year; 'Irish twins', Tim would call them (*slang; offensive*). Now they're a tough-looking twosome. I recall there's another couple of older lads, too. They're hard nuts, like Cerise, so I'm glad they're not here right now. JoJo is the eldest. She's always seemed softer than the rest of the Musgraves, somehow.

Now I wonder if there's something to that.

'OK, how about I ask you?' Before Cerise rejects the idea outright, I add: 'It's for India.'

Something changes between us, I'm not sure what. It's like someone lets the air out of the older woman. Cerise meets my gaze, one pierced eyebrow raised, as if she appreciates my chutzpah, even if I am otherwise pathetic to her. *Go on*, her gesture seems to say.

'You call JoJo by a different name these days?'

Cerise's expression sours. She rolls her eyes at me. The answer in her mind is clearly in the negative, followed by a few expletives, but the kids are with her so she says nothing.

I continue. 'Does JoJo like to be called Jenny?'

Cerise takes a sharp intake of breath, which descends into a hacking cough. I take this as an affirmative. But seconds later, the older woman dashes my hopes.

'No.' Cerise clicks her fingers at the kids and the dog. They all turn, grumbling, towards the block of flats. 'Look, JoJo don't need the trouble, alright?'

'So there *was* trouble. Between my sister and JoJo?' I confirm. 'What was it about? Please, let me talk to her.'

Cerise looks at me, puzzled and irritated. 'She ain't here.'

I persist. 'When will she be back?'

'She won't. She's too good for us now.' There's a faraway look in Cerise's eyes, suggesting pain. She dampens it quickly, not the type to show vulnerability. *Just like my mother.*

'Where does she live now?'

Cerise watches her kids file into the block. 'JoJo's made something of herself. She don't need you digging around what's past, especially when she's worked so hard to distance herself from all … *that.*'

'All what? Cerise, please!'

But Cerise turns her back on me. She shuffles across the green, ignoring my shouts after her. I give up, watch her disappear inside. As she goes, I realise with a start what I saw flitter across her rigid features as she regarded me, possibly for the first time in her ferocious life.

Pity.

Twenty-two

The Coach House is quiet as I let myself in, bar the noise of Tim loading the dishwasher. I can't see Mum anywhere. I hover on the kitchen threshold. Tim stares out the window. His expression is glassy, like he could shatter any second. He snaps to attention as I amble in, wipes the sink, spraying it with antibacterial cleaner, even though I've done it only that morning.

He offers me a too-wide smile. 'Hello, love.'

He'll ask me in a moment if there's anything I want, anything he can do for me. He could cook me some eggs; fetch me a glass of water? Men like Tim want to look after women, help them, comfort them. It's how they feel useful, needed. Even as a rebellious teenager, angry at the world, I loved how safe Tim made me feel. He was always *just there*, ready to make tea or dispense hugs.

Right on cue: 'So, when's term starting? Next week? Do you need me to drop you at the station?'

'About that.' Embarrassment makes the room grow warm. I've managed to avoid the subject before now; it hardly seemed important. Another flash of that night I was out drowning my sorrows while my sister lay dying pierces through me.

Tim's gaze settles on my face, and he understands immediately.

'You lost your job?' His brow furrows. 'But I thought you were at that school until Easter?'

Yes, me, too. I shrug. 'Cutbacks, I guess. Last in, first out.'

Now Tim sighs, his hands massaging his forehead. 'You should sue them, it must be breach of contract or something.'

'Doesn't work that way for supply teachers.' I keep my voice light, trying to change the subject. 'Anyway … I've managed to get into India's laptop.'

But Tim's glum demeanour deepens. He sits down in a chair, eyes screwed shut. His body is rigid with stress. I've never seen him respond in such a fashion. He stays quiet, so I break the silence.

'I'm going to find out what happened to India.'

Tim speaks through gritted teeth. 'We *know* what happened to India.'

I can feel the hard edge in his voice but still feel compelled to make him understand. 'No. We don't. India wouldn't kill herself, she—!'

Tim jumps up from his chair as I say this. He takes the two or three steps across the small kitchen, invading my body-space. I flinch away from him, shocked. My stepfather has never laid a hand on me in the twenty-five years I've known him; he's barely even shouted. Yet in that instant I feel certain he is going to grab me by the shoulders. *Is he going to shake some sense into me?*

Then, at the last possible moment, he stops himself. His voice drops several notes with shame. But he still makes his appeal.

'Poppy, *please*. Think of your mother.'

I recover my nerve. 'I *am* thinking of my mother. We all deserve the truth!'

Tim's eyes look skywards. He shakes his head, as if he cannot believe what he's hearing or I am a lost cause. *Maybe both.*

He steps away from me and leans on the counter, as if he can't support his own weight. Seizing my chance, I take the stairs from the kitchen two at a time, towards my room on the third floor.

On the landing, I glance sideways towards my parents' bedroom. The door is open. Mum, so active before the funeral, now lies on the bed. She's fully clothed, facing the wall. I go into the room, expecting her to sit up. She doesn't.

'Mum?'

She doesn't stir. Perhaps she is asleep. I negotiate around the bed, towards her side. I see her eyes are open. She's staring at the wall, her lips mumble something I can't hear. *Lost in the past.*

'Oh, Mum.'

I sit down on the end of the bed. I put one hand on her leg. She's wearing tan tights; there is the static feel of nylon under my fingertips. More tears well up behind my eyes, that familiar stab of pain in my throat.

'I *will* find out what happened to India.' I repeat, hoping this might pique her interest, if only to have a go at me, like Tim did. But Mum does not move, nor give any indication she knows I'm there.

I get up and drift towards my own room.

As I go, I feel the familiar vibrating tingle in my pocket: India's phone. I snatch it out, hoping it is Jenny.

It's an email notification. I open the inbox, expecting yet more spam. I stare for a second, hardly able to take in the username. There is no subject line, because I had not specified one. It is a reply to my question, 'How did you know my sister, India?'

The email is from Blithefancy.

I press my finger on the screen, opening the message. The pessimist in me expects it to be bad news. Perhaps Blithefancy didn't know India in real life. Maybe she or he just read India's blog. It *has* to be yet another dead end, doesn't it?

It takes me a moment to decipher the real message, versus the semantic noise in my brain. I take in the words, at last:

'Quicker to explain in person. Am in Brighton too. Meet me @ the Prince Albert, tonite, 9 pm (or as close as I can make it 2 then). I WILL be there.'

I do not hesitate. I tap out a reply straight away, hoping my response gets through before Blithefancy logs off again: 'See you soon.'

Twenty-three

New Year's Eve. I am dressed up. It feels wrong, going out like this, just days after my own sister's funeral. But I've watched enough detective movies to know I need to blend in at the Prince Albert. It's a well-known meat market and dive of a pub, between Kemptown and The Lanes. I recall going there as a teenager: it was frequented by horny teens looking for hook-ups back then.

So I've raided India's wardrobe again. Even though it makes no sense, I haven't wanted to take more of India's stuff than I need to. I arrived without luggage, and I've not managed – or rather, felt like – going shopping for more clothes. So I've taken a few pairs of my sister's leggings, Mum being so much shorter than me.

Now, I discover India developed a taste for the flamboyant and punky in my absence. Some of the garments still have the tags attached, never worn, bought from online alternative clothing stores. There are dresses with rips cut out of them, plus tops and skirts held together with safety pins and buckles. Shoes with heels you could break your neck in. If India went to the Albert with Blithefancy, then this must be the type of thing you wear to a place like that nowadays.

I am relieved to find my options are limited. Though India and I are – *were* – of similar heights, I am considerably broader across the shoulders and fuller in the bust, like our mother. What's more, my feet are way too big for any of India's insanely high heels. My own boots will have to suffice.

Eventually I find a red tartan mini-skirt with chains hanging down from the belt loops. I team it with a black vest top that has a zip across the bust. I unzip its teeth: sure enough, my cleavage is on display. I regard myself in my sister's full-length mirror. I stifle a laugh. I look ridiculous. *I am too old for this shit.*

I pull the clothes off again and find a silver-grey mini-dress at the back of the wardrobe. It's made of t-shirt material, and, like everything these days, is decorated with sequins – more a day dress than one for going on the pull – but I'm past caring. Maybe I can jazz it up.

I pull the dress over my head. As I'm a larger build than India, it's much more figure-hugging, but that works. I grab some of India's make-up, slapping on some foundation, some silver eye shadow. She only has bright-red lipstick, but that's a bridge too far for me, so I slick on some salve instead.

As an afterthought, I grab India's black kohl eyeliner and ring my eyes with it. We shared a similar colouring, so I brush my hair into a knot on the top of my head, tying a scarf around it in a bow as I've seen her do. From a distance, I could *be* India. That will help Blithefancy to recognise me.

I pull on one of India's old leather jackets. I note there is a sugar skull painted on the back. It must have been too big for her, because it fits me perfectly.

Blithefancy can't miss me.

The night over the city is starless; cloud obscures the sky. My boots crunch on the frost on the ground as I make my way towards the seafront. As I progress, I can hear bells on the pier; the sound of pennies cascading into the slots; the buzzer of the ghost train shrieks. The tide laps the pebbly shore below.

Matthew said once that, if you're ever lost in Brighton, you don't need to look. All you have to do is walk downhill and you'll always end up by the beach. When I was fifteen and he was nearly eighteen, we'd gone on our first date – *to Gay Pride, of all things* – and got separated. I didn't have a mobile phone back then, so I spent ages looking for Matthew among the riot of colour and people on stilts that is the procession and after-party in the park.

After an hour of searching, I remembered Matthew's advice. I made my way downhill, sure by now I'd never find him. Yet there he was, waiting under the archway, hands in his pockets, the big yellow letters of Brighton Pier over his head. Now, I can see teens milling about there, the next generation, unaware and uncaring about what's gone before. Why should they? *No time like the present.*

I turn down a side street. I can see the Prince Albert straight away. It's changed. The outside of the building is decorated with specially commissioned graffiti, forming a rainbow even in the dim evening light. On one of the walls is the bar's Twitter username in neon paint, surrounded by stars and hearts. The pub is sandwiched between a shop with its shutters down and a bar that Australian ex-pats frequent. I hear their accents, harsh and twanging in the cold air, as I stalk past.

After two or three minutes, I'm at the head of the queue. A small female bouncer appears in front of me. She's wearing a suit, her earpiece looped around her tiny neck. She's shorter than I am, Korean descent, maybe, with a buzz cut.

She looks me up and down with obvious appreciation. 'So. Not seen you here before?'

I flash her a dazzling smile. 'My first time.'

She smirks. 'We'll be gentle with you.'

She holds out both hands. I realise she wants to check my bag. I undo the clasp and show her I have no contraband. She nods, waves me in.

Inside, I discover there are two areas. The first looks like I remember it: an old soak's bar, smelling of beer and old cigarettes. There's some beaten-up leather sofas, along with scarred oak tables, chairs and booths.

But that's where the similarity ends. There's more graffiti on the walls, plus plastic-flower garlands lining the bay window. Elaborate curtains have been fashioned around a giant TV screen, which is off. Rainbow flags are strung up across the room, looping around the bar and over the pool table. EuroPop plays loud. A sculpted Adonis pulls pints, rather than shaking cocktails like Tom Cruise.

Everywhere are seated couples. Many of them with their heads close together, so they can each hear what the other is saying, or steal a kiss on the sly. I don't fail to notice the vast majority of the couples are the same gender.

So the Prince Albert is an LGBT joint now.

My eye settles on a corkboard near the bar. On it, flyers for cabaret acts, Gay Pride events and various support groups. At the top of the board, someone has scrawled a handwritten message, just in case any tourist barflies still don't get it:

'We're here. We're queer. And we will serve you beer!'

If I'm surprised, it's not because it's an LGBT bar. I've lived in Brighton most of my life. I've grown up seeing same-sex couples together: in the street, on posters, carved in sculptures and emblazoned as public art. Brighton has led the way for LGBT-friendly spaces, so it stands to reason this community continues to expand.

What surprises me is that India was frequenting a place like this. I feel certain I never had any hint my sister could be gay. I cast my mind back. I recall she brought boyfriends to the house when she was a teenager. But maybe those boys were a phase. Or maybe India was bisexual. *How the hell would I know?*

I move through the first bar, weaving my way past tables and chairs. A couple of people look up and smile as if they recognise me; but then avert their eyes when they realise I am not who they think I am. *India, no doubt.* Good. Blithefancy *will* find me.

I reach the door to the second bar. I push on it. I discover it's a fire door and soundproof. A wave of loud music hits me in the chest as I cross the threshold.

The beat feels like it's travelling the length of the floor, enveloping me in a ball of noise. My ears ring. I suppress another laugh. *I really am getting too old for this shit.*

After taking a moment to acclimatise, I drift around the room. My eyes alight on everything in it. The back wall is all mirrors, to give the impression that the bar is bigger than it is. On the stage, an impressively tall drag queen lip-syncs to a Kylie song; the audience lap it up. Faces blur in the darkness, contrasting with the tiny glittering spotlights of the giant disco ball overhead.

A young boy, fresh-faced, just out of his teens, walks towards me. He smiles. As he draws nearer, I realise he is perhaps in his early twenties ... and female. Her build is small, diminutive. She gives me a lazy smile. A chancer.

'Buy you a drink?' She has to speak right into my ear, so I can hear. She smells spicy and definitively masculine, but her skin is smooth, like porcelain.

I smile. 'I'm not into women.'

My admirer scowls. 'I'm *not* a woman!'

I realise my error. 'I'm sorry...'

But my admirer has already turned away, my words snatched by the pounding music.

I feel a finger poke me in the small of my back. It's what India always used to do to get my attention. I swing around, sure for a dumb moment my sister is standing behind me. In that instant India is alive to me and I'm so glad to see her.

But of course it's not her.

It's another young woman. She's shorter than me, but much skinnier. I notice her clothes are a little baggy. She's wearing a black top with bell sleeves, plus a long black skirt slightly on the big side. Like mine, her eyes are ringed with kohl. She has added a black teardrop under one eye, a spider web drawn crudely on her other cheek. She's wearing black lipstick to match, and a long red wig that looks like doll's hair.

'Blithefancy?'

The goth girl nods. She has pale, brown-gold eyes under her pasty white make-up. She hesitates, then indicates with a hand we should go through to the other bar. I see her lips move, but her words are snatched away by the music.

'Come with me,' she is saying.

Twenty-four

On the dashboard, his mobile vibrates, the LED shining upwards, creating patterns of light on the windscreen. *She Who Must Be Obeyed* again. He grits his teeth, ignores it. She can wait.

For once.

He turns his car down the dark street. Parks, avoiding streetlamps directly overhead. He has the perfect spot. Cloaked in shadows inside the car, facing away from the venue, he can take in the scene via his rearview mirror. The building is bathed in orange light, revealing all. Out the front, a big bouncer and a much smaller Korean woman, also in black tie, wait. Both their faces are impassive.

The Prince Albert pub.

He jumps as a carouser outside slams both hands on the windscreen. The guy is bearded, yet wears a dress, a feather boa around his broad shoulders. Sensing his antagonism, the bearded man utters a hearty chuckle, audible through the glass. His companion attempts to peel him away.

Inside the car, he pulls a face, then makes an obscene hand gesture at the reveller. *Fucking queers.* The reveller finally shuffles off with his boyfriend, a tall, thin waif of a lad, bare, tattooed arms and eye-wateringly skinny jeans. They meander towards a small queue of similarly dressed attention-seekers.

Tension pulls his body into angular shapes. Sensing the stress in his forearms as he grips the wheel, he lets go and flexes both hands. His wrists roll with a satisfying *crack*. He does the same with his shoulders, limbering up. He's had to do this so many times; there's no telling how it might go. He waits for the queue to clear a little more, then gets out of his car.

He presses the key fob as he goes, the alarm chirrups behind him.

He strides across the road, his sights on the Prince Albert. He barely flinches as he's almost knocked down by a student on a pushbike with no lights, who swears at him. This draws the eye of the lady bouncer, who, despite being literally half his size, squares up to him, her arms in front of her in a mock 'street' pose.

'Hey … it's Ken! Lost Barbie, honey?'

'Outta my way.'

The Korean bouncer kisses her teeth. 'Y'see, that's not the way it works.'

She indicates her brick shithouse of a partner behind her, who appears in his full view for the first time. He doesn't remember seeing him before; he must be new. He's surprised to find himself looking up at him. With his height, that doesn't happen often. The doorman is huge.

He regards both door people, deadpan, his fury hidden as always. 'You want money, that it?'

He makes a show of taking a money clip from his back pocket. He waves the roll of notes at both of them: *How much?*

The Korean flashes him her pearly whites. 'How about … a million?'

He sighs. 'Now you're being ridiculous.'

'Then no deal, hombre, piss off!' The Korean sweeps her hands to the left, gestures for him to step aside.

Behind him, he can hear the renewed babble of intrigued voices. He doesn't turn around to look at the freaks and queens. Instead he meets the eye of the male bouncer, who has not spoken once, yet has not moved his gaze.

'You like a lady boss? Figures.'

The door to the pub is agonisingly close. Maybe if he can get the big man to swing a punch his way, he can duck under and squeeze through.

'You a giver? Nah, a receiver, I can tell. Pillow-biter.'

But the doorman shrugs. 'Hey, don't knock it 'til you've tried it, love.'

There is a chorus of guffaws and heckles behind him now. He knows when he's beaten. Grudging, he moves aside, allowing two women holding hands to wander past. One gives him a mock-sympathetic smile. She takes a paper flower from her hair and attempts to tuck it behind his ear. Exasperated, he bats her hand away. The decoration falls to the pavement. She and her girlfriend seem to find this hysterical.

'Chill out, fella. Life's a lot more fun,' she advises, before disappearing through the glass doors.

Ever the opportunist, he surges forward after her. He hopes to slip through, before the male doorman can grab him.

It's not to be. A meaty hand grabs his left arm. He throws a right hook in response that finds only air; the other guy dodges it with ease. The doorman pushes his left arm up behind his back, almost between his shoulder blades. He bares his teeth in pain, but refuses to cry out. It's been a long time since he's been beaten in a fight; even longer since he was bested straight off the starting blocks. He flinches in expectation of another blow.

But the male doorman does not kidney punch him as he expects. The huge bruiser pushes him forwards. He falls to his knees, arse in the air, prostrate. He throws both arms out to steady himself before his forehead connects with the bumper of a car parked near the kerb-side. Cue more laughter behind him.

'I like him better like that,' the Korean bouncer quips.

Adrenaline and embarrassment flooding through him now, he stands, brushing his jeans down. He does not look behind him, at the goading faces. He sucks in the night air, attempting to calm himself.

In his pocket his mobile rings. He pulls it out, not even bothering to check; he knows who the caller is, after all. But his thumb finds 'reject', followed by the 'off' button. As the phone powers down, he resolves to go home. He can deal with her wrath another day. *Fuck this shit!*

He stalks back to his car.

Twenty-five

Frog King

I dream when I am awake. Do you?

In my dream, I chase a golden ball across a meadow. In its green centre, a pond. There is a name written on the ball. I know I will need to catch the ball to read it. But every time I reach for it, it strays out of my grasp. My treacherous foot kicks it ahead of me in the dew-laden grass.

The golden ball hits the pond in the meadow's centre, creating ripples on the top of the stagnant water. The pond looks so beautiful, but now I've disturbed the surface I can smell the rot: sweet, stomach-churning bile in the air.

He brings it back.

Wide facetious smile, pebbly skin. He's smaller than me, yet his strength undulates through his forearms. He is not to be underestimated. He is unpredictable, despite his size.

He clenches the ball in his webbed hands, curious at my desire for it. The name on the ball is turned towards him, so I still can't read it. Frustration courses through me, but I force myself to smile.

He doesn't know why I want it so badly. He is oblivious, unaware of his place in all this. Which gives me courage.

'Give it to me, now,' I demand. My voice is loud and clear, like the fresh water in the nearby brook that I can hear, but not see.

His smile vanishes. He spits out the words, each one dropping from his amphibian lips like acid. I feel them on my skin, burrowing into my flesh like maggots.

'They'll never let her go.'

India

POSTED BY **@1NDIAsummer**, 10 December 2016

36,559 insights ↲ **SHARE THIS**

   ↲ **_writerchic88_** likes this

   ↲ **_Emz2011_UK_** likes this

   ↲ **_markotron_** likes this

   ↲ **_Alfie98_** likes this

   ↲ **_warriorwasp_** likes this

   ↲ **_Milliecat_456_** likes this

      ↲ **_Blithefancy_** likes this & reblogs this from 1NDIAsummer, adding: _my shining name!_

   ↲ **_lilyrose06_** likes this

Twenty-six

Grateful, I follow Blithefancy back into the front bar. Though the music seemed loud in here when I came in from the street, compared to next door it now feels sedate. The soundproof door swings shut behind us, muffling the decibels in the room beyond. I breathe a sigh of relief. *Yep, I'm old.*

Blithefancy leads me to a booth at the side of the room, near the bay window. The young woman then sits opposite me, her hands folded primly in front of her on the table. I don't remember to ask her if she wants a drink. Courtesy, consideration, all other thoughts go out the window.

'So. You're Jenny?'

She opens her mouth, but no sound comes out. She nods, instead.

I get straight to the heart of the matter. 'You were my sister's girlfriend?'

'No!' Jenny seems shocked by this idea. Then she remembers I have no clue who she is, or what's been going on. 'We were ... close. But not romantically.'

I absorb this. Jenny's golden-brown eyes contrast with the pasty-white make-up she's wearing. She is a classic beauty: high cheekbones; square jawline leading to a dainty chin.

'How did you meet?'

'We've known each other a long time.' Jenny's pronunciation is particular. Her vowels and consonants are rounded, almost studied. I wonder if I can hear the trace of an accent there, but I'm unsure. My memory stirs, bringing with it an old adage: *The rain in Spain falls mainly on the plain.*

'How long?'

'I don't know … a long time. Since we were kids.' Jenny grabs a beer mat and starts shredding it with her long nails.

'She never brought you to the house.' I'm sceptical, but I try and keep my tone level, neutral. She must not think I am accusing her of anything. I don't want her to clam up.

'My mother didn't approve.' Jenny continues to tear the beer mat in front of her.

I'm confused. 'Of you?'

Jenny meets my eye again. 'Of India.'

If I expected that talking to this enigma would bring me insight, somehow now I feel even more lost. I mull over Jenny's words.

'So India *was* gay?'

Jenny rolls her eyes. 'Either/or is all you people understand. Only ever two options. Male or female. Gay or straight. Why not both? Why not none?'

You people. Irritation prickles me, but I let it go. I know how words can trigger and cajole a reaction from others; I've seen it many times, in my classroom. Jenny is mining for one from me. But I won't give her the satisfaction.

I attempt to change the subject, back to the matter in hand. 'Was it you, on India's voicemail? The night she died?'

Jenny's mood sours abruptly, like Matthew's did on the phone when I asked him to help me jailbreak my sister's laptop. 'Yes.'

'"You shouldn't have waited for me," you said. What did you mean by that?'

Jenny sighs. She moves one fingernail to her eye. She remembers her elaborate make-up, is careful not to smudge it. 'I was supposed to meet her that night.'

'Where?'

'At Brighton station!' There's something unpredictable about Jenny. She turns her attention towards those around us, as if she's bored of me. 'If we couldn't meet here, we'd go there. But that night I missed her.'

I press on. 'Did she seem suicidal, when you saw her last?'

'No!' Jenny seems outraged at the thought.

I take advantage. 'She'd been prescribed antidepressants and was referred to a psychiatrist. Did she tell you that?'

Anger overtakes Jenny. 'She was not suicidal!' She leans towards me, resentment etched on her pale face. '*You* weren't here. India was fine. I *know*.'

'I believe you.' I reply.

Jenny's scornful expression softens. She seems relieved to be taken seriously. She takes a deep, juddering breath. 'I miss her.'

'Me, too.'

Instinctively, I reach forward, place my hand on hers. She leaves it there for a moment, her eyes focused on something far beyond our booth. 'They don't understand.'

'Who don't?'

She's back with me. Jenny's eyes stare at me and she shivers, before averting her gaze once more. Then, as if embarrassed, or not used to contact, Jenny jerks her hand away from mine. She places it in her lap under the table.

'India was murdered.'

She mutters the words so quietly, I barely trust my own ears. At first I think I have misheard. I've wanted to hear these words since I came back. I open my mouth, accusations on my tongue. How can I trust this girl? Suspicion, dark and red, floods through me. Maybe Jenny knows India was murdered because *she* was the one who pushed her from the bridge!

'How do you know that?' I demand.

Jenny's pale-brown eyes meet mine again. Her tone is incredulous. She can't believe she has to say it. 'Because India would never kill herself?'

I sigh. 'Sorry. I know. It's just … I worry it might be because of me.'

Now the words are out there. I can't unsay them. *This is my fault.* The ugly thought that bloomed in my brain the night I found out about my sister's death has now taken root. It's sent out spores into my chest, grasping my heart and throttling it.

I was the one who caused the rift between us. *Could India have been so lonely she could have taken her life?* I cast my eyes downwards in shame. I expect the mercurial Jenny to tell me to stop thinking about myself.

But Jenny is distracted. Adonis appears at our table. He leans down, whispers something in her ear. Jenny's eyes widen. She grabs her bag, pulling her long red wig from her head and shoving it inside. Underneath, her hair is black, poker-straight and shoulder-length. It's only a little shorter than my own.

'I have to go.' Jenny hurries out the booth, her hair a shield over her made-up pale face.

'Wait!'

But she turns away from me. I watch her go over to the bar with Adonis, his hand at the small of her back. He pulls up the bar hatch and lets Jenny through. She disappears out the back.

Adonis turns on his heels and tends to other patrons at the bar, his wide, innocent smile on display. Like nothing has happened.

Confused, I look towards the bay window. Through the flower garlands, I can see a fracas outside.

A small crowd has gathered. I can see the Korean bouncer laughing, her breath steaming. The male doorman surges forward, but then dips out of my sightline. I stand, but beyond the glass, yet more people gather, obscuring my view. I can hear muffled jeers. I wait a few more moments, but as the small crowd disperses, whatever they were looking at disappears as well.

No one is waiting for a drink as I approach the counter. Adonis's attention is on me straight away.

'What can I get you?' He smiles, but I'm aware he's cagey. His eyes flit all over me, trying to size me up.

I don't order. 'Jenny a friend of yours?'

He doesn't miss a beat. 'She's a regular, yes.'

Adonis leans on the bar like Matthew did at Elemental. He's perhaps as tall as Matthew, but that's where the similarity ends. This guy is white, thinner, slighter, blue-eyed, blonde. His hair is carefully sculpted and gelled, a crew cut. Both his arms are heavily tattooed. They're not scrawled, hand-drawn prison tats like the big doorman's outside, but vibrant with colour and detail.

'Jenny here a lot, then?'

'As often as she can.' Adonis picks up a hose and squirts some soda water into a glass.

'So you would have seen my sister with her?'

Now I finally have the barman's attention. He regards me with those baby blues. He clocks the dress I'm wearing, or perhaps he finally realises the family resemblance. I see in his eyes what I saw in Cerise's: *pity*.

'Sometimes,' he admits. He drinks. He holds the tumbler like it's a champagne flute, pinky finger extended. *It's so hot in here.*

I'm surprised. 'Not every time?'

Adonis shakes his head. I'm about to ask another question: about why he helped Jenny escape, or where she went. But a couple of customers come up behind me. Adonis's gaze flits to them as they bark drink orders over the noise. He turns his back to me, so he can serve them.

An impulse grabs me. I take a quick look around, ensuring no one's attention is on me. Then, as Adonis leans down to grab something towards the opposite end of the bar, I duck under the counter hatch without opening it.

I speed through before anyone sees me, into the back room.

Twenty-seven

I don't know what I'm expecting to find.

It's a small kitchenette. There's a fire exit directly opposite. It's not alarmed. I open it to see what's out there. Behind the building, there is a deserted car park. As I could have predicted, Jenny is nowhere to be seen. *Long gone.*

I let the fire exit close shut again, remaining inside the back room. My eyes dart around, taking the place in. To my left, there's a food-preparation area and a sink. A selection of mops and brushes stand next to it. On the counter in front of me, a plate and cup rack, plus an industrial-sized glass washer. Its metal lid stands up, empty, waiting to be loaded and set off again. To my right, there's a large bottle of hand wash, some tubs of cleaning chemicals, plus two catering-sized drums of tea and coffee, as well as a couple of crates of mixers. On the wall is a selection of the staff's coats and bags.

Then I spot it.

A black bag shoved in between two large boxes of crisps, near the sink. On the side of it: a local gym's name. It might be Adonis's. He would have to work out a lot to maintain that physique. Maybe I can find out something about him, his connection to Jenny.

I can hear Adonis's hearty laugh from out front. I should have a few moments yet. Hurrying, I grab the bag and unzip it. There's a crumpled wad of black clothes inside. I pull them out, expecting a tracksuit or similar. But it's not.

It's a black top with bell sleeves. A long black maxi skirt. Perilously high heels. And that long red wig, like doll's hair.

Jenny's.

I don't have time to puzzle this out. Adonis opens the door to the kitchenette. Caught in the act, I freeze where I am.

But the barman's head is turned away from me. He's still deep in conversation with someone in the bar itself. Not seeing me, he moves back towards the voice, letting go of the door. It swings back, leaving me alone again.

That was close.

I know I won't be so lucky a second time. I shove Jenny's clothes back in the bag, returning it to where I found it. I race to the fire exit and slip out, just as the kitchenette door opens again. *Phew.*

Outside, I run away from the Prince Albert, across the car park. I pause as I make it back to the front of the club again, unseen. I stop, panting and exhilarated. Standing in the biting night air, I feel a surge of adrenaline coursing its way through my veins. I'm almost woozy with it.

Jenny is real.

I thought uncovering this fact would bring me an answer. In a way, it has: like me, Jenny thinks India didn't kill herself. It feels good to be taken seriously, even if Jenny has no more proof than I do. But I don't believe that.

I'm certain Jenny knows more.

I dodge drunks in fancy dress (and in various states of undress) as I amble downhill. All around me, Brighton erupts with New Year's Eve party-goers. I remember Matthew's emotionless face in the churchyard after India's funeral, but somehow I still want to tell him my news.

Elemental looks different at night. I wander inside, pushing against warm bodies as I go. People peer at me as I shift past. A couple of men smile at me. I take no notice.

The bar is busy; New Year's Eve is one of Brighton's most popular nights outside of the main season. The black lights are on, making everything white shine luminously; teeth and t-shirts and jewellery are bright in the dim, blueish-tinged darkness.

I make it out of the crush near the door into an empty space by the bar. A harassed-looking redhead fulfils drink orders for two men in suits. She's not alone: there's also a young bloke behind the bar; a geezer – all chewing gum and swagger. He's clearly not interested in work. He leans on the counter, a lazy smile on his face, attempting to chat up a young blonde woman who twirls a straw around a glass. She averts her gaze from his, coy.

Behind them, there's a group of young bucks playing drinking games. They erupt in cheers and beat on the tabletops with their tattooed fists.

I can't see Matthew anywhere.

It must be a live music night. On the stage is an Alanis Morissette wannabe with panda eyes and long, curly hair. She strums an acoustic guitar while waving her body left and right in erratic half-circles. 'Alanis' caterwauls her way through an angry song about a man who is not good enough for her. I wince as she attempts – and misses – a painful high note, before her song finishes.

The small audience gathered around the stage claps politely, more with relief than esteem. Alanis doesn't seem to notice. She bows twice and waves with both hands as she leaves the stage, a wide smile splitting her features in two.

Just as I'm thinking about phoning Matthew, he appears on the stage. He's wearing a white shirt that glows in the bar light, the cuffs undone and rolled back to the elbow. He approaches the microphone, unaware of the effect he's having on the women – and a couple of the men – down the front, by the stage. He never did have a clue how fit (*adjective, British slang.* attractive. Related words: hot, sexy) he is.

Matthew mumbles something about a song he wrote, only for someone to heckle him. It sounds a good-natured taunt, but Matthew's eyes flash with anger. Just as quickly, his vitriol disappears. He shrugs, launching into a witty piece that's half song, half performance poetry.

Within moments people are clapping along and laughing. I'm glad, but also taken aback. I knew how talented Matthew was right from when we were teenagers. Yet I'd never been able to get him to do anything about it. He wouldn't even take music lessons. The spectre of his father's disapproval dissuaded Matthew from the arts: as far as Alan Temple is concerned, music is for poseurs. Better to get a 'real' job like his: buying and selling and building.

As Matthew entertains the growing crowd around the stage, I wander over to the lazy young guy behind the bar. The redhead is still run off her feet and he's still desperate to hook up with the blonde woman. I know he will be easy to mislead.

'Hi.' I lift up the bar hatch and slide through, so I'm standing next to him.

The young barman's gaze flits from the blonde woman's ample chest to my face. He's irritated at being interrupted. 'You can't come back here…'

'I know, I know.' I'm apologetic, all smiles. 'But I'm with Matthew. He said to go through to the back and wait for him.'

'He did?' the young barman just wants me out the way. He looks across the bar. Matthew is still on the stage and has just announced a second song. 'Fine.'

I grin and go through. I catch the redhead's eye as she pushes yet another glass under the optics. She regards me with suspicion, but doesn't say anything. She's far too busy picking up the slack.

I find myself in a large version of the kitchenette behind the front bar at the Prince Albert. In this one, there's a kitchen porter in a white chef's jacket and checked trousers stacking the dishwasher. She's a girl of perhaps seventeen or eighteen, no make-up. Her hair is tucked under her checked bandana.

I front it out, giving her a wide smile. This is obviously good enough for her, because the teenager lets me continue without comment. I crash through the next door and find myself in a corridor with two doors leading off.

Both are open. On the left, I see a small dressing room, next to the stage entrance. Alanis sits there, her guitar across her lap. Her eyes are closed in rapture, as if she's meditating.

The other door leads into a small office. It's little more than a broom cupboard; no window, and just enough room to fit a desk and chair, plus a rack on the wall, filled with paperwork. I know it must be Matthew's.

I go inside, closing the door behind me. I sit down on Matthew's chair and wait for him.

Twenty-eight

'What are you doing here?'

Twenty minutes after I begin my vigil, the door opens. Matthew appears to deposit his guitar. He doesn't seem particularly surprised or annoyed. He's not welcoming, either.

I try and mask my disappointment. 'I wanted to see you.'

Matthew props his instrument against a slim-line filing cabinet I haven't noticed. He leans against the wall. 'So, Poppy Wade. What can I do for you? Only I am very busy…'

Hurt pools in my chest. *So that's how he wants to play it? Fine.*

'I thought you'd like to know: The girl – Jenny? – the one my sister wrote to on her final blog post … she's real.' I feign nonchalance as I lean against the desk, my body inches away from his.

'OK…' He's humouring me.

Irritation prickles the back of my shoulders. 'No. I mean I've met her. *Tonight.*'

Matthew rubs his face with his left hand. I can hear the scrape of bristles under his palm. 'So, what does this prove?'

Even I am forced to admit he has a point. 'I'm not sure … yet.'

Matthew still stares at me. He reaches across the tiny space and grabs for the bow in my hair. It unravels. My hair falls in soft waves around my face. He nods almost imperceptibly, as if to say: *That's better*.

Embarrassed, I try to change the subject. 'I went to see Cerise about JoJo.'

'I told you, Jenny's not JoJo.'

I think back to the strange, secretive goth-like girl I met an hour ago. The pale, white make-up, the red wig … her black, shoulder-length hair underneath. JoJo has a completely different bone structure, different-coloured hair. I hate to make comparisons, and as much as it pains me to say it, Jenny is far, far more attractive than India's old friend.

'I know. I still think JoJo's hiding something, though.'

'Like what?'

'I don't know. If I could just talk to her...' As I say this, I see something shift across Matthew's face. 'Do *you* know where JoJo lives?'

'No.' He says, his expression earnest. 'But...'

'Matthew?' I prompt.

He exhales. 'JoJo works at The Obelisk. She's one of the hotel's PAs.'

So Jabba JoJo really *has* moved up in the world. I envisage Cerise, her fierce pride in her eldest child. The Obelisk is one of the biggest employers in Brighton. The hotel and restaurant must employ more than a hundred and fifty people. Waiters, porters, drivers, chambermaids, cleaners, admin, bar and kitchen staff are all required to keep such a huge machine ticking over.

'JoJo lives at the hotel?'

'That's not for me to say.' Matthew steps away from me now, his back against the wall. Literally and figuratively.

So she does then. The space between us feels charged. Matthew's gaze flickers from my face to neck, back again. The temperature in the room seems to rise by several degrees. My brain throbs in time with the muffled music of the bar beyond, straining against my skull.

I lose the fight with myself. I reach forwards. But Matthew's hand shoots out and grabs my wrist, preventing me. His fingers close around my flesh. His fingertips feel worn, scratchy. His big brown eyes are sad, not angry.

'I'm sorry,' I whisper, 'I should never...' I can't bring the words into being. None are adequate.

Matthew draws me closer to him. He presses my body against his, his flesh stiff against mine. I am transfixed, confused by how the tables have been turned on me. I'm following his lead, when before it was always mine.

Matthew growls in my ear. 'Why did you have to come back?'

He has one hand on my waist, his other now on the back of my neck, holding me still. I know he won't hurt me, but I am still in his power.

And I like it.

'For India…' His grip on my neck tightens and I flinch. I say what I think he wants to hear. 'I came back for you, too.'

But his expression remains stony. Uncertainty creeps through me. I can't deny the thrill of it. Matthew has never behaved this way with me before; he's become someone else.

I try another tack. 'Look. I get it, OK?'

'I don't think you do.'

In a single fluid movement, Matthew turns me around. I'm now facing away from him. He moves me towards the desk, but not before he sweeps his other arm across it. Items go to crashing to the floor: an out-tray, more paperwork.

Before my brain can catch up, Matthew bends me over the wood. My palms lie flat on the table surface, him pressed up behind me. He places one foot between mine, prises my ankles apart.

'What the hell?' I struggle a little, but it's just for show. In the mirror shine of the desk, I can see the smile on my face.

He still has one hand on the back of my neck. The other finds it way inside my sister's silver dress, grabbing my nipple.

I arch my back as he traces the bumps of my spine in my neck with one finger. He moves both his hands to my breasts, his breath hot on my cheek.

He looms over me. 'Do you get it now?'

I get it. He is in charge. Matthew's hands encircle my waist. He grabs my hips, pulling me to him, rubbing me through my dress. I moan. But then…

There's a knock at the door.

Distracted now, Matthew gives a low groan. He lets go, calling out behind him, 'One minute!'

I stand up with as much dignity as the sudden about-turn will allow. Matthew adjusts his crotch, rolls his shoulders.

I smooth down my wrinkled dress and realign the top of it. Matthew waits for me, then unlocks the door and wrenches it open, his body language still rigid.

It's the teenage kitchen porter. Her expression is poker-faced. If she's guessed what we might have been doing, she gives nothing away.

'Lou says get out front 'cos Reuben's a lazy twat.'

Another smile tugs at Matthew's mouth. 'That's a direct quote, is it?'

The teenager shrugs, unapologetic. Matthew looks to me, holding one arm out towards me. For a moment, I think he's going to sweep me to his chest and hug me like he used to, one arm around my shoulders.

Then I realise: He's shepherding me out. My cheeks burn. *I am dismissed.*

I swallow down my embarrassment. 'Anyway. Thanks for the information.'

Matthew is cool as ever. 'You're welcome.'

Matthew's smell of tea tree and aftershave invades my senses as he squeezes past me, leaving me on my own.

Twenty-nine

I dream of the Prince Albert, filled with black light like Elemental. The dance floor heaves with bodies. Strobes give the appearance of lightning, illuminating faces as I struggle to focus. Somehow, I know my sister is in the crowd, with Jenny. My eyes can't find either of them. Instead, I see only Matthew in the middle of the surge of the bodies.

He's looking right at me.

Matthew is Medusa. I feel frozen in place, my limbs turned to stone. I can't look away. I don't want to. His white shirt is luminous, like a beacon; so are his eyes. He smiles. His teeth are impossibly white: wolfish, almost canine. Strobes flash around us like a warning.

I know I shouldn't go to him, but I can't help myself. Even though I'm asleep, I know the physical response my body is undergoing is real. I awake, bathed in sweat, heat pours from between my legs.

'You get off, if you want.'

I blink. Sitting in the booth in the arcade, the petulant squawks of seagulls outside filter into my consciousness. Tim appears next to me, a bucket of coppers trailing from his hand.

'You sure?'

'Don't take two of us. The place is dead.'

Tim doesn't turn in my direction. He wanders over to the penny-falls machine, shoulders hunched, as close to a physical rendering of 'miserable' as a man can get. He kneels down beside the machine, unlocking its back with one of the many keys on the ring on his belt.

'Well, why don't you go … sit with Mum?'

Returning to the booth with the bucket, my stepfather looks at me without seeing, a wistful look etched on his features. 'She doesn't want me,' he says.

Of course she doesn't. She only wants India.

'We all just need time.' Even as the words leave my lips, I can hear them for what they are: hollow.

But my stepfather's attention is already elsewhere. I grab my bag. Tim opens the booth door for me. He pats my shoulder absent-mindedly as I pass.

I wander through the glass double-doors of the arcade and out onto the pier. Below, the sea is grey, choppy, silt churning through the water. I walk back towards the concrete of the seafront.

A few of the kiosks and stalls are open now, but the majority of them sit idle. I lean against a nearby kiosk's colourful, padlocked front door. The tide is out, far in the distance, leaving pebbles and twists of seaweed stranded.

The seafront is uncommonly deserted, even for a weekday. A figure with a metal detector runs his machine across the shale, but from this distance, he is far enough away to seem like a matchstick man.

The only thing standing between the headland in the distance and me is The Obelisk, reaching its black marble pillar high into the air, a single shaft of sunlight spearing down from the white sky, shining off its tip.

The wind behind me, buffeting me along, I set off towards the hotel. The tinny bells and rattlers on the moored boats below send a metallic, out-of-tune song after me. Teeth chattering, I race up the steps to the hotel and dive into the revolving doors. As I'm forced to shuffle at sedate pace, I flush as a blast of warm air envelops me and my body temperature tries to adjust. The revolving doors spit me out into the vestibule, my face bright red. I must look deranged.

The concierge who lolls at his post barely takes any notice of me. In his late thirties, he reminds me of a young Alan Temple: ambition exudes from every pore. But I am of only minor interest to him. He can see I am not The Obelisk's regular clientele just by glancing at me. *No tips here.* Just like the seafront beyond, the hotel is deserted. Nevertheless, I feel compelled to explain my presence.

I flip my straggly hair out of my face. 'Hi. I'm looking for the restaurant?'

The concierge smiles back, out of politeness more than anything else. He nods in the direction of a glass foyer beyond the reception, clearly marked BAR & RESTAURANT. Sheepish, I slope past, but as I do, he makes a fist in the air, as if to say '*Yes!*' I freeze. He remembers himself, looking around the hotel reception, just in case. I see then that he has an earpiece in his left ear, a surreptitious cable under his collar. He's listening to some game. Embarrassed, I rush into the bar.

Crossing the threshold, I look around, expectant. The place is empty. No one sits at any of the restaurant tables. Did I really believe JoJo Musgrave would be here, waiting for me? I must have, because a perverse disappointment lances through me.

There is just a young barman behind the huge, black-marble bar. He gives me a forced smile as I meander towards him. He is stacking a tray of clean shot glasses under the counter. I can smell lemon detergent wafting from the tray.

'Hi. JoJo Musgrave in today?'

The young barman's fake smile wilts. He has no idea who I'm talking about.

'Maybe later?'

He shrugs: 'Sorry. I'm new.'

Me too, I want to say. Except, am I? Everything seems so familiar, yet so markedly different. I feel as if my old life has been demolished, like our old flat in Hove. My new life seems like it's made of dust and chunks of old brick, recognisable yet impossible to put back together. *Now what?*

'Can I get you anything?'

I glance back towards the reception, which is still deserted. I won't make it past the concierge into the hotel itself. I resolve to wait. I sit down on one of the stools at the bar and flash the young barman a wide smile.

'Sure. A Coke, thanks.'

Half an hour creeps around the clock face as I drink my Coke. Some early diners appear in the restaurant, eager to get a seat in one of the booths with a view of the beach. A writer sets up in the corner, nodding to music playing in his headphones, only pausing to look up from his laptop occasionally, as his coffee cup is refilled by a young waitress with a glass jug and a bored expression.

A professional with a knotted scarf and bare arms, no jacket, drifts in. He taps his phone and barks drink and lunch orders. (**Hipster**, *noun.* A wearer of beards and ironic t-shirts; thinks he's better than you.) But the young waitress takes it all in her stride. As she slams his toasted panini in front of him, I find myself hoping she's spat in it.

Another hour passes, the restaurant fills up. A hubbub of conversation surrounds me. I know I have to admit defeat. I can't rely on chance any longer. I will have to go and look for JoJo … even if that means running the risk of getting thrown out of The Obelisk.

I amble back out of the restaurant. The reception of the huge hotel is moderately busy now. A small queue of people waits to check in. The concierge chatters to an old couple, who try and communicate with broken English and strong Eastern European accents. No one pays attention to me. I flit through reception, past the elevator, the freight lift. I make it through a side door.

I'm in.

Thirty

I discover I am in a service corridor. Last night, Matthew said JoJo was one of The Obelisk's PAs. She must have an office. Where would that be? There are no helpful signs, like you might find in a hospital. *Typical.*

Up ahead, a couple of teen boys in the black-and-white junior uniform of The Obelisk staff appear out of another door. They look at me but don't challenge me. They're carrying boxes. From one, a banner trails. They crash through more doors.

I hang back then follow them. But they don't end up at any offices. Instead, we're in a large, echoey room on the ground floor. Expensive oak-block flooring booms under my feet.

I'm in The Obelisk's ballroom.

The staff inside are preparing for an event. Streamers, shaped balloons and bags of favours in boxes line the room. I grab a flyer from a box on the nearest table to me. It reads: SPRING BALL, about a week from now. I recognise it, of course. The Obelisk holds one every year, as a celebration of Jayden Spence's birthday. It's a display of obscene opulence: anyone who's anyone will be here.

'What do you want?'

I am caught in the sights of a middle-aged event planner. She's a stocky woman with a confident stance: broad shoulders swept back, head held high.

'Nothing. I…'

My words trail off as I spot JoJo, wielding a staple gun. A couple of lads carry chairs over to her. She wraps chintzy-looking fabric around each one, before stapling it in place. She hasn't seen me.

The event planner's attention is diverted. Her hawk eyes spot someone doing something wrong. The older woman descends, rebuking a small, thin blonde teenager to my left. I'm already forgotten.

No one else's eyes on me, I hurry over. 'JoJo?'

She freezes at the sound of her name. As she turns, her eyes roll, but less in annoyance than resignation. JoJo looks over to another Obelisk senior staff member, who nods: *He's fine for the minute.*

JoJo's gaze falls on me, resentful. 'Come on, then.'

She flicks her limp red fringe out of her eyes, then picks her way around the boxes. I fall into step with her, and we disappear through another side door marked STAFF ONLY and somehow, we're back in reception.

My eyes blink at the assault of light and noise. It's even busier now: main check-in time. The concierge is now engaged in banter with a tall model type, who has a small dog in a bag. Porters push wagons loaded with suitcases and bags. I shuffle after JoJo, back into the restaurant.

JoJo sits opposite me in a booth. 'I've got ten minutes.'

Her arms fold protectively across the whole of her upper body. I struggle to connect this young woman with the child I knew. Her skin is still bad, her pale face pasty, her hair thin. I can make out patches of hair dye at her temples. I try to silence a cruel voice in my head: *She might be plain, but she is not ugly.* As if that justifies my lack of charity.

'What happened between you and India?'

Whatever JoJo was expecting to me to say, it wasn't this. Her animosity and suspicion seem to deflate. 'You really don't know.'

'Know what?'

JoJo feels inside her waistcoat pocket. She pulls out a pouch of tobacco, a pack of Rizlas. I recall the Facebook profile photo of India at the festival, a garland in her hair, hand-rolled cigarette in her hand. *So JoJo must have taken that picture.*

'It was over that blog of hers.'

My brain casts over the various codenames I saw on India's site. So one of the entries must refer to my sister's ex-best friend.

'What was the problem with it?'

'She thought she was a detective or something.' JoJo deflects her gaze from mine, concentrating instead on rolling her cigarette. *Nervous.*

I aim a well-placed jab. 'You have something to hide?'

It works. JoJo's eyes flash, anger in them for the first time. 'It wasn't like that. Bitch slut-shamed me to everybody.' She winces, remembering India is dead. But her anger and frustration win out. She lowers her voice. '...And I mean *everybody*. Not just online, though that was bad enough. She tried to lose me my job here, too!'

I try and process these details. 'Slut-shame' jumps out at me. 'Why?'

JoJo blinks. 'Oh, so it's my fault? Victim blaming, great.'

'No, that's not what I meant.'

Anger and hurt boil under the surface of the girl opposite me. Looking at JoJo, I can see the sweet, easy-going teenager I remember is gone. In her place is a combative young woman. I am reminded of Cerise, always on the offensive.

I take the plunge. 'Do you know Jenny?'

JoJo's lip curls in derision before she can check herself. 'Yes ... No. Sort of.' She puts the rolled cigarette in her pocket.

I'm patient, though I don't feel it. 'Which is it?'

'I know *of* her. We didn't exactly all hang out.'

I press on, trying out a theory. 'You were jealous?'

JoJo looks at me askance. 'Why would I be jealous ... of *that*?'

I try and keep my tone neutral. 'You sound like you don't like her.'

'I don't like either of them.' JoJo's voice is lofty, filled with a devil-may-care contempt that actually reveals that she cares very much indeed. 'Anyway, India reckoned she was gay now.'

'You sound like you didn't believe that.'

JoJo shrugs. 'Doesn't matter what I believe. India made that clear.'

An uneasy pause falls between us. With JoJo's anger receding, I can feel the trail growing cold. I am anxious to keep hold of the thread.

'So. What kicked it all off?'

JoJo looks like she's about to jump out of her chair, storm off. But she doesn't. I wonder what could have happened to JoJo in the last four (*nearly five*) years to change her so radically. Or maybe I just had her wrong, all those years ago.

'There was a man. Someone I shouldn't have got involved with.'

Join the club, I want to reply, thinking of Matthew's taunting touch the previous night at Elemental. I wait, expectant as JoJo fiddles with her lighter. For one sickening moment, I wonder if she means Matthew. *Surely not?* But then a vision of Matthew on the bench at the churchyard spears its way into my brain: *People change.*

'I knew she'd go off on one. But to do *that* … to *me*?'

'What did she do? Tell me, exactly.' I'm going through the motions, playing for time. I worry I already know the answer.

'Put my picture on rating apps…' She sees my confused look: 'Shitty platforms where strangers can go on about how ugly you are. She got me trolled on Twitter, tried to get #JoJoMusgraveisaslut trending. She doxxed me as well.'

'Doxxed?'

'Shared my personal information online. I got all these self-righteous moralistic pricks – *strangers!* – contacting me, telling me what a slut I am. Some of them even called here. That's when it got really bad. But they couldn't fire me, not for this. I checked. And I'm not ditching my career, not because of that … *bitch*.'

JoJo's lip trembles. I can see the struggle etched on her face. She's in her own little world, remembering the arguments between her and her childhood friend. All the wrongs that can never be put right now.

'Who was the man?'

'No one you know.' JoJo is defiant, guarding her secret jealously.

Now I can see the teenage girl she was. But JoJo would have seen Matthew with me at the Coach House all those years ago, more than once. Hope burgeons in my chest. *Maybe her clandestine lover wasn't Matthew, after all?*

I try another tack. 'Show me a picture, then.'

JoJo grabs her phone from her pocket, slides through her photos. She turns the handset around, almost sulky, like I'm a parent demanding proof. I brace myself.

But as I'd hoped, it's not Matthew.

It's a white guy. He's in bed, bare-chested. His mop of blonde hair is mussed, falling over one half of his face. I've seen him before, but he's smiling this time, propped up on his elbows, looking directly into the camera.

It's Jayden Spence.

Thirty-one

Ugly Sister

Stubby fingers, chipped nail polish. Friendship bracelets, greying bra straps pinching rounded flesh. Ribbons on your DMs, honesty in your eyes.

Where did it all go?

You gave it all up for him.

Is he worth it?

You thought you could step out of your skin, be transformed. You shed us all like a snake would, seizing on what you wanted, squeezing for all you were worth.

Even when you felt the give of brittle bones, ground to powder, you would not let go. You thought you could rise above us, become Lady of the Manor, but now you are alone.

Who you are deep inside will always follow you.

Is he worth it?

India

POSTED BY **@1NDIAsummer**, 3 December 2016

32,110 insights ⏎ **SHARE THIS**

⏎ **writerchic88** likes this

⏎ **Emz2011_UK** likes this

⏎ **markotron** likes this

⏎ **Alfie98** likes this

⤺ **_warriorwasp_** likes this

⤺ **_Milliecat_456_** likes this

   ⤺ **_Blithefancy_** likes this & reblogs this from 1NDIAsummer, adding: _She can't get away with it!!!_

⤺ **_lilyrose06_** likes this

Thirty-two

'Take a picture for us.'

I rolled my eyes as I looked up from my desk, my Art History homework, my English Lit revision cards. I was revising for my A Levels, I wasn't interested in India or any of her dorky friends, like JoJo. India was experimenting with make-up; she was going through the inevitable orange phase. JoJo's flushed round face was framed by pigtails. A pair of tweens, dressed in clothes a tiny bit small, their pre-pubescent bodies changing daily.

India stood over me, holding her phone, a hopeful look in her eyes. For reasons I don't know even now, I wanted to crush that hope out of her. Perhaps because I was older, so I could. Or, more likely, because she had bested me at something else that I don't remember now, so I was getting my own back.

'Take a selfie, I'm busy.'

'We've got loads of those! Pops! Take a nice one … For us … Pretty please??' India grabbed one of the heart-shaped scatter cushions from my bed and hit me lightly in the chest with it.

I totally overreacted. Perhaps it was exam stress or hormones or both, but even as I did it, I knew I was going too far. It was like I was watching myself from above; I was powerless to stop myself. I leapt up from the bed and grabbed India by the arm. My fingers pressed hard into her flesh. I screamed something at her and frog-marched her across the purple carpet of my bedroom, propelling her out of my face, my space, whether she liked it or not. JoJo trailed after us, her eyes wide, her mouth a perfect red 'o' of shock. I slammed the door after them both and leant against it.

'I'm telling Mum!' I heard India burst into tears on the other side of the wood. She rained fists on the door. 'You bitch!'

'Yeah … bitch!' JoJo echoed.

This was enough to get my back up all over again; her words preventing me from going out and apologising. I was jealous of India and JoJo. I knew that even then, deep down. That was the real reason I hadn't wanted to take the picture of them, arms draped around each other, posing for the camera. India and JoJo were so close when they were kids; they'd been like sisters.

Ugly Sister.

JoJo is not a pretty girl, it's true. But India was always fiercely loyal to her oldest friend. It wasn't like my sister to make such a cheap shot. But worse than just writing an angry blog post, it seemed that India set out to destroy her ex-bestie. She even tried getting JoJo fired. It seems totally out of proportion from my sister. I recall JoJo's bewilderment, her betrayal and anger that can now never be resolved.

How could JoJo targeting Jayden Spence have changed India's feelings for her so radically? Had Ana written it, it would make more sense. JoJo (and Jayden) wronged her, carrying on behind her back. And it wasn't just Ana's partner JoJo had tried stealing either, but the father of her child: the little girl Ivy.

I am perturbed at my sister's blog's disgust with her oldest, childhood friend. What could be the reason for it? As far as I am aware, India did not know Ana that well, if at all. Would my sister really burn JoJo over one mistake? Though India was always somewhat high-handed in her morals, it's difficult to fathom why she would choose them over her best friend.

I imagine the shit storm (*noun.* Scandal. Related words: fiasco, train wreck, clusterfuck) that must have erupted when Ana got wind of the affair. Then there would have been Alan Temple's rage at some chav bitch taking advantage of his little girl. I shudder.

It can't be much better for JoJo now. I recall her trembling defiance over not leaving The Obelisk. The Temples must have applied extreme pressure on the Spences. So JoJo Musgrave really is her mother's daughter, hanging on by her nicotine-stained fingernails.

But JoJo had claimed she was at The Obelisk all night on 22nd December, tending to an office Christmas party for one of Brighton's many big insurance companies.

There must have been a hundred people there, how's that for an alibi? Her face was triumphant, delighted to prove me wrong. She also let me know she'd already given a statement to the police, too: DS Rahman, no less – our own family-liaison officer.

JoJo cannot have been the one to push my sister from the bridge. But who else could it have been?

After another quiet evening and a fruitless attempt to get Mum to eat anything, I manage to coax her to drink some hot chocolate. Tim arrives late from the arcade, exhaustion carved into his features. Every night he meets my gaze first, the unspoken question in his eyes: *Any change?* I usually answer with a barely discernible shake of my head, but tonight I present the empty, cold cup as if it's a trophy.

'Maybe she's turned a corner.'

As soon as the words trip off my tongue I realise how false and wooden they are. Perhaps these clichés and platitudes are lurking in the wings, ready to jump into our mouths and make us say them. Time heals all wounds? What a crock.

A wan smile tugs at my stepfather's lip. 'Maybe.'

I go to my room. Unable to sleep, I gravitate back towards my sister's laptop. I open Google and type in 'The Obelisk Resort'. The Spence family's visages fill the screen. Gordon Spence stands behind a chaise longue, his tapered fingers on his wife Olivia's shoulders, as if holding her still. She is wearing a sleeveless dress and a pained expression beneath her uber-white smile. Her eyes turn upwards, cat-like.

Next to his mother is Jayden, hands in his lap, slouching against the back of the chaise longue. He looks like he's just rolled out of bed; maybe he has. Like his father, he's wearing a tie, but it's much looser and his cuffs are undone.

Gordon and Olivia Spence are new money, like the Temples, so spared absolutely no expense in raising their only child. Born out of privilege like that, a little prince like Jayden Spence was used to getting his own way. His arrogant expression in the photo seems to confirm this. I'm more certain than ever that it was him at the cemetery, the day of my sister's funeral.

Ana sits poised next to Jayden. It must be an old photograph, because Ana's stomach is rounded with the swell of pregnancy. Like Olivia Spence, she looks as if she'd rather be anywhere but in that room, in front of the camera, playing happy families. They all look like mannequins. Stiff. Unreal. False.

The Temples probably closed ranks on the Spences when news of Jayden's affair with JoJo broke. The fallout must have been one of the first consequences the playboy had ever had to face. Jayden would have found himself subject to the bewildering fury of Alan Temple. Maybe even his own parents, as well. No one likes a scandal. It's said that Gordon has always been careful to try and 'erase' any of his own past misdeeds.

Could Jayden or Gordon have 'erased' my sister?

Since I'm online already, I type in the URL of my sister's blog: www.1NDIAsummer.com. The little wheel of doom goes round and around, before settling on a 404 message. FAIL. I sigh, thinking the Wi-Fi has timed out on me. But then I notice I have full bars at the top of the screen. *What the hell?*

I retype www.1NDIAsummer.com into the browser.

Another 404 message.

Trepidation settles over me. Could I have deleted the blog by accident? *Surely not.* I may be bad with computers, but even I can avoid the big DELETE button on the dashboard.

India's blog is gone.

But how?

I've read about how nothing is 'really' deleted online. There must be a way of getting India's blog back. I grab my mobile, press redial. I don't care that it's late and neither does Mike, because he answers within one ring this time.

'My sister's blog is gone. Have you done something? Like … from afar?'

Mike slurps something through a straw before he answers. He sounds exasperated, as if he were expecting my call.

'Yeah, I frequently delete stuff to make annoying clients come back. It's my world-domination plan. I'll be Bill Gates five years from now.'

I grit my teeth. I need his help, after all. 'Then how do you get something back that's been erased?'

I can hear the tip-tapping of keys. 'Check the cache.'

'What the hell is the cache?'

Ten minutes and four explanations from Mike later – plus a quick read of eHow – I think I know how to restore the blog. I thank Mike and hang up. Taking a deep breath, I copy and paste the code he emails me into the browser. It all looks like gobbledy-gook to me. *Whatever.*

I click on it, then press the shift key.

Nothing.

I take a deep breath. I call up another browser and try that.

Again, nothing. *Shit!*

I feel panic surge through me again.

'If whoever deleted the blog knows what they're doing, they won't have left a trace; the cache will be empty,' Mike warned.

Wait. Maybe Jenny can help me?

I type in www.blithefancy.com. I expect to find Jenny's single-page profile of the sugar skull, plus the email contact button, as I did just forty-eight hours earlier.

It's been replaced with a 404 message, too.

'Fuck!'

Feeling sick, I open my emails, searching for Jenny's email address. It's info@blithefancy.com. I fire off a test email and press SEND. It bounces back in an instant, complete with yet another 404 failure notice.

I can't believe it. I have no way of getting back in touch with

Jenny. And I need to see her again. I gulp in deep breaths, attempting to calm my anxiety. It's OK. I can go to the Prince Albert and look for Jenny there, right? *Right?*

But then another realisation hits me, something my panic-addled brain has refused to accept until now.

If India's blog is gone and so is Jenny's online profile, the evidence points to one very obvious conclusion.

Jenny deleted both.

Thirty-three

The boy slumps in the passenger seat, arms folded. Wind whistles off the beach and buffets the car, as rain pelts against the windscreen. The hypnotic swish of the wipers slides across the glass as the boy's eyes, harsh and accusing, reflect in the rearview mirror. A magic tree hangs from it; the counterfeit pine scent pervades the car, like their unspoken words.

This time, he found the boy wandering down on the pebbles underneath the palace pier. His black jacket was perched on his shoulders like a cape. Seeing the boy dressed like that reminded him of a time when he himself had felt free. He'd been perhaps eleven or twelve, no older. He'd ridden his bike with friends, no helmet. Back then, his only protection had been his hood on his head, billowing out behind him as they'd all pedalled pell-mell down the steep hill towards the seafront.

He sighs as he recalls the whistling of the air past his ears, the feeling of lightness in his shoulders and chest, his cry of joy as loud as the gulls overhead. It seems like a million years ago. Just remembering the feeling brings a stab of grief so hard it feels like a punch to the solar plexus.

The boy cut a strange figure on the beach in the dying sunset. Almost regal. His arms were wrapped around his scrawny chest, as if hugging himself. There was a smell of vinegar and chips in the air; hot fat from the donut stalls above. Bright lights shone down, but rather than illuminate him, the boy was still mostly cloaked in shadow, dressed as he was, all in black. Only his eyes reflected the light. Like a cat.

The boy did not run from him. *For a change.* Instead, he sighed and offered up his slender wrists, as if for handcuffs. Not a word was spoken. In response, he took a deep breath, dampening his hot frustration. He betrayed none of this on his face.

He turned and led the boy back to the car. The passenger door thudded closed behind them like a coffin lid.

He looks over at the boy now. The weight of the boy's stare makes him anxious, though he is unsure why.

'I don't want to have to do this, either, you know,' he tells the boy, his voice soft, cajoling. Almost pleading.

'Then why do you?' By contrast, the boy's voice is clipped and clear, piercing the silence and clawing at his heart.

As a band of orange streetlight journeys over the vehicle, the boy's face is lit up in that feral snarl, so like his mother's. But as this thought flowers in his brain, he pushes it back down. Just like he always does.

He grips the steering wheel. 'You know why.'

'You can stop all of this.'

India's words. She had come to him, again and again, begged him to listen. But he already knew everything she had to say, and it didn't change a damned thing. Life is simple to girls like her: black or white, left or right, right or wrong. She'd thought all it took was making a decision, being brave. Then it was over, like tearing off a Band-Aid.

If only.

Some things never end. They just morph and mutate, according to circumstance. He has dreams like this: He's chewing gum. At first, it's pleasant, minty. But then it changes. What was refreshing, now feels abrasive. It starts to sting his tongue as it expands. It's sticky and viscous, gluing his teeth together. He forces his mouth open, yanks desperately at the gluey mass. It comes out in strings. He pulls at it, but somehow it's connected to the back of his oesophagus. He gags. Still it grows; he can never pull enough of it out. As quickly as he clears it, there is more. He wakes choking, heart racing, clawing at his own throat.

But the boy does not seem aware of his discomfort. Instead he grips the ripped car seat. Whatever connection they had is lost.

The boy picks at the upholstery. 'I'm an embarrassment, right?'

'I never said that.'

Shame floods through him. How many times has he wished this was all different; simpler; the secrets and lies gone? But she decreed what they all had to do. They had to play the game; the penalty was simply too high to deny her. Besides, he owed her. He knew that. He can't escape it.

'You didn't need to!' the boy hisses, one part disgust to two parts hurt.

The boy turns away, puts one bare foot up on the dashboard. Behind the wheel, rage blossoms where shame was just seconds earlier. He grits his teeth, bats at the boy's foot, trying to knock it from the dashboard. But the boy bares his teeth at him like an animal and swipes back at him, nails nicking the flesh on the back of his hand.

'Put your shoes back on.' The words come out as a dark growl.

The boy is belligerent. Unmoving. 'Why?'

He yanks on the gearstick, grinding to a standstill in the middle of the road. If there was any traffic behind them, he would have caused an accident. But it's a weeknight in January, out of season and before nine o'clock. The whole of the seafront is deserted. Only a dog walker, hunched into their anorak and making their way towards the steps behind an exuberant collie, turns and looks momentarily; then makes their way down to the beach.

Behind the wheel, he rounds on the boy, his own eyes flashing this time. A dark shadow jumps out of him, swells within the space between them.

'Put your shoes back on. Now!'

The boy's bravado vanishes. Eyes glassy with tears, he blinks furiously. He grabs each boot, pulls each one back on. Raises both palms in defiance, though his gaze finally casts downwards. The boy knows his place; when he is beaten.

They drive the rest of the way in silence.

Thirty-four

'Pops … Poppy!'

Light floods my room. My eyes blink as the curtains are yanked open. I groan, dazed for an instant.

Framed by the window, Tim is a silhouette in the grey morning light. 'I can't find your mother.'

I sit up on one elbow, perceiving rather than hearing the fear in my stepfather's voice. In an instant, sleep skitters away from my brain like cockroaches from a filthy kitchen when a light is turned on. I swing my feet out of bed and stand, my nighty falling back down, sparing my modesty. From Tim's tone, I know what he's thinking. *Mum has gone out, intent on doing the same as India.*

I try not to let panic infect my voice. 'OK. Well … maybe she's in the bathroom?'

'No.' Tim's tone is testy, irritated. *Obviously he has looked there.*

I still attempt to placate him. 'Perhaps she's just gone to the shop?'

Even as the words leave my mouth, I can feel the lie in the air. When not lying on her bed, vacant, Mum has wandered, aimless and restless, around the Coach House. She's been here and yet not; lost inside herself. Tim took her to the doctor, but it made little difference. Mum has been an automaton these past few weeks, unable to process her thoughts or surroundings.

With sickening clarity, I know, deep within in my bones, my mother's sudden disappearance means *something*. There is no way she could have just fancied a walk, or noticed by herself we're out of milk.

Oh, God.

'I'm going to check.'

Tim doesn't need to say where. I know where.

The bridge where India fell.

'Can you go into town and look? I'll drop you.' He goes back downstairs to grab his car keys, while I pull on some clothes.

We sit side by side in the car in silence, the air heavy between us. Tim's eyes are focused on the road, his knuckles white as he grips the steering wheel. With a pang, I see how deeply this has affected him. *My poor Tim, the only real father I've ever known.*

After he has dropped me off near the seafront, I stare at the tide on its way out then cast my eyes across the beach. It all seems so clear: Fate has thrown my family together. Now the same ruthless hand seems intent on tearing us apart.

Today is an unfathomably sunny day, blue skies. The beach is deserted but for a woman and her kid, throwing a ball for a dog. The young boy, of about nine, trots behind her. He drags a large branch of driftwood as the dog runs away full pelt. As they wait for the animal to return, the woman puts one arm around the boy. He jerks it off in the blasé way kids do, as if he expects her to be there, always. But she won't be.

I stride towards Elemental. I don't know where else to start. I know Matthew doesn't care about me, but he came to my sister's funeral. *Maybe he'll help me look for Mum, for India's sake?*

It being daytime, Elemental is not busy. Approaching from this angle, I see there is a raised beer garden on decking to the left of the building, with steps down from the street. I pick my way across the slippery, rain-sodden wood.

All of the French windows are closed. Through the glass, I see the teenage kitchen porter appear from the back. She carries a tray of nachos to a bearded patron in his mid-twenties. He smirks as the porter dumps his food in front of him. To the left, the redhead barwoman lolls on the counter, scrolling through her phone.

I reach for the handle of the first French window, but then I hesitate. In one of the side booths I can see Matthew sitting with his father.

The two men don't look like they're full-on arguing, but it *is* a heated discussion. Matthew's back is to me, but his shoulders are hunched. He throws his arms in the air. Alan Temple shakes his head, draining the last of his Scotch. The older man looks as unkempt as ever. There is a cigarette tucked behind his ear.

Not for the first time, it strikes me how little the Temple kids look like their father. There's more resemblance between Tim and me. We have similar features, even if we don't share blood ties. When we were kids, Ana would call Alan 'Our *white* father'. The way she said it was as if the three Temple kids had a black patriarch out there somewhere and Maggie had installed Alan to bring them a notch up the social scale.

Inside Elemental, Alan's face cracks with a wide smile. He pats Matthew's back, between his broad shoulders. Matthew turns at last, standing: he dwarfs his father. In contrast, he is not smiling. He looks furious, like he might reach forward and grab Alan by the lapels of his wrinkled suit.

Then I catch a glimpse of her, behind them.

Mum.

She appears from the beach-side door, next to the bar. I don't understand how I could have missed her on the shale outside.

But there's no time to figure that out now. Mum seems disoriented, confused. The redhead behind the bar smiles. But my mother ignores her, drifting past the counter like a ghost. Mum wears no shoes: she's not carrying them, nor does she have a bag with her, or a cardigan. She leaves wet footprints across the floor tiles. Her bare arms, feet and legs look purple with cold.

She's looking straight at me.

Determined, Mum marches towards me. I struggle to think what I could have done – or more likely have *not* done. *Do I deserve her wrath, this time?* My mother's temperament is changeable, difficult to stay one step ahead of.

But then she veers off to the left. I am confused, then realise the setting sun is behind me. It glances off the glass, effectively creating a one-way mirror. My mother hasn't even seen me. It was just an illusion. A curious mix of relief and disappointment courses through me. If Mum wanted to have a go at me, for whatever reason, it would have been the first time she'll have noticed me in days.

But it's not to be. The redhead catches up to my mother. Mum stops, as if she's forgotten what she's doing. My heart aches at how she's been diminished. I grab the handle again, but before I can open the French window, everything changes.

My mother spots her quarry. With a silent screech behind the insulating glass, my mother launches herself at him, hands hooked like claws.

Alan Temple.

I yank the door handle. The soundproof barrier is gone instantly. Alan makes no attempt to prevent my mother from raining blows on him, shrinking away from her instead, holding his arms over his head.

My mother's shrieks reverberate around Elemental. The redhead, the teenage kitchen porter and the bearded patron look on in horrified fascination. Matthew attempts to grab my mother's hands.

But he misses. Like a wild animal, my mother whips around. She scratches his cheek with one of her long nails.

'Mum … Mum! Stop!'

I grab her from behind, by both elbows. Mum stiffens against me, at the feel of my touch, the sound of my voice. She arches her back, trying to shake me off.

But I am too strong for her. She screams something, but I can't make sense of the words … Not yet. Then Mum slumps, all the fight leaving her.

'Crazy … *bitch.*' The redhead breathes heavily, as if she's just finished a cross-country run. She snaps a finger at the teenage kitchen porter. 'Call the police!'

'No, don't.' Alan Temple sits down in the booth, his face pale with shock. He looks up at Mum, dazed. She's staring beyond him, at nothing. 'Get her home.'

Alan pats my arm in thanks, absent-minded.

The redhead can't hide her incredulity. 'You can't be serious…?'

'Enough.' Alan pulls a handkerchief from his pocket and gives it to his son.

Matthew doesn't know what it's for, then touches his cheek. He sees blood on his fingertips. Then his gaze moves from my shoeless mother, to the wide-eyed diner and the rest of Elemental's idle staff.

'OK, back to work,' he says.

Begrudgingly, the other two women shuffle off.

Matthew looks to me for explanation. 'What's going on, Poppy?'

'I don't know.'

My reply is automatic. I wasn't able to understand my mother's words as she'd screamed them. And I was tunnel-visioned, intent on preventing her from doing Alan any serious harm.

Yet now, minutes later, Mum's shrieks resonate in my ears, and I hear her words, as clear and as confusing as ever:

It was you. It was always you.

Thirty-five

Tim arrives at Elemental to pick up me and Mum. As my stepfather arrives in the deserted café bar, his face is a picture of relief. But his expression swiftly turns to horror when he sees how vacant Mum is. He attempts to embrace her, but Mum's arms stay by her sides. She mutters to herself wordlessly again, talking only in her mind, *but to whom?*

'Oh, love.' Tim kisses the top of Mum's head. There are tears in his eyes. 'Let's get you home, yeah?'

Matthew appears at the bar to watch us go. I take in his inscrutable expression. Matthew is not looking at my mother, or Tim, but me.

'I'm sorry about … earlier,' I say.

'S'fine.' Matthew looks to Mum now and forces a smile, the words wooden and uneven in his mouth. 'Hope you feel better soon, Kirsten.'

Mum's head turns towards Matthew, her senses returning to her. It's like only his voice can gain her attention.

'Don't you feel sorry for me, boy. *Don't you dare!*' She raises a finger, pointing it in Matthew's direction.

Matthew's brow furrows in confusion. I take Mum's arm, but she jerks it away, tutting like a child. I throw an apologetic look over my shoulder at Matthew as we leave, but the bar is deserted again.

The doctor who is also a family friend arrives at the Coach House again. He shuffles in with his cane and converses in low tones with my stepfather. My mother sits in her chair and stares at the sideboard.

I sit on the stairs, trying to eavesdrop, but only picking up every second or third word: '…self-harm … crisis … respite.'

After an hour, I drift to the doorway – to make my presence felt, even if I have nothing to add. I discern that it's been agreed my mother will not be sectioned, but might perhaps agree to a 'little break' at the hospital and go in voluntarily? Same difference. *Just words*, like Matthew said the day we'd buried my sister.

So the doctor asks Mum in a falsely cheery voice what she would like to do next. He emphasises it's *her* choice and she doesn't have to do anything against her will. But my mother is not herself: she seems neither scared, nor against the notion, simply apathetic. Through the doorway, I see her shrug. Consent, of sorts. Another phone call is made.

Unable to do anything else, I go upstairs and pack my mother a bag. I don't know how long she is going for. Two or three days? A week? A fortnight? Yet again, I am cast into a situation where I don't know the protocol. Do I pack normal clothes? Or pyjamas, like someone would wear at a 'normal' hospital, as opposed to a psychiatric institution (*noun*. Asylum. Related words: loony bin; nuthouse)? I end up grabbing a selection of clothes, so she can choose. I add her toiletry bag, her Kindle on top – in case she feels like reading.

An hour after this, a tall woman with a long face strides towards the doorway. She's got the type of smile that lights up a room, her shoulders free from the hunch of worry. She's not in a white coat, nor any uniform that connotes a medical background. An ambulance does not accompany her. She is in her own car.

The woman sweeps into the room and looks straight at my mother. She speaks only to her, as if the rest of us don't exist.

'Hello Kirsten, I'm Sue. I hear you're having a hard time?'

I want to snort. *A hard time?* But I don't. Psych professionals like Sue must have a doctor's case full of understatements to cover every scenario and eventuality, designed not to trigger the patient.

Mum stands, her arms wrapped around her upper body. Tim places her coat around her shoulders, but she makes no effort to thread her arms through.

Sue looks to Tim. 'You're hubby, are you?'

Tim nods. A relieved smile plays on his lips, but a stab of guilt twists it downwards again. I can see the thoughts and emotions flicker across his strained features. *He doesn't want Mum to go. He wants to her to go. He doesn't know.*

Sue senses it too, because she pats his arm. She must have seen this reaction before. 'She'll be OK.' Sue gives me her radiant smile as I step forward, Mum's bag in my hands. 'I'll take that, shall I?'

But I don't want to let it go. Not yet. 'It's OK, I'll come out with you.'

Sue nods, extending an arm towards my mother. Mum takes it, striding out of the Coach House with her. She does not look back at her husband.

I pause to shoot a sympathetic glance at Tim, but he's turned his face away. The doctor has one hand on my stepfather's shoulder, as if he alone is holding him up. Should he let go, Tim will slump to the floor, his body unable to support him. I want to run over and hug my stepfather, but I don't. Tim is old school. It would probably break him. He cannot be vulnerable in front of me.

So I race out after Sue and my mother. I clatter down the steps of the Coach House, handing over Mum's bag. I give Mum a peck on the cheek, plus an uncustomary embrace. Mum recoils from my touch, then remembers to hug me back. I can smell her floral scent and momentarily, she's my mother again. She rocks me, rubbing my back.

'I love you, darling.'

'I love you, Mum.'

But when Mum lets go, that lost look is back in her eyes. She glances from me to Sue, waiting for direction.

Sue leads her round the passenger side of the car and helps her get in, fastening her seatbelt for her.

Sue slides in behind the wheel, winding the window down. She winks at me. 'We'll take good care of her.'

Sue sets the car in motion, doing a three-point turn. I wave to my mother, but she's gone again, staring out the side window like she did in the funeral car.

I watch the car retreat down the road, not moving but staying outside long after the vehicle has gone.

Thirty-six

At the hospital, there are more consultations for my mother. It is agreed Mum is not responding to medication the way they've hoped. Sue arrives, a familiar face, asking if there's anything specific – 'other than the obvious' – that could be troubling my mother? Tim shakes his head, baffled.

I tell Tim I think Mum knew India had been living what I euphemistically call, 'an alternative life'. But Tim surprises me and says they'd both known India was gay.

'When did she tell you?'

Tim sighs. I can see it written all over his features: *Does it matter?* But he goes through the motions, for my benefit.

'Not sure. Two, maybe three years ago.'

'Why didn't either of you tell me she'd come out?'

'Because that's India's news.' Tim is diplomatic, as ever. He doesn't make return accusations like Mum would have: *You should have called her and talked to her properly, asked her about her life.* I can feel the sting of the truth of this myself.

This avenue of enquiry closed, I think instead of India's blog. I speculate whether Mum could have known about whatever my sister had been up to with it.

So I read the codenames out to my mother when Tim is not at the hospital with her, searching for recognition in her eyes. I get none. I don't share my concerns with Sue. I'm scared to, in case my mother is an accessory, somehow. But Mum can't be involved. *Surely not.* Mum's behaviour with Alan and Matthew *has* to be the product of a mind gone awry after the tragedy of losing India … nothing more, nothing less.

To counter these uncomfortable thoughts, I consider the leads I have so far. The blog deleted, I pore over my written notes instead. JoJo is *Ugly Sister*, but India's blog is addressed only to her, not Jayden Spence as well. JoJo might be shady, but she has an alibi. She was caught on CCTV and in front of a hundred witnesses at The Obelisk the night my sister died. I know DS Rahman himself has checked this, too.

I concentrate, try to think like a gambler would. Growing up around the arcade, helping Tim with the slips, I've become used to measuring life in odds and likelihoods. 'All's fair in love and war … and money!' Tim would quip, before emptying buckets of change into the coin sorters for the bank.

So, maybe Jayden could have had my sister erased in revenge … for breaking him and Ana up, making their relationship 'complicated', as Ana calls it on her Facebook profile? Maybe Jayden Spence is one of the other names … The Wolf? Frog King?

If I were a betting woman, I would put money on Jayden being Frog King. He was the type to play the Big I Am. He'd survey his kingdom, doing the least possible while ensuring his minions did all the heavy lifting. And as I already knew, he'd been distracted, playing away with JoJo. I recall the ball in my sister's dream. The words of the frog – 'They'll never let her go' – come to mind, and suddenly something clicks.

I know whose name is on the ball.

Thanks to Gordon's love of publicity, I know where the Spences live. It's a palatial, gated complex near Brighton Marina, made up of three large Victorian converted houses, linked together. I take a bus across town and stand outside the opulent, extravagant gates (the Spences have even created their own family crest, for God's sake). It's as if Gordon Spence has composed a list of everything you might find in a gazillionaire's home and then demanded it be built.

The buildings spring up like majestic white mushrooms from a perfectly tended lawn. There's a swimming pool, a decked area and a gazebo. There are servants' quarters and a riding stable, even a petting zoo. I can see a pot-bellied pig, a couple of ducks and a llama wandering about. A young woman with raven-black hair and a farmer's gait slings feed into a trough. The animals waddle over.

On the lawn, there's a selection of children's toys: a swing, a slide, a sandpit. I don't have to imagine Ana's little girl here. I recognise some of the state-of-the-art play equipment from Ana's Facebook photos.

Security is top notch. A camera stares down at me from above the gates. Before I can even press a buzzer, a hoarse, male voice with a clipped accent barks from the intercom near my elbow.

'Do you have an appointment?'

'Yes,' I lie, though my stomach flips. 'I'm here to see Ana Temple.'

'Name?'

Crap, they've got a list. I give up on the game, knowing they've found me out. 'OK, look – I need to see Ana. Two minutes. Send her out here, if you prefer?'

'Nice try.' There's no warmth in the voice on the intercom, his tone steel. There's no way he'll be letting me in. 'Move away from the gates, please.'

Cursing, I do as I am told. I wander down the road a few steps. I sit on the kerb and wait, watching as the afternoon sun sinks away into the horizon. Dusk comes early. I scroll through India's phone. A couple of social-media notifications, neither important. More spam, newsletters.

Still no message or call from Jenny.

Around six, a couple of cars leave the Spences'. I spring to my feet in readiness, but I don't have time to run up and slip through the gates unseen as I hoped. *Damn it.* Frustrated, I kick the road, still on the wrong side of the barrier.

A voice behind me attracts my attention. 'Can I help?'

The voice is heavy with accent. Eastern European, maybe. I turn to see the woman who was tending to the petting zoo. I notice the gate has a pedestrian exit, too. She's wearing a threadbare fleece, jeans and wellingtons. Her black hair is threaded with premature grey, her forehead creased, lips chapped.

I give her a wide smile. 'I've come to see Ana?'

But I am thwarted again. 'Ana not here.' The woman pulls the pedestrian exit shut after her. The metal of the gate clangs with finality.

'She's out?' I say, hopeful. 'Is she with Matthew, maybe? At Elemental?'

The woman shrugs. 'Dunno.' She strides off ahead of me, forcing me to race after her.

'Are you saying Ana *doesn't* live here?' I demand, falling into step with her.

'She not here for weeks.' The woman takes a packet of cigarettes from her breast pocket as she stalks down the road on long, skinny legs.

'She's moved out?'

The woman lights her cigarette. The end glows in the growing darkness. 'Dunno. Good night.'

I stop, helpless, as she disappears down the road. I recall Ana's relationship status on her Facebook wall: 'complicated'. But where do women with children go, when their relationships are in trouble? Easy.

Back to Mum and Dad.

Thirty-seven

I walk the twenty-five minutes it takes to cross town to the Temples' faux-Tudor mansion, Coy Ponds. They've been here ten years, but I haven't been welcome for half that. It's an impressive place, but next to the Spences', its white-timbered frame looks like a dolls' house.

I trudge across the mini-bridge over the well-stocked pond that leads into two smaller ones, the whole design perfectly symmetrical. In them, carp shimmer under the water. The garden is busier than the Spences', too. I have to tread a slalom course around a selection of shrubs, trees and garden ornaments: fairies, dragons, even a wishing well. Maggie Temple has always believed in magic and happy endings.

I knock on the front door.

Ana must have been expecting someone else, because she opens the door with a wide smile. Behind her, the little girl appears. Curious, the toddler's wide brown eyes stare up at me, as she holds onto Ana's skirts. Motherhood suits my old friend.

'Ana…!'

Her face sours as she attempts to shut the door. I put my foot in the way, cursing as the tough wood slams on my flesh. There will be an ugly bruise there in the morning.

'India was in love with you, wasn't she?'

That's enough to make her stop. She regards me, agog: her mouth falls open, her perfect white teeth on display. 'What the hell are you talking about?'

I feel my pet theory beginning to dissipate. Ana is no actor; and you can't fake that kind of reaction off the bat. I press on, anyway; perhaps Ana was never aware of my sister's infatuation.

'She split you and Jayden up, right? Saw her chance, with him playing away. Because she had feelings for you!'

Pain throbs through my bruised foot. If life were a cartoon, my foot would grow to twice its size, with big red arrows pointing all around it. But I push my discomfort down and concentrate on Ana.

She rolls her eyes. 'I haven't seen India in ages. I hadn't even talked to her!'

My theory shatters, *Tom and Jerry*-like, to china pieces on the floor. My sister never struck me as a hopeless romantic, adoring someone from afar. And she was almost twenty-five, not a shy schoolgirl. So, OK, perhaps my theory for why India had shamed JoJo was incorrect; but maybe the end result's still the same.

'Did India come to you about Jayden's affair with JoJo … *before* she put it on the blog?' I wince, sure Ana will try to slam the door on my foot again.

But she doesn't. Ana swallows down her resentment, her hand on her little girl's head. I realise she is trying to keep her cool, for the child's sake.

'No,' Ana confirms at last.

I dive straight in, before I can think better of it. 'So, where was Jayden, the night India…?'

Ana's eyes bug. Behind them, the cogs of her brain work overtime. It's clear she has no idea, but is trying to remember.

'With me,' Ana says finally, a defiant smile on her lips.

She doesn't fool me. 'You're lying.'

'Oh, whatever, Poppy.' There's venom in Ana's words. 'I'll say this once more: Leave. Us. Alone. Now get your foot out of my door.'

I lean forwards, bracing the door on my elbow before she can shut it on me again. 'I saw Jayden at the funeral. Watching us. Why would he do that?'

Ana's face twists in that feral snarl of hers. 'Maybe he wanted to make sure India was dead!'

I don't rise to the bait. 'Did Jayden get rid of India? For telling everyone about JoJo?'

Ana's eyes are shiny with rage, or tears, or both. 'You're deluded. What the hell is this? You feel guilty you weren't here, so you're trying to make up some conspiracy to fit?'

'I'm not making it up!' I silently implore Ana to hear my certainty, to recognise the possible truth in what I'm saying. We were close, once. She owes me the benefit of the doubt. 'The girl India wrote her note to – Jenny? She *does* exist. I've met her. Now the blog is gone and…'

'Would you listen to yourself? India's gone, Poppy!'

The little girl whimpers at our raised voices. Ana remembers herself and leans down for her daughter, but the toddler flinches away. This brings Ana's ire in my direction a second time.

'Now look what you've done!'

Ivy breaks away from her mother, through to a room beyond. I hear another voice in there, a male one. I seize on this.

'Is Jayden here…?'

I try and force my way into the hall, but Ana's hands grab me by the shoulders. She's surprisingly strong, forcing me back over the threshold with ease.

'This isn't over!' I shout.

Ana flashes me a facetious smile. 'Oh, just piss off and play detectives somewhere else.'

My aching foot removed from the entrance, the door is slammed shut in my face. I stand on Coy Ponds' front lawn, wondering what the hell my next move should be.

Thirty-eight

There's a bitter breeze in the winter night air. It whips along the seafront, bringing rubbish with it. The beach is deserted, dusk slithering up its banks. As I return to the Coach House from Coy Ponds, I catch sight of The Obelisk again. Dark shadows surge over both piers. There is a twinkling of neon lights from the takeaways and bars further along the beach.

As I wander across the beach towards the massive hotel resort, I see activity in the big, glass reception. The concierge talks to a tall woman with a beehive hairdo. He's smiling, but she is the stern type and looks less than amused. She stalks out of the doors, towards a taxi waiting on the forecourt. I recognise her as the event planner of the upcoming annual spring ball to celebrate Jayden Spence's birthday.

That's where I can find the elusive playboy.

I pray I haven't missed the event. I whip my phone out of my pocket and call up The Obelisk's website on its little screen. I wait as it loads, impatient. I click on the ticket icon and baulk at the price. *How much?* I've already lost my deposit on my London flat, as well as my few belongings that were still back there. I received a multitude of notices from my landlord, the last telling me everything was going in a skip. *It's all junk anyway.* I'm just glad Tim isn't about to throw me out and that I've a little money saved.

Another thirty-six hours pass. There is still no word from Jenny, despite my repeated checks of my sister's phone and laptop. I keep hoping it's all just a big mistake. Maybe the server did something wrong? Maybe India's blog will come back, or at least Jenny's Blithefancy profile with the sugar skull. Yet every time I type in both website addresses, I am rewarded only with that infuriating 404 message.

With no other lead, I give in and buy a ticket to the spring ball. I borrow a dress from Mum's wardrobe this time: green, with silver piping, it's a little short but I decide I can pull it off. Tim is underwhelmed when I announce I'm going to The Obelisk Ball. I expected him to be angry, to wonder how I can party with both my sister and mother gone. But he does not seem to notice, even when I ask him for a lift down to the resort because I am not used to walking in my mother's wedge heels. Tim drops me off without a word, like I'm a teenager going to the prom.

Adjusting my wrap, I teeter across the hotel's front car park, anxious to get out of the cold breeze blowing in from the beach. I run over possible scenarios in advance. What if Jayden isn't there? The ball is just an excuse for his father to play the big shot, so maybe his son won't bother turning up. That would be a disaster. Or perhaps Jayden will be there, but with Ana? That could be even worse, given the scene at Coy Ponds.

I make it into The Obelisk without incident. I hand over my ticket and mingle with the countless other guests, both resident and nonresident. The hotel seems alive with music and talk. Party-goers take up every available space. People chatter and amble through the communal areas, stopping in reception, on the stairs, on the mezzanine.

The event's decoration is impressive: everywhere streamers and ribbons; translucent helium balloons full of glitter; even live statues on podiums. These patient men and women are painted gold and silver, waiting to shock guests by moving suddenly. People flinch in readiness, delighting in the anticipation.

Warmth creeps up the back of my neck and down my sides as hundreds of bodies circulate around mine. In the air, the acrid smell of metal oxide pricks my nostrils as masked performers trace colourful swirls with indoor sparklers. The bars are full, the main restaurant heaving. I feel hundreds of eyes upon me. A lone female, I discover my very presence causes ripples through the crowd as they part around me. Anxious to withdraw into the shadows, I take up residence at a side bar just beyond the main ballroom.

I am sure that if Jayden is here, he will have to pass me at some point. I turn to the barman to order a drink. It's the kid with acne from earlier in the week. I order and the young barman leaves a contour bottle with a pink straw in front of me. As I glance behind me, checking for Jayden, I see JoJo stalk past. She carries a tray of canapés and gives an exasperated look when she spies me, before disappearing into the crowd.

My gaze settles on various faces, masked and not. The music swallows the hubbub of chatter of all except those closest to me. I hear a laugh as someone brushes up against me. Big hands hold me in place as a man attempts to navigate his way through the crush, past me. I look up.

'Poppy. What are you doing here?'

Matthew.

His right hand grips my arm. He's wearing an expensive suit, his tie loose around his throat like his father. There's a five o'clock shadow on his chin.

He is alone.

I am torn, both wanting to speak to Matthew and to search for Jayden. I dally a moment, but the latter wins. I attempt to jerk my arm away from Matthew, but his fingers dig, harder, into my flesh.

'I asked you a question.' Matthew looms over me.

I glance up at him. 'It's a public event.'

'Hardly your thing, though.'

'People change.'

Matthew raises an eyebrow. 'Touché.'

I glance down at the crowd milling around us. I can see Maggie and Alan Temple standing on ceremony, smiling and laughing with other party-goers. As ever, Maggie looks immaculate in a beautiful red silk dress. Alan looks like he's been dragged through a hedge backwards. Yet they're easy in each other's company, their bodies close.

'You can't be here.' Matthew moves his gaze away from me, scanning the crowd. I don't know who he's looking for, but I can guess: Ana. So she must be here.

'You don't get to tell me what to do.' Despite my anger, I like the touch of his fingertips on my skin.

'Sure about that?'

As Matthew says this, an involuntary shiver makes its way down my spine. I am unnerved, just like I was during our interlude in his office at Elemental. His fingers clench around my arm. Suddenly he's moving, forcing me to go with him.

'Look. I just want to speak to Jayden…'

Matthew's jaw tightens. He does not turn to me. He does not release me, even when I try to struggle free.

'You can't do this! Matthew!'

But Matthew doesn't listen. I strain against him now. But he increases his grip, pushing me in the opposite direction.

As we go, I catch sight of my quarry, walking away: Jayden Spence. An unlit cigarette dangles from his mouth. The playboy exchanges words with a dumpy guy with grey hair, who has an arm slung around a tall woman with an elaborate stole. Jayden walks towards a side door.

He's not with Ana.

I turn my body in Jayden's direction, determined to follow him. But I can't fight Matthew; he's too strong for me.

I recognise where we're going: towards the front doors of the hotel. *He's going to eject me!* I renew my struggles, to no avail. But before Matthew can open the big glass doors, someone materialises out of the crowd in our path. I hear him groan behind me: *busted*.

'Poppy. I told you to stay away.'

Ana.

Thirty-nine

Ana wears a 1920s-style dress. It's short and beaded on the front; there's a feathered headband in her hair. Her long, shapely legs are bare. On her feet are shoes that would cost a normal person a week's salary. She looks amazing and knows it; millenials would say that she *got swag (adjectival phrase.* Sophisticated. Related words: cool, smart).

For some, it might be difficult to believe Jayden chose to play away with an awkward girl like JoJo, when he had a woman like Ana at home. But I know better: Ana's confident veneer is just a shell, as easy to crack as the skin of ice on the fountain in front of The Obelisk. Perhaps JoJo was a welcome distraction from Ana's many neuroses, or maybe Jayden just took what he wanted, because men like him do.

I grin benevolently at Matthew's sister. 'Ana. Lovely to see you.'

Ana affects a bored sneer. 'Really.'

She catches sight of her brother's inscrutable expression, his hand on my arm. Caught out, he lets go of me.

Her eyes narrow. 'Are you with her?'

'No!' Matthew says, perhaps a little too fast. *Or is that my imagination?* 'I didn't want you to have to see her, that's all.'

The air between them crackles with resentment. I've seen scenes like this play out before, so I know better than to attempt to intervene. Disagreements between the Temple siblings can be epic; they always build up with a pressure cooker's intensity, and can become physical. The more Ana pushes, the more Matthew retracts. Then, when his back is finally against the wall, he erupts. It isn't pretty.

'You're going backwards, Matt.' Ana pokes the flesh of my arm with one of her ridiculously long talons. There are nail jewels on every single one. I swallow back a retort.

'I told you, I'm not going back to her.'

Despite the way the argument is going, I am heartened. So I must have been the subject of previous discussions between them. Did Matthew tell her about our moment in the office at Elemental? Or did she guess? (**Twin Fu**, *noun*. Spooky shit where your other half knows what you're doing, even before you do it.)

Ana puts her hands on her hips. 'You remember what *she* did?'

But Matthew is stone-like. His shutters are well and truly down. 'You remember what Jayden did?'

Ana's face crumples, like Matthew has dealt her a body blow. Her relationship is a very sensitive subject, as I deduced. But she recovers quickly.

'That's different. Jayden's just another twat who can't keep it in his pants. *She* ran out on you when you had *cancer*, Matt!'

In an instant, I'm transported back four (*nearly five*) years. The smell of antibacterial hand gel; the low, hypnotic whirr of the chemo machine; lights and alarm bells. Sickness permeates the air, loss hovers in every corner of the ward. Patients smile as painful cannulas are forced into their hands. They offer words of encouragement to one another, deliberately ignoring the spaces where another person once sat, telling themselves it's just a cancellation. *Not another death*.

Facing Ana, fury makes me flush. 'That's not *why* I left! You know that. You both do – right, Matthew?' I throw my appeal at him, sure he will validate it. But, like in the office at Elemental, I am disappointed. Matthew shrugs, almost imperceptibly. He won't look me in the eye.

It's the confirmation Ana needs. 'He needed you. But off you went, gallivanting round London, leaving us to pick up the pieces. Selfish bitch.'

'It wasn't like that,' I insist. 'I was going anyway! We *both* were. Matt decided to stay...'

'Yes. That was your cue.' Ana enunciates each word slowly, as if I am a child. 'Guess you missed it.'

Anger pricks my skin. 'Look. I'm going, OK?'

Matthew opens the big glass door for me. I stalk out, without a backward glance at the twins. The noise from inside is muted as the door closes behind me. I totter across the car park, like I'm going home. As I reach the parking barrier, I stop.

I steal a glance back at The Obelisk. I can see Matthew and Ana still by the doors, but now deep in conversation, their backs to me. Matthew puts a hand out, brushing his sister's arm, but she jerks away, as if she can't bear him to touch her. She watches him disappear into the throng, before stalking off in the opposite direction.

I lean down and pull my heels off, my bare feet flinching as they touch the cold tarmac. When I saw him in the crowd, the playboy had an unlit cigarette dangling from his mouth.

I know where Jayden is.

Forty

I sidle past a service entrance to another backroom area, ducking behind a pillar. A hungover chef staggers out with a bunch of bags and cardboard. He shoves it all in the compactor and presses a button. I wait until he's gone, then make my way around The Obelisk's peace gardens, towards the smoking shelter beyond.

'Smoking shelter' is a misnomer. That word brings forth notions of shacks in pubs with roofs made of corrugated iron, plus broken benches and dog ends littering the concrete. But like everything else, The Obelisk's smoking shelter is a work of art. It's more akin to an ornate bandstand, its posts carved with tiny, intricate designs in gold and silver.

Just as I hoped, Jayden Spence is holding court there. A small cluster of all-male sycophants stand around him, lapping up his every word.

'So yeah, obviously, blud. I told him to go fuck himself.'

Jayden's hangers-on erupt into peals of laughter. His voice is reedy, plummy and slightly musical, the unmistakable timbre of someone who's had a wealth – *literally* – of education. But despite his accent, Jayden's words are more *street* (*adjective*. Common. Related words: rough, poor) than he looks. They seem false and stilted on his tongue, like a non-native English speaker's.

I sit down on one of the baroque seats nearby to eavesdrop. I look over at the group of men. I stare shamelessly at Jayden. I nod, as if I'm entranced by everything he's saying. As some other bore drones on in his ear about contracts, Jayden catches sight of me in his peripheral vision. I avert my eyes, feigning embarrassment. When I look back, I can see him grinning to himself, like he's hit the jackpot. He believes my bluff, just like I knew he would. *Men like him always do.*

Two minutes pass. His cronies find themselves dismissed, as Jayden focuses his sights on me. Beyond the smoking shelter, the weather has taken a turn for the worse. The hairs on my arms prickle. The shelter is open, glass-topped. I can see the stars through the panes as raindrops hammer down on them. Jayden appears by my side on the bench.

'Haven't seen you around here before?'

Even I can't suppress my mirth. '*That's* your opener?'

'Innit. True though.' Jayden pulls another cigarette from a silver case with his initials engraved on it.

I let the question stand. I know him but he doesn't recall me. Ana got together with him long after I left Brighton. I just smile at him, watching the wheels of his mind spinning round. As far as the likes of Jayden Spence are concerned, all women want them. All he need do is divide them into two categories: the ones he wants and the ones he doesn't. And he wants me. He makes no secret of that. He takes me in, looking me and up and down, approving. I flutter my eyelashes and flip my hair like a prize pony.

'I don't remember putting you on the guest list.'

I offer a girlish laugh. 'I bought a ticket.'

He offers me a cigarette, but I decline with a shake of my head. He's not paying any attention, though. It's just a ruse to move his whole body towards me, into my space. His breath smells sour: whisky and ash. I force myself not to shift away from him in distaste.

He places one hand on my thigh. I let him. That little voice in the back of my head pipes up again: *Now what?* India's face swims into my mind. Could the hand on my leg right now be the same one Jayden used to push my little sister from the bridge? I suppress a shudder.

'My name's Poppy.'

Jayden purses his lips. 'Oh, I know who you are.'

It all happens so fast. The playboy drops his cigarette and grabs my right forearm in the same movement. He grips my wrist and twists my flesh. It causes me to cry out in pain. He is strong. I'm caught completely off guard.

'This is about India.' So he *does* remember me, after all. 'Am I right?' He twists again, making tears spring up in my eyes. 'I heard you'd been sniffing around. I don't like ambushes, *Poppy Wade*.'

Raw anger kicks in. I know how to handle scrotes like Spence. Growing up with a suspicious mother like mine, who saw threats everywhere, I'd opted to take self-defence classes, just to get her off my back. I'm glad of them, now.

I turn my free hand into a hook and drive it hard into Jayden's side. His eyes roll in agony. He lets go of my arm and falls to one knee, both hands in the small of his back, where I know my blow must be reverberating.

I'm not finished. I backhand him across the mouth. *Bitch slap* (*noun*. A blow with an open hand. Related words: strike, whack). He whimpers like the coward he is. He falls backwards on his arse, both arms raised in surrender.

I stand over him, triumphant. 'Hey, *blud*, don't treat women like shit!'

As I stare at the crumpled playboy at my feet, sound registers: clapping. Confused, I look up.

There's a flash of movement and someone appears in the smoking shelter. But not from the hotel side door. He appears from the grounds, like I had. Out of the darkness, like he's taking form from the shadows.

Matthew.

Forty-one

'Reckon he's had that coming for a while.'

Matthew leans against one of the smoking shelter's ornate posts. I shrug, unable to speak for a minute. I'm wired; my body is still twitching slightly from the fight.

I note an almost predatory gleam in Matthew's eye at the sight of the blood on his brother-in-law's face. His suit is drenched with rain. Matthew must have been standing watching beyond the smoking shelter for a while. I realise: *He is pleased I've hurt Jayden.*

'Fuck you, Matt.' Jayden hisses.

Matthew smirks. He grabs Jayden from the floor, lands him heavily on the bench.

Jayden groans and touches a hand to his mouth. Blood on his fingertips: a split lip. 'She's a crazy bitch!'

'True,' Matthew concedes. He catches my eye and smiles, the first real warmth I've had from him since my return. I smile back, despite myself.

Jayden's head jerks from me to Matthew, like a Wimbledon match. 'Oh, so you two are back together, are you? Brilliant. Can I go now?'

'No!' Matthew and I say this together.

Jayden regards us, his face dark with petulant fury. I decide to grab my chance while I can.

'Why did you come to India's funeral?'

'I didn't. Not exactly, anyway.' Jayden stays where he is, slumped on the bench, one hand still clasped to his aching back. He shoots an appealing glance at Matthew. 'I just wanted to see Ana, innit. She wasn't answering my texts or picking up the phone.'

I look to Matthew to confirm this.

He casts his mind back, then nods. 'It's true. He waited for her afterwards.'

But I'm not willing to give up, just yet. 'Where were you, Jayden, between six and nine on the 22nd December?'

The playboy regards me, slack-jawed. 'Are you for real? What is this Miss Marple sh—?'

Jayden's words cut off as Matthew looms by my side, arms folded, the threat obvious. *Any excuse.*

Jayden raises his eyes skywards. 'Fine!'

The playboy digs in his pocket. I think he's going to pull out yet another cigarette, but it's his mobile. He taps the buttons, scrolls through his diary app.

'I was … here. It was the Marchand Christmas party.'

I recollect JoJo telling me the same. I look to Matthew again. 'Is he telling the truth – was he here?'

Matthew shrugs this time. 'No clue. You'd have to ask Ana.'

Another stalemate. She's already told me Jayden was with her.

'Even if he was here, he could have left and then come back, right?'

'Whoa, whoa, are you saying what I think you're saying?' Jayden's drink-addled mind finally catches on. 'You reckon I killed India. For real? Jesus!' Jayden shakes his head, as if he can't quite believe it, forgetting his own unprovoked violence towards me just minutes previously.

'You got motive.' I find myself saying. A phrase lifted from a TV show.

Jayden sighs. 'Yeah, yeah, OK: I admit it. I hated India. She nearly screwed me and Ana up for good…'

Matthew butts in, his visage a ferocious snarl. '*You* nearly screwed you and Ana up for good.'

Jayden hawks a gob of bloody phlegm at Matthew's feet. 'Like I could get a look in, "little bro"!'

I assumed Ana deleted Jayden's pictures in a fit of pique, once she learned of his infidelity. But maybe Jayden just didn't figure that highly on Ana's radar? I've seen only that one picture of him on Ana's Facebook profile, compared to countless photos of Matthew and, of course, her daughter, Ivy. It could explain the affair: he wasn't getting what he wanted from Ana; she was freezing him out?

Jayden regards Matthew, whose face is full of scorn. Jayden's expression is curiously triumphant. 'We're over it now, anyway. Life's good.'

'You're lying. I know Ana's moved out.' I enjoy the renewed panic in Jayden's eyes.

'OK, OK! We're still working on it.' Jayden admits, his visage now as sulky as a twelve-year-old boy's. 'But we're making progress. Why would I screw that up months after the fact by killing your bitch of a sister?'

Matthew's gaze meets mine, requesting permission. I nod, without hesitation. He lands another blow on Jayden, this time to his stomach. I see Matthew's lip curl with a disconcertingly delighted sneer. Jayden doubles over, air deflating from him with a rasping moan.

But whether I like it or not, Jayden has a point. It doesn't seem likely that an empire like the Spences' would place itself in jeopardy over something that is now public knowledge. *Why would he kill India after she'd told everyone about him and JoJo?*

'How do you know Jenny?' I demand.

'Jenny who?' As Matthew raises another fist, Jayden gives a weedy shriek: 'I know lots of Jennys, man! Don't hit me again! Which one?'

Which one? Well, isn't that a question. I can feel myself beginning to grasp at straws. 'You got any Jennys working here, at The Obelisk?'

Jayden looks at us with wide eyes. 'I dunno...' The playboy flinches from another blow from Matthew that doesn't come. 'Maybe! You'd have to ask my dad. He does the hiring and firing.'

I have an urge to walk back into the ball and grab Gordon Spence by the lapels. 'And where is your dad? Is he here tonight?'

'Dubai.' Jayden snivels, wiping his nose with a sleeve. 'Went yesterday. Check if you don't believe me! My mum's with him, OK?'

A sense of anticlimax settles over me. I look to Matthew. 'We're wasting our time.'

Matthew's gaze is still on Jayden, the shadow of violence still on his face. His shoulders are tense, his hands balled into fists by his sides. I'm unnerved. I've never seen him in such a pose before. It's as if he's having to concentrate on *not* hitting Jayden again. *He must really hate him.*

'What the hell does Ana see in him?' I take Matthew's arm.

He looks at me, remembering I'm there. 'Beats me.'

We turn our backs on the wilting playboy. I pick my bag up from where it fell on the shelter floor and grab my shoes. The rain has now downgraded to just mizzle (*noun, dialect.* Light rain. Related words: drizzle, shower); the air and grass are alive with moisture under my bare toes. It's cold, but not unpleasant. My feet sink into the muddy ground. I have to pick my way across the lawn with exaggerated steps, half leaning on Matthew.

The grass becomes concrete. We've made our way around the massive building, back to the car park. I stop, suddenly world-weary. My sister's words come back to me: 'You will be free … as I am, now.' Maybe it *was* a suicide note. Perhaps, like Ana said, I'm making up conspiracies to fit.

As if he senses my disquiet, Matthew stops and cups my face in his big hands. 'India wouldn't want you to torture yourself like this.'

Matthew brings his lips to mine. As I close my eyes, I see my sister. India laughs and runs across a beach. She's wearing the long, hippy skirt with the bells from her Facebook picture. She wheels around in a circle, her head thrown back at the bright-blue skies overhead. India loved life. Deep inside me, I know that. Nothing could have affected her so radically as to change that. The image shatters like glass. I turn my face away from Matthew's, taking a moment to compose myself.

'I'm sorry, I thought…?'

I look back at him: his expression seems open, vulnerable. Any trace of malice is gone. I grab his hand, pulling him to me.

We kiss again.

He envelops me in his big arms. I breathe him in, as if I can absorb the whole of him. His lips are soft, though his chin is scratchy. He tastes of beer as his tongue moves into my mouth. I can feel his heartbeat, pressed against his hard chest.

'C'mon, let's get out of here.' Matthew's voice is playful.

Holding hands, we race back up the seafront towards his car, away from The Obelisk.

Forty-two

I don't ask where we're going. I don't need to.

Matthew does not drop me at the Coach House. Instead, his car cuts through Brighton's streets. At night and out of season, they are all but deserted even now, at the weekend. Beyond, the neon lights of the business park glitter. A handful of youngsters appear from a pizza joint and hoot at someone else across the road.

The clock on the dashboard reads just past midnight. Looking at Matthew, his hands on the wheel, he seems so familiar, yet so different, too. But I've known him the best part of twenty years. I lost my virginity to him; lived with him. *This is Matthew,* I remind myself.

We arrive at a modest, white converted building about a fifteen-minute drive from The Obelisk. An apartment block. Matthew pulls in to an adjoining car park and we get out of the vehicle.

'You live here?'

There's a small front lawn, a couple of washing lines, a kid's pedal truck abandoned on its side. It's less than Matthew is used to at Coy Ponds with his family, but I'm not really surprised. Matthew never really went in for the trappings of wealth. Our flat in Hove was far worse than this.

'I'm on the top floor.'

'Oh, the penthouse?' I tease.

'Hardly.'

Matthew lets us in through the front door, which opens with a code. There's a spacious hallway, a small stained-glass window and a door that leads out to a back garden. To the right, a number of pigeonholes for post. On the left, a stairway with a large, curved banister. I follow Matthew up. The building is higher than it looks: three, four, five storeys.

Finally, we're at the top. There is only one flat up here. Matthew stops outside a scarred door and lets us in. It opens directly onto a large kitchen/living area. Through a doorway, I can see a compact bedroom, a double bed. As I might expect from Matthew, everything is pathologically neat, just so. He gets this from Maggie. I recall the inside of Coy Ponds always looks like a show home, despite the mad jumble of ornaments on the lawn.

He opens a cupboard. 'Do you want a drink?'

But I'm bored of pretending everything is innocent between us. 'Not really.'

Matthew reaches out and grabs my waist. He pulls me to him and towards the bedroom. Contrary as ever, I pull in the opposite direction, forcing him to use more power than he should need to. I can feel the sinews in his arms contract.

I smirk at him, as if to say, *Now what?*

He pushes me against the wall outside his room. His weight is on my chest, pinning me there. I couldn't resist him if I wanted to. But I don't want to. I want him so bad I can feel a ball of heat exploding within my stomach. It works its way out of me, between my parted legs. I feel him harden. Material strains against my thigh.

Forceful, Matthew kisses me. He pushes his tongue into my mouth. I can't breathe. One hand finds my breasts; I'm not wearing a bra. Matthew's other hand finds its way under my dress, between my legs. His long fingers press past the thin material of my knickers. Two probe inside me and an involuntary moan emanates from my throat.

He hooks his thumbs in my underwear and yanks them down. I hiss. It is not unpleasant; I'm just surprised. Matthew lets go of me and stands back, appraises me.

I am wrong-footed again, my knickers round my ankles. I tense. Have I just fallen into another trap, like in the office at Elemental? I expect him to sneer at me, to tell me to go.

But he doesn't. My green dress is hitched up; I smooth it down. Still unsure of his motivation, I decide stepping out of my underwear is the least awkward option, so I do. My face betrays none of my inner turmoil.

'Matthew…'

'Quiet.' His tone is cold, a stranger's.

I'm shocked, but I can't deny the thrill. Another smile twitches in my lip, but I bite it back. He pulls me into the bedroom.

I observe as Matthew pulls his keys from his jacket, undoes his watch. He dumps them both on a cabinet. He unbuttons his shirt, lets the material flutter to the floor. He was always well built, but he's put on more muscle since I saw him naked last. My ego makes me wonder if he's spent more time in the gym in order to get over me. I reach out to trace one of his developed pecs with my fingers, but he slaps my hand away.

'Wait,' he orders.

That anticipation surges through my stomach again. All the time he stares at me. I don't tear my eyes away from his. He unbuckles his belt and undoes his trousers, lets them fall.

I avert my attention from Matthew's stomach. I grab the hem of my dress and yank it over my head. I stand before him, stripped. Defiant. I dare him silently to tell me to go.

He steps forwards, his gaze travelling down my naked body. He holds both hands either side of me, like a magician. I am desperate for him to touch me, to feel his skin on mine, but he doesn't. *Yet.*

'You got yourself into this.'

His hands move closer. I don't say anything as I let him lightly trace my breasts, my waist. He leans towards me and whispers in my ear. 'Say it.'

I obey him, obstinacy deserting me for once. 'I got myself into this.'

Matthew's impassive expression finally melts. He smiles.

I let him fold me in his arms. For a microsecond, I'm outside of the moment. In my mind, I see Ana's Facebook picture: Matthew in hospital, being comforted like a boy by Maggie.

But then I'm back. I grab for his boxers with one hand. We both stumble. I find myself walking backwards as he pushes forwards, towards the bed. I let myself fall back onto it, him on top of me.

'I missed you.'

Before I can reply he clamps his mouth back on mine. He moves upwards, his weight on my chest again.

He thrusts hard into me.

I gasp as he buries his head in my neck, biting me. His nails rake the skin on my sides. He pinches one of my nipples, making me cry out. He is unapologetic.

My hands find their way to his shoulders. I hold onto him, not wanting any space between our bodies. He grinds into me, but we both know it can't last long.

I cross my legs around him, over his back. He grabs my hips as I raise them off the bed. He speeds up, taking a sharp intake of breath as if trying to brace himself.

Then with a grunt he's done. He collapses onto me and stays there.

A contented sigh escapes me. I feel the impetus between us evaporate with the rough clasp of his touch.

Matthew rolls off me, stares at the ceiling. I prop myself up on one elbow and stare down at his face. His expression seems conflicted. He turns his face away.

The consultant's voice was soft. 'It's not a good tumour.'

Like there are any good ones.

She was a second-generation Chinese woman. Her voice was a strange mixture of a London accent and clipped vowels from speaking her native language at home. She hated telling us this, so she tried to buoy us up with forced optimism.

'Good news is, we caught it early. Prognosis is very good. Nine out of ten, OK?'

The consultant reached forwards, put a hand on Matthew's arm. She then outlined treatment options for us: surgery and chemotherapy. It all seemed so straightforward. *Doing it would be the hard part.*

'What about kids?' Matthew said.

The consultant averted her eyes, her answer obvious. *There would be no kids.* His face twisted with anguish.

I looked at Matthew, surprised. I never knew he wanted a family. We'd never discussed it. Anyway, I didn't care. I just wanted him well again. *My Matthew doesn't belong in this world.* How could he be so gravely ill? He was barely into his thirties; the fittest and healthiest of all of us. *It doesn't make sense.*

But it would never make sense. Cancer never does.

Nine out of ten. Prognosis very good.

The consultant's gaze was serious; she tried to bore her message into us, but it bounced off.

'Shock and trauma are centred in the kidney,' she said. Her expression was wistful, as if she was retelling a bedtime story, though I saw a glimmer of belief in her eye: 'Tumour can change people, if you let it.'

Now, Matthew and I lie in the darkness, not speaking, our bodies no longer touching. Back then, Matthew's love seemed like a Springer Spaniel's: *enthusiastic, loyal, bright.* Now, Matthew's temperament has been replaced with a more lupine quality: *suspicious, aloof, angry.*

Everything we had seems lost. But it isn't cancer that's done this to us.

It's me.

I want to say something, but I can find no words. *Words don't really mean anything, do they?* He does not attempt to hold me like he might have once.

There's space in the bed, a chasm of history between us as we both drift off.

Forty-three

Mirror, mirror on the wall … who is in charge of it all?

You, of course. They dance to your tune, try and keep up with your demands. But they will always fail. Their efforts will never be enough, especially his.

Your outside shell is deceiving. Your love is blinding, all encompassing. Those who worship at your altar fall to their knees in front of you, awed by your presence. But your love always comes at a price. They must give up parts of themselves to become a part of you.

Rebellion is not tolerated. Instead, you insist Jenny does not exist. You don't seem to trust your own eyes. Or maybe it is her beauty that offends you? And she is beautiful. But you tell her she is nothing, deny her. She scratches her skin, trying to uncover the real girl inside, but finds only blood and bone and hurt … You say you love her, but refuse to set her free.

Or is it *my* blood that runs in her veins, too?

Perhaps both. Twenty-five years of lies lead to this.

But your days are numbered. Deep down, you know this. It's why you have him doing your dirty work for you. Bringing Jenny back to your toxic folds, warning me off. Yes, I know a threat when I hear one.

So here is one, for you.

Let her go. Or I will be that voice, for Jenny.

Unlike her, you can't stop me.

India

POSTED BY **@1NDIAsummer**, <u>27 November 2016</u>
<u>29,266 insights</u> ⏎ **SHARE THIS**
> ⏎ ***markotron*** likes this
> ⏎ ***Alfie98*** likes this
> ⏎ ***warriorwasp*** likes this
> ⏎ ***writerchic88*** likes this
> ⏎ ***Milliecat_456*** likes this
> ⏎ ***Blithefancy*** comments: *ugh, sum ppl – IM me xx*

Forty-four

'So, has there been anyone else?'

Matthew woke in a better mood. He brought me coffee, kissing me on the lips like he used to, as if we'd never been apart. But now, with my enquiry, his shutters come down again.

'What does it matter?' His tone is accusing, his expression irritated, as he pulls his head through a t-shirt.

My gaze flickers to the brown scar on Matthew's side, before it disappears out of view. It's neat, keyhole. I think he wanted me to see it, to gauge my reaction. Even though I Googled the images at the time, I still thought the scar would be bigger. Yet it seems so small, for something so life-changing.

I smile uncertainly, trying to keep the mood light, 'Just curious.'

'For God's sake, Poppy, it's been nearly five years. Do you think I've been living like a monk, or something?' Matthew's voice is gruff as he pulls a pair of trousers, neatly pressed, from the chest of drawers, 'I know *you* can't have been.'

I'm stung at the inference, even though it's true. I remember the wandering hands of D, the night my sister died. The various men before him, after Matthew and I split. Though I went looking for sex, I never wanted anything serious. I barely ever wanted a second date. Just someone to warm my bed, take my mind off the stress of work. The guys I met were fun, but they weren't Matthew.

I try and keep my tone playful. 'Maybe not, but no one measured up.'

To you, I add silently. I want him to smile now, say the same back to me. Then we can laugh and lie back down on the bed together. *That's how it's supposed to work.*

If Matthew can read my thoughts, he's not letting on. He yanks on his jeans, one leg, then the other. He says nothing.

Put out, his unresponsiveness exacerbates my hostility. 'Why didn't you defend me to Ana, at the ball?'

Matthew's expression is impassive again. 'She has a right to her opinion.'

Resentment flowers within me. I always knew the depth of Ana's rage at my actions. But she seems to have conveniently forgotten that just a few weeks before Matthew's diagnosis, I'd been offered an unconditional offer at Goldsmith's University to do a postgrad course. We'd been making plans to move to the capital together, before Matthew's test results came back with the news that would blow everything apart.

I try and keep a lid on my fury now. We've been down this road before. Many times. 'I still wanted you to come with me. You *were* coming with me!'

'Things changed.' Matthew's back is to me. He busies himself, grabbing socks from a drawer. He sits on the bed to put them on, deliberately not looking me in the eye. 'You left me behind.'

I'm aghast. 'You *know* I didn't. I would never…!'

'And yet you were gone, exactly when I needed you.' Matthew's voice is flat, not accusatory. Somehow that makes it worse.

'I wanted you to come with me,' I repeat, stubborn as ever.

Matthew finally regards me, his expression withering. 'How could I? I had cancer.'

But I'm not taking that. 'There are hospitals in London, for God's sake. Better ones, probably, than here!' I can't believe how we've fallen into the past so readily. 'I would've looked after you. You know I would.'

'I needed to stay here,' Matthew sighs. 'Look, it was your choice: stay or go. You left.'

Here we are again: *The Ultimatum*. It has always been about *my choice*, never Matthew's. But I didn't have a choice, not really: the very fact I still wanted to go was held against me. Not just by

Matthew, either. Ana; even India. Both of them reckoned they knew what was best for *my* boyfriend, what *I* should do.

I could understand it from Ana, as she was his twin sister. But *my* sister lectured me endlessly, telling me Matthew would do the same for me. *But how the hell would she know?* She'd never known the inflexible side of Matthew, or the part of him that would run back to Mummy whenever there was trouble.

Choking down my anger, I turn my back on Matthew. I grab my stuff off the floor and sweep through to the bathroom. I lock myself in the tiny room. I debate quickly about taking a shower, but decide against it. I'd only have to put dirty clothes back on. I want to get out of here as quickly as I can. I splash water on my face and slick my rumpled hair, before yanking my dress and shoes back on.

Like the British-Chinese consultant said, Matthew was lucky. They caught the tumour early. It would be a question of battening down the hatches and getting on with chemo, yes, but we could handle it! Together, as a couple. *Why didn't he believe in us?*

So I left and began my postgrad course. I felt certain that Matthew would join me inside of a month. I even made enquiries at Brighton hospital, asking what would happen if he wanted to move his treatment. They said it would not be a problem; London was only up the road, after all.

But Matthew didn't join me. Instead, I found myself in a Mexican standoff: he wouldn't budge, so neither would I. I tried to follow his progress, first via my parents ('We can't get involved, Poppy'), then via India, who wanted to give me a piece of her mind every chance she got. As far as my little sister was concerned, it was simple: *Come back.* Mum and Tim wouldn't intervene with that either, waiting patiently for us all to sort it out like adults.

But I was too stubborn. I sent Matthew cards, gifts, letters. They came back, returned to sender, unopened. I tried texting and emailing him. No reply. Before long, I backed off, still sure Matthew would have a change of heart.

He didn't.

As I appear from the bathroom, I see Matthew is dressed for work. He looks tired and stressed. It's all I can do not to walk over to him and put my head on his shoulder, make him wrap those big arms around me just like he used to. But that's all changed. I don't know how.

'Matthew…'

I will him to turn from the window, look at me. I can feel the words bubbling up, about to spill from my lips. I want to tell him that last night it seemed like we slipped back into the past, in a *good* way. We rediscovered each other, called each other back from the brink. I want to tell him I should have come straight back to Brighton, tried to salvage our relationship.

That it was my fault.

For some obstinate, pathetic reason I stayed put in London. It wasn't as if I even had much to stay for: I was unable to get a long-term teaching contract after my postgrad. So I lived like an overgrown student; the best I could afford was that crappy studio flat. Now I've been fired, and I've ended up boomeranging back to Brighton anyway.

But he doesn't turn his head. His plea hisses through his teeth – part anger, part sorrow. '*Don't,* Pops.'

It's like a blow to my breast. That sense of connection I felt to Matthew last night has broken. Maybe it was all just my imagination. Perhaps Matthew really is a stranger to me now?

Saying nothing else, I stalk out, slamming the front door after me.

Forty-five

I traipse through the streets, still dressed in the clothes of the night before, black rings of smudged mascara under my eyes. *The Walk of Shame* is imprinted on me, for everyone to see.

An elderly woman sits outside a greasy spoon in the frosted, pre-spring air, a newspaper in hand and a dog at her feet. She looks up at me as I wander past. I brace myself for the judgement in her eyes as she drinks me in. Instead, a smile plays at her mouth as her attention drifts back into her own memories. I wonder whose house she crept from, and back to where. To her parents'? From a lover's to her spouse's? Only she can know.

I let myself back into the Coach House, expecting the third degree from Tim. But my stepfather is not seated at the table, nor does the stench of a freshly lit cigarette permeate the air. I call out ahead of me, just like I always do, but no voice answers back. I'm relieved. I grab a drink of water from the tap. As I see a blurred reflection of my face in the aluminium sink, a flash of Tim comes to me; the jagged stress in his voice, the anxiety making his body form squared-off shapes. I close my eyes and it's gone again.

As I drain the glass, I feel, rather than hear, footsteps overhead. It's Tim's heavy tread. I move towards the stairs, rest a hand on the banister. I hear his low voice mutter something, as if he's talking on the phone, or to himself.

Then there's a loud crash, as something heavy thuds against the far wall of the stairs. It's thrown with such force it hits the banister on the opposite side, then crashes towards me. I duck, just as a shower of clothes rains down on me, followed by a suitcase, which hits me in the shoulder. It's light and empty, so I'm unconcerned for myself, especially as the silence is broken by a loud, guttural howl of despair from upstairs.

Alarm and fear jump through me. 'Tim!'

In a blink I'm at the top of the stairs. My eyes widen at the sight of my stepfather. He's wearing yesterday's clothes, rumpled and stained. His eyes are bloodshot, his face flushed with drink, yet it's ten o'clock in the morning. His usually neat hair, parted at the side as long as I've known him, stands on end, making him look deranged.

'Tim … Tim, stop!'

My heartbeat flutters upwards as my stomach sinks. *Is it Mum?* I want to say. Yet I can't summon the words to my lips. Tim makes no indication he's seen or even noticed me. He's in his own world.

Helpless, I watch him through the door of my parents' bedroom. Ornaments crash with a tinkle of ceramic against the wall, breaking as they drop to the skirting board. He grabs the bottom of their bed and overturns it, that animalistic shriek of desolation now mixing with fury.

'Bitch!' he yells.

I flinch as if stung, though I know it's not directed at me. Tim never swears – and certainly not derogatory language about women. Instinctively, I realise Tim's display is about Mum, though not in the way I feared. She might not be dead, but she has abandoned him. Nevertheless, hearing the vitriol in my stepfather's voice, heavy with outrage, is deeply disquieting. Tim roars into the air again and I watch him stamp one foot through the back of the bedside cabinet, then sweep my mother's make-up brushes and perfume bottles off the dressing table.

Finally, he's done. He collapses to his knees and erupts in noisy sobs, his shoulders shaking like a child's. Somehow, this is even more alarming than everything I've just witnessed. Tim never cries. At that moment, I want to turn on my heel and disappear into my room. A treacherous voice in the back of my skull even tells me he would prefer it that way.

Instead, I creep forwards. Place a hand on his shoulder. He grasps for me, for any kind of comfort. He puts his burly arms around my legs. I untangle myself from him and kneel beside him, letting him rest his head on my shoulder. I can feel his tears soaking through my stupid green dress. I wish, not for the first time that morning, that I had stayed home with Tim last night, rather than go to the spring ball.

'I'm sorry, Tim,' I murmur and I mean it.

Not just for going out, but for underestimating the pain he has been in. For Mum. For India. For always thinking of Tim as the strong one.

For everything.

Forty-six

There is still a rhythmic thumping on the bedroom door; it makes a cross-rhythm with the pulse in his head.

She was not meant to be here. She returned with the little girl, claiming to have forgotten something the toddler simply couldn't live without.

So she caught them red-handed, manhandling the boy into the kitchen. She made threats then, saying she would call the police and that she didn't care about the consequences – *anything had to be better than this!*

He had to wrestle her phone from her hand. She gasped as he threw it against the wall. It broke into two pieces, which skittered across the tiles of the luxurious hallway.

But her shock did not last long. She came at him with those nails of hers. He grabbed her by the armpit, arm extended so she couldn't reach his face. He then braced himself against the big oak banister, dragging her up, step by agonising step as she bucked against him, kicking at his shins all the way. She's chunkier than she used to be, so it wasn't as easy as it once had been. She snarled and spat, screaming about how much she hated all of them; that she was going to *fucking kill him if he did this sohelpmegod!*

Making it up onto the landing, he bundled her and the child into the bedroom. But she came at him as he closed the door. He had to push her head and then her talon-tipped hands back through the gap. He held onto the doorknob as she rattled it back and forth, shrieking yet more pointless threats. Finally he turned the key, locking her inside.

He can hear the toddler crying in her cot, where he's put her, her pudgy hands clutching the rails. The toddler howls in sympathy with her mother as she kicks the bottom of the door, a tattoo of resentment.

He massages his temples before leisurely making his way back down the stairs. He knows what is waiting for him in the kitchen. His foot hits something; he's kicked it across the tiles again.

He sighs and stops, retrieving the pieces of the fallen phone. He dawdles, attempting to fix the pieces back together. The battery goes back in without an issue, but the fascia is smashed in two. He makes a mental note to buy her another. He knows he can't buy her love, but perhaps she might forgive him eventually.

He just wants to keep them all safe.

'Get a wriggle on!'

The call is for him. The other woman's voice is thin, reedy, demanding. She wants the back-up – his heft behind her words. His heart dips into his boots. He doesn't want to open the door to the kitchen, but his treacherous feet move him forwards regardless. He can still hear the beat on the door upstairs, a non-stop tempo leading him to the battleground. He braces himself and pushes the door inwards.

'Just look what you've made me do!'

Her voice is scolding, harsh. She stands, her thin form a shadow in the bay window. She extends an arm and the bangles on her skinny wrist clink, like the keys on a prison warder's ring.

But it is not him she is speaking to, now. In the centre of the room: the boy. Dressed in black again, no shoes. He sits on the only chair available, his hands clutching either side of the seat. He knows instantly the woman has forced the boy to sit there. He has folded his body over, his chest on his lap, legs drawn in, as if he hopes to hide himself from their gaze. The boy's eyes stare down at the black-and-white tiles beneath their feet.

He turns to look at the damage. Drawers pulled out, thrown on the floor in anger. Several chairs and the pine table upturned. The vase of lilies has crashed and broken on the floor, yellow pollen and petals floating on the tiles, the water making its way in squared off patterns through the grout. A collection of paperwork, scattered, some sticking to the floor in the puddles.

The woman circles the boy on the chair, her lips pursed, silent. Then she sighs and kneads her eyes with the heel of her hand.

'What are we going to do with you, eh?'

The boy does not speak, nor give any indication he's heard her. He doesn't move a muscle. Face still towards the floor.

He remembers being in this position, too, literally and figuratively. He learned what he had to do to win her favour again. He fell onto his knees on the tiles, threw his arms around her bony legs, begged her forgiveness. If he could squeeze a tear or ten out, he did it: the uglier he cried, the more hiccups and snot, the more she liked it. It made her feel needed. Important.

He tries to send the boy a telepathic message: *Just give her something. Anything. Play the game.*

But dry-eyed, the boy does not move.

'I said…' The woman moves forward and grabs the boy by the hair at the nape of his neck, forcing him to sit up straight; '…what are we going to do with you!?'

The boy bares his teeth in pain. But he does not cry out. He lets go of the seat, both his hands to the back of his head, to try and relieve some of the pressure on his hair roots, threatening to tear from his scalp.

A cruel smile flickers on her face then and she twists. Finally he yelps. This seems to satisfy her and she lets go.

'The boy's learned his lesson…' he begins, but is silenced when she raises a talon-like nail at him. She is not interested in hearing from him. She never is. She might need him, to help deliver her punishments and penalties; but ultimately, she is in charge.

'I've told you, so many times…! What will it take?' Her gaze falls on the fallen cutlery drawer, upside down near her feet. Its contents are spread out before her: a selection of knives and forks and spoons; a couple of curly drinking straws with cartoon characters.

She zeroes in on what she wants: a pair of scissors.

With the smile of a greedy child swiping the last biscuit, she grabs them from the floor as she bunches the boy's hair, still grasped in her other hand.

'Perhaps this will make it obvious!'

With a shriek, the boy realises, too late, what she is doing. He kicks into action and jumps up from the chair. As he turns, she waves the bunched hair in his face like a fan, before letting it go. It cascades to the kitchen floor.

The boy reacts like she's sucker-punched him in the gut. His knees buckle and he falls to the floor, emitting a high-pitched, mournful wail. He gathers the hair towards him, a fruitless endeavour; a pitiful sight.

She throws the scissors down on the counter. She pants, as if she's been running. She's enjoyed this.

His disgust must show on his face, because suddenly her eyes are back on him. She reaches forward, grabbing at his arm with her sharp nails; they prick his bicep through his shirt, but he meets her eye.

'*You* should've prevented this,' she hisses.

He jerks his arm away, enjoying the surprise in her eyes, the sight of her as she wobbles and falls against the countertop. Unable to look at the boy, who is still on the floor, he turns on his heel and sweeps out of the kitchen, into the hall.

The front door is open. The other man stands on the step, half in, half out, as if afraid to come in. Maybe he is. He can hear the thud of the door upstairs, the boy's pitiful weeping, the baby's low grizzle. The bad feeling, the vitriol, envelops the house like fog.

The other man forces some authority into his voice. 'What's happened?'

But he doesn't reply. He shoulders his way past the other man and out of the house, leaving them all in his wake.

Forty-seven

I lock myself in the Coach House bathroom and step out of my dress. It forms a silky green puddle on the tiles. I turn on the tap and rub a hand over my face. I roll my neck and shoulders, feel the tension in them. Emotional exhaustion seems to catch up with me as steam billows all around. It obscures my reflection in the mirror.

In my parents' room, Tim had snapped back to normality with worrying aptitude. He smiled, rubbing tears from his eyes. He patted my shoulder, as if it was me that needed comforting. The message was clear: *I'm fine now.*

Words hung in the delicate air between us. I knew if I chose the wrong ones, they would come showering down sharp and lethal, like glass.

I forced normality into my voice. 'So. You going somewhere?'

I meant the suitcase and clothes that had crashed down the stairs. Tim feigned ignorance. Attempted a joke.

'Thought I'd have a clear out, you know.' A ghost of a smile pulled at his lip as he ran a hand through his thinning hair. 'Never could stand all this matching Laura Ashley shit.'

But I wasn't going to run with that. 'Mum is coming home … isn't she?'

At the mention of my mother, Tim seemed to sag, like a huge weight was pressing on his shoulders. I regretted saying anything, but I didn't retract my query.

Tim sighed. 'It's … complicated.'

'What does that mean?' Dread pierced through me again. I felt like my family was unravelling, yet I was powerless to stop it.

Tim grasped my face between his rough palms. 'Whatever happens Pops, you're my girl. You got that?'

I didn't know what else to say, so I dipped back into The Big Book of Clichés and Platitudes. 'We'll get through this.'

Tim nodded. 'Let's hope so.'

Now, in the bathroom, I wipe condensation away from the mirror and examine my reflection. My lower lip twinges. There's a small, red bite-mark at the base of my neck, another one on my left breast. Finger marks on my hips.

People change, Matthew said.

I spent years fucking Matthew. He never left a mark on me in all that time. Matthew no longer seems the safe guy he was. He now seems mysterious, even potentially dangerous. Being with him now is like entering a maelstrom. I say the word at the mirror. It looks like I'm saying 'male storm'.

The water as hot as I can bear, I slide into it, the tap still running. I take a sharp intake of breath as my flesh is almost scalded. I submerge my whole body, right up to my neck. My pale skin instantly turns red, tingling below the waterline.

I turn the tap off with my foot, leaning back to wet and lather my hair. As I slide back up, I catch sight of more marks. This time, on the inside of my thigh. Matthew's thumbprint, where he pinched me and held me down. I can still feel his hands all over my body, like he wants to possess every inch of me. Do I not like this new, shadier version of him, then? Part of me might be perturbed, but surely that's only because I knew how he was. *Before*. The other part of me welcomes this unexpected change.

I want more.

I sigh, and force my thoughts onto a more pressing, if no less confusing path. I take stock of everything I've learned so far. Jayden and JoJo are another dead end. Working at The Obelisk the night of my sister's death gives them both an alibi, plus I have to admit: Jayden killing India *after* she's told everyone about the affair seems a little counterintuitive.

Yet Ana looked stricken when I asked her about Jayden and where he'd been the night of 22nd December. At the time, I'd seen that as panic, confirmation Ana didn't know where he was.

I therefore jumped to the conclusion that my old friend was giving him a false alibi. But what if it was the other way around? Maybe she was trying to account for her *own* movements that night.

I have to go back.

Forty-eight

I pick my way across the lawn at Coy Ponds, around the ridiculous ornaments. I don't want to have to talk to Ana again. And if going to Coy Ponds seemed like a painful trip back into the past the last time I visited, now, after my night with Matthew, it is excruciating.

I knock, hoping that by some miracle Matthew might answer the door, while praying he doesn't. I know there is little chance he will. He already told me at his flat that he only sees his family when necessary and usually only for Ana's sake, such as when he attended the spring ball.

'What do you want now?' Ana appears unsurprised to see me on the doorstep again. This time, she appears to be alone, the little girl nowhere to be seen.

I dive straight in. 'I talked to Jayden.'

I'll give Ana credit, she doesn't flinch. 'And?'

'He was working that night. At the hotel. Lots of witnesses, apparently.'

Only now does Ana's ice-maiden veneer crack. A triumphant smile spreads across her face. 'Told you.'

It's now that I move in. 'Funny thing is, he never mentioned you were there.'

'Well, I was.' Ana tries to front it out. 'I spent most of the night in the office. Helping with the admin, that kind of thing. We had a few problems with the suppliers for the Marchand party.'

Her words seem too pat, rehearsed. 'Is that what you told the police?'

It's as if she abruptly deflates. She nods.

'And Jayden backed you up?' I try to keep the surprise out of my voice.

Ana purses her lips. 'You better come in.'

She stands aside, permitting me across the threshold. I amble through, into the large, marble-floored hallway. An ornate staircase sweeps its way up to a mezzanine landing. Downstairs, off the hallway, there is a selection of closed doors. Directly opposite us, another door is ajar. I glimpse black-and-white kitchen tiles before it closes, seemingly of its own accord.

I turn sharply to Ana. 'Who's here with you?'

'No one.'

But I don't believe her. I march across the hallway, my boots clacking on the ostentatious flooring. I grab the kitchen door handle and wrench it open.

Who I'm expecting, I'm unsure. My eyes glance around the large deserted space, alighting on the sink, the countertops, the back door. As with everything at Coy Ponds, there isn't an item out of place. In the centre of the room, a wooden table and chairs, typically homely, almost *Waltons*-esque. It's utterly at odds with the rest of the décor, all chrome and aluminium and sparkling surfaces.

I turn back towards Ana, who stands behind me, arms folded, as if to say, *Satisfied?* She turns and opens a door to her left.

I follow her into a grandiose living room, though, just like the rest of the house, it looks more like something out of a magazine than somewhere anyone actually does any living. The colour has changed since I was last here four (*nearly five*) years ago, plus the room seems bigger. I realise that the Temples have extended the ground floor of the house, taking a small patch of garden, but installing two sets of gigantic patio doors.

Beyond the glass, the grass is beautifully lush and green, and although it's early in the year, there are plants in flower in various pots. I wonder what harsh chemicals have achieved such colour. It reminds me of Ana's hair, the chemicals that she once used, and Maggie still does.

Why did you stop relaxing your hair? I want to blurt out the words, but stop myself. I feel embarrassed. I'm not here for that and it's none of my business. I was fascinated by black hair when I was younger, even wanting to dive my fingers into Afros or newly straightened hair. Like I had the right; like it was mine.

Shame ripples through me at the memory. It was Ana, grabbing me by the wrist to stop me, who made me realise my trespass. But not only that, I felt the sore scabs on her scalp: gummy scales around her roots.

'Why do it to yourself?' I demanded.

Ana smiled, but there was no humour or goodwill in it. 'So I can look like you, of course.'

Her stare penetrated mine, made me feel like a thousand ants were crawling on my skin, but I didn't know why. I dismissed her comments as a bad mood, or because she didn't like me hanging around her and Matthew all the time. She was always a jealous person. Now, I'm not so sure that was it, but I can't put my finger on why.

'I wasn't with Jayden, OK?' she says now, sitting in an armchair. She crosses her legs, her arms still folded defensively across her chest.

I betray nothing on my face. 'Where does Jayden *think* you were?'

I perch on the edge of an overstuffed sofa, stiff with anticipation. Ana regards me, brow furrowed. She wrings her hands. Whatever she wants to tell me, she has already thought better of it. Finally, she sighs.

'He thinks I was here.'

I process Ana's words, understanding their implication immediately. *Jayden thinks Ana was alone the night my sister died, so he's given her an alibi.*

'I know it looks bad.' Ana's face is in her hands; she's avoiding looking at me. 'India tells me about Jayden and JoJo, drags us *all* through the mud, then a couple of weeks later she ends up dead. That's why I said I was at the party, with Jayden.'

'But you were here, alone?' I prompt.

Ana nods. 'I swear on my girl's life, Poppy, I never saw India that night.'

'And I have to just take your word for that?'

Ana throws her hands up in the air. It's clear she has nothing left.

I fancy I can feel the sincerity in her gaze. Indecision grabs at my gut. 'OK.'

I feel Ana's relief pour out of her as I concede; it's palpable in the air.

I don't want her to get complacent, yet, though. 'But I'm warning you, if I uncover anything else dodgy to do with you and India, I'll be going straight to the police myself.'

Ana gives me a hasty nod. 'Thank you.'

So I leave, curiously dissatisfied. I've either done the right thing, or backed away from my first big lead. All the same, if I tell the police Ana lied on her statement, but she still *isn't* responsible for India's death, my accusations could send the investigation off at a mad tangent. They might even derail it altogether. Then the real perpetrator might not be found at all.

Perhaps discretion really is the better part of valour.

For now.

Forty-nine

'Matthew's not in,' the redhead says as soon as I approach the bar at Elemental.

I barely hear her words above the caterwaul of Nirvana, though the accompanying shake of her head makes her meaning obvious.

It's a Sunday night and the bar is dead. A couple of women, a bottle of red wine between them, prop up the bar. The jukebox blares nineties' grunge. A couple of lads fiddle with their pint glasses, not speaking. They don't look the women's way, even though they laugh loudly, attempting to get their attention.

I lean towards her, shouting in her ear. 'He in later?'

The redhead just shrugs. *How the hell would I know?*

Irritated all over again, I stalk out of Elemental, climbing the concrete steps back to the seafront. The inshore breeze is up again; it whips along, yowling in my ears. I can barely hear anything. I duck my head down, putting both my hands in India's red hoody pockets, hurrying up the road and into The Lanes where there is more shelter from the bitter wind.

I don't consciously head anywhere, but all the same I arrive outside the Prince Albert. I wonder if the Korean bouncer will let me in again, but she's not there, and I am waved through without a second glance by the two male heavies on the door. A Sunday night before seven, they need all the paying clientele they can get.

I look around the near-deserted bar, hoping Jenny might magically reappear, or at least Adonis. The music is much quieter, though it is still an endless thumping baseline. It sets my teeth on edge, reminding me, once again: *Too old for this shit.*

I go to the bar and wait. I'm in luck. Adonis emerges. He chatters away as he stacks glasses. He doesn't recognise me until his gaze settles on my face.

He sucks in a breath. 'Jenny's not here.'

'I can see that.'

I indicate I want a Coke. He fetches one and slides it across the bar top to me. I put some coins down.

'How about you call her and let her know I'm here?'

'Don't have her number.' Adonis seems to slump. Perhaps he fears a confession might pour out of him, against his will.

'I think you do.' I point to a nearby booth. 'I'll be waiting there. OK?'

I sit down and wait.

'What do you want?'

After about twenty-five minutes, Jenny finally materialises next to me. Her goth get-up has clearly been thrown on in a hurry: just her red wig, sunglasses indoors. I take her in. She's wearing street clothes: jeans, plus a short-sleeved t-shirt that's a little tight. The material hugs not only her small, almost pubescent breasts, but rides up over a small roll of fat around her middle I haven't noticed before.

'Why did you delete India's blog?'

She freezes. 'I had to.'

'Why?'

'Someone made me.' Jenny hangs her head. A curtain of red wig-hair falls in front of her face.

'Who?'

'I can't tell you.'

Another stalemate. I sigh. 'OK. What *can* you tell me?'

Jenny wears no white make-up this time, nor are her fingers adorned with those wicked-looking talons I'd seen on them that first night. There's glue on her stubby fingernails, which are all bitten down to the quick.

Even in the dim light of the pub I can make out that Jenny's skin is darker than mine, though lighter than Matthew's. Perhaps she's

Asian. *Is this why her mother didn't approve of India?* White girls and their 'alternative' lifestyles and Western ideals do not always mix well with more traditional families.

'India didn't give me any details … she just said she had something to tell me.'

Jenny keeps looking to the doorway, then back to Adonis at the bar. His eyes never leave us, even as he serves pints of beer to a lesbian couple. They stand at the bar with their arms wrapped around each other's waists, their hands in one another's jeans back pockets.

'OK.' I bite down my frustration. Jenny seems skittish, like a horse. I don't want to spook her, drive her away again. 'You were meant to meet her at Brighton station, but you missed her. Right?'

'Right.'

'What were you meeting her for; something specific?'

Jenny sighs. 'She said she needed to meet someone before me. And that then she was going to tell me something.'

I absorb this. 'That's it?'

'That's all I know. I swear. But then she ended up dead. Don't you think that's a bit funny?'

I do. Jenny seems relieved to be taken seriously. Behind us, a big man ambles down the steps of the Prince Albert, and Jenny shoots up from the booth. But it's no one she knows. She visibly wilts again, gathers her thoughts.

'I have to go.' She pats my shoulder absent-mindedly then moves away.

I watch her weave her way between the tables. She disappears through the bar hatch again, Adonis lifting it up for her. He glances over at me with a stern, forbidding look that reads, *That's your lot, now.*

But it's not. As Jenny touched my left shoulder, her right arm reached across me, so I could see there was a tattoo on the inside of her forearm. It was small, but beautifully done: an intricate design made up of many colours. I've seen the same design before, on Jenny's profile and on the back of India's leather jacket.

A sugar skull.

Fifty

I emerge from the Prince Albert, back into the cold night air. I don't want to go back to the Coach House. I'm not ready to give up my wild goose chase just yet. Jenny's words ring in my ears. As well as Jenny herself, India was meeting someone else the night she died. *But who?*

Dusk falling, from The Lanes, I make my way through the narrow little streets, back onto the main thoroughfare. The shops' shutters and doors are closed, the lights off or dim in the main windows. The wind is cut off here. I begin to hear ambient noise once again. Muffled voices and music filter out of a pub. Shadows and lights flicker ahead of me on the wet, red-brick pavement.

I make my way through the labyrinthine, narrow streets. I dodge between jewellers and cafés, outside chairs and tables stacked in neat piles. I hear laughter. It's a group of lads, younger than me. They lounge on some benches in a little square, holding budget beer bottles. They catcall and jeer as I trudge past them. I daren't approach them.

I amble back downwards, finding myself at the seafront again. It's still quiet. A couple of groups of revellers walk briskly against the harsh wind coming off the beach. They disappear down the concrete steps to the bars below. I pull my phone from my pocket, selecting a picture of India.

I sidle up to a couple of teen boys. They're seated on a groyne, sharing a cigarette and a plastic bottle of cider. I turn the phone around, so they can see the picture of my sister.

'You seen this girl? Maybe just before Christmas?'

My expression is earnest, desperate. It makes the boys shrink away from me, their eyes wide. Both drop over the side of the groyne onto the beach below, laughing.

'*Please!*' I shout after them, even though I know my efforts are fruitless.

A trio of young women walks towards me now. They're unconcerned by the cold, despite their bare arms and legs. Handbags dangle from their shoulders and arms, hands tucked under armpits. I step into their path as they attempt to dodge me.

'Did you see this girl? It would've been just before Christmas?'

Two of the girls part and walk around me, but one of them stops in front of me. She's about twenty, dressed in a vest top and short skirt, with fuck-me boots. Her hair is scraped up in a vicious ponytail, a cigarette dangles from her cherry-red lips. She regards the picture on my mobile of my sister, as if struck by the sight of it. Hope crystallises in my stomach spreading into my chest. But then she cackles and waves a dismissive hand at me.

Crushed, I turn away from her. I let the wind push me along the seafront. The wind buffets around me, deafening me against the sound of voices, even the lapping tide on the beach behind us. I walk on blind, trusting my body to take me where I need to go. I cross the road again and make my way past the Odeon, the Travelodge, more bars beyond it.

I weave my way through a hen party staggering out of a nightclub on Queen's Road. The hen is dressed in a bandeau top and skirt held together by safety-pinned 'L' plates. She's crying, holding onto the maid of honour. The second woman is doing all she can to hold them both up, despite wearing eight-inch heels. Another girl lurches forward and vomits onto the pavement, splashing her own shoes. The rest of the party, drunk and loud, yell at a bouncer who says they won't be coming back into the club. One of them attempts to eyeball him. She is as tall as him and maybe as wide, but the bouncer seems unconcerned. Her bluff met, the big lass gives up, telling him his club is shit anyway.

But still I don't stop. Up ahead, I can see my destination. My mind catches up with my body at last.

Brighton station.

I make my way past night buses and food carts selling bangers and burgers. I pass through the station's automatic doors. An assault of noise and light bounces off the glass-panelled roof. Overwhelmed, I finally come to a halt. I sense other people stopping behind me, then working their way around me.

Some late commuters wander through from the London train, their eyes and expressions weary. They drag small suitcases of work behind them. Most of the shops' and cafés' shutters are down, but one still has its doors open and lights on.

Apart from these regulars, the station seems fairly busy. There must be some kind of music festival going on. I see a disproportion-ate number of teenagers with backpacks, camping rolls and t-shirts splashed with the names of rock bands. They loiter everywhere, wide grins on their faces as they take in their freedom.

Transport Police in their neon-yellow jackets, their collar radios bursting with static, usher the teens along. I understand: the teens are supposed to leave; they must have come in with the last train. But there are hundreds of them and eight police officers. Authority figures or not, it's going to be a slow night for the adults.

I approach one of the officers. She's much shorter than I am; she looks like a harassed child, her jacket too big for her. She attempts to move on a group of four of five lanky youths. They stare down at her with amused expressions. One of them holds a six-pack of lager, forbidden in public spaces. He smirks at the police officer and cracks open a can anyway. The police officer looks up as my shadow falls on her.

'Yes, can I help you?' She doesn't really want to help me. And who can blame her? She's tired and stressed and wants to go home.

I show her my phone, the picture of India on it. 'Did you see this woman, on the night of 22nd December?'

The police officer seems relieved to be distracted from the poten-tial confrontation with the teen boys. She takes my phone from my outstretched hand. But there's no recognition on her face.

'What date did you say?'

'22nd December.' I take a deep breath so I can steel myself to say the words, 'There was a death on the line that night.'

It's the prompt the police officer needs. I see insight flash in her eyes, which then roll as she attempts to cast her mind back.

'A girl *did* jump the ticket barrier and run out of the station. I was on the train, I saw her through the window. I told my colleagues this at the time. Why are you asking?'

'And you think it was this girl? She's … she was my sister, you see.'

The police officer's expression changes, looks more kindly. 'Yes. I remember the guard's whistle went and I had to get off the train, pronto.'

'Did you see anyone else with her?' I think of Ana, whether it could have been her India was supposed to be meeting.

The police officer shakes her head. 'Not with her, no. But she was running away from someone. She was shouting. Something like, "No chance!" or "You had your chance"! I'm not sure which.'

My mouth feels dry. 'A woman?'

The police officer blows out her cheeks. 'No. A man. She was on the main platform. He ran after her, but he got stopped by a guard at the ticket barrier.'

This unexpected revelation feels like a punch in the gut. If the police officer told her colleagues about this, why didn't they do anything? Wasn't this important information? Then another thought occurs to me: Could it have been Matthew? *Please God, no.*

I take a deep breath. 'What did the man look like?'

'White male. Middle-aged.'

My heart ricochets in my ribcage with relief. It can't possibly have been Matthew, then. Could the police officer mean Jayden Spence? 'Middle-aged' means different things to different people. Jayden's about thirty-five, forty at the most. The police officer is in her early twenties by my guess; she might think of Jayden as 'older'.

'Was he fair or dark?' I don't want to hear it.

'He was dark.'

The police officer pokes a pin right through my theory. Jayden is blonde. There's no way anyone could mistake him for dark-haired, particularly not in the bright lights of the station.

She puts her hand on my sleeve. 'Look, I told the investigating team all this at the time. If they thought he was an important witness, they would've found him by now. It's hard, I know. You want to know why your sister did it…'

I pull my arm away from her touch, scowling at her. But I don't have time to argue with her now: an unwanted thought is buzzing in my head like a bluebottle. It refuses to leave. This time, I have to breathe life into the words so its toxic eggs hatch.

'Was he short, tall? Fat, thin?'

'Short. Nice face.'

'How short?' I hold my hand out flat: *Taller or shorter than me?* The police officer gestures a hand towards my shoulder height. I feel those talons of trepidation tighten in my chest, ready to strike.

I know who was chasing my sister at the station the night she died.

Tim.

Fifty-one

'Are you OK ... Pops. Poppy!'

I struggle to raise my head from my folded arms. The room spins as a pounding bass line cracks through my skull. I sit up, too fast, as a palm touches the small of my back. A dark silhouette peers down at me. The black lights illuminate the whites of his eyes and teeth, the pale shirt he's wearing.

'Matthew.' I croak, the music snatching my words away.

I glance around, confused momentarily. I'm in Elemental. It's not busy; just a handful of patrons at the bar, five or six more in the booths. I don't recall how I got to the bar, or how long I've been here. It feels as if in the station, only moments ago, I blinked; and now I'm drunk, a row of five or six shot glasses and two or three long glasses in front of me, all empty. Despite my intoxication, an adult, sober voice inside my mind tuts just like Mum would: *Mixing your drinks? You'll pay for that in the morning, girly.*

In response, nausea flip-flops in my belly. Pain hits me in the solar plexus. Bile rises, hot and forceful up my gullet. I lurch to a standing position, hand to my mouth, eyes watering.

Matthew says something I can't catch as a drumbeat thumps. He ushers me towards some swing doors; on the aluminium sign, the letters 'XX', plus the female symbol. The toilets. I surrender myself to his guidance and stumble across the threshold. It's deserted inside. I see Matthew's concerned expression in the mirrored walls as I kick the nearest cubicle door open.

I collapse to my knees. I feel Matthew's hands in my hair now, pulling it out of the way for me as I hug the bowl. The pain in my chest and stomach twists as hot vomit surges from my mouth.

I'm shocked as bright-blue liquid spews forth into the toilet water, before my brain catches up and connects with the fuzzy taste of peach schnapps and lemonade. It's just the blue colouring of curacao liqueur. I must have been drinking Blue Balls cocktails. Great. Tomorrow, I really am going to be hangin' (*adjective*. Hungover. Related words: rough; morning-after-the-night-before).

'That's better,' Matthew says.

Words fill the space between us. Irritation floods through me now; I want to ask him how the hell he would know if I felt better or not. Chinks of memories pierce me as I'm forced to lean over the toilet bowl again:

> *FLASH* – I stagger, mindless, back down the hill from the station; Elemental's aluminium-and-blue sign acts like a lighthouse in the dark;
>
> *FLASH* – I walk straight up to the bar, slamming a note on the counter; drink flows, the first goes down easily, just as they always do;
>
> *FLASH* – I flirt with that young geezer who loves himself behind the bar. I see teeth, the start of a tattoo on his neck, disappearing under his shirt collar. Behind him, the redheaded bar manager, her mouth twisted in disapproval…

Matthew had not been in Elemental when I arrived, I was sure of it. Perhaps his redheaded bar manager had called him, told him to fetch me? But then I'm chucking my guts up again, my body purging itself of alcohol.

Finally, there is nothing left. My body spasms involuntarily. More sour saliva fills my mouth. I gasp for air, taking in the smell of toilet cleaner and stomach acid. I jerk my hair from Matthew's light grasp and attempt to stand. I'm wobbly; he grabs my elbows as my knees buckle.

I try to say thank you, but a deep sigh emanates from me instead. I lean against the cubicle wall, exhausted, my eyes fluttering shut. Matthew strokes the curve of my jaw with one of his rough palms, then kisses the top of my head.

Blackness.

*

I wake with a start, heart hammering. I'm alone, just in my knickers, tangled up in the duvet. A brief recollection shoots through me and my stomach plunges with shame. I woke again in the car, heart racing as he tried to park outside the Coach House. There were no lights on, the house cloaked in darkness.

'I can't go in there!'

In the car, I strove to catch my breath, struggling to find the words to explain to Matthew. Dreams of Tim had followed me into drunken oblivion, I told him. I'd been with the young policewoman, back at the station. Just like she'd said, Tim had appeared at the ticket barriers. Anger had contorted his mild face; he hadn't looked like my stepfather anymore. In the nightmare, I'd felt those cold claws of terror inside my chest and turned to run … But in that brief second, everything changed, as dreams are wont to do. Next I'd been flying over the city, pinpricks of light beneath me, like stars fallen to earth. Too late, I realised I was not flying, but falling. Like India, I plunged from a railway bridge, Tim's grave expression looking down on me as I plummeted.

In the car, Matthew's brow furrowed, but he did not press me for details. He turned the key in the ignition. We set off again across Brighton, through the deserted back streets. I felt safe again as the orange streetlamps coursed over the car; the mesmerising flashes of lights soothed me, lulling me back to sleep.

I perked up when Matthew parked outside his flat. My mood soared from one end of the scale to the other: despair to jubilation. I made it into the flat with Matthew and proceeded to take off my clothes in a ridiculous striptease. Then I looped my arms around his neck, trying to kiss him.

But Matthew smiled, determined not to take advantage. He peeled my hands away, laying me down on the sheets, drawing the duvet up under my chin like I was a child. I was petulant then, telling him there was no way I could go to sleep.

Then I blinked and sunk under once more.

Pulling myself up from the plump pillows, I can hear Matthew's muted tones. Thinking someone else might be in the next room with him, I wind the duvet around myself and venture towards the door. He's framed as a dark shadow in the window, the light in front of him. He's bare-chested, his back to me, the phone to his ear.

'I just think…' He stops as the person on the other end of the line interrupts. I can see the tension emanating from Matthew's whole body as he grips the handset. 'Yes, I get that. But—'

The caller cuts in again. I can hear the high pitch; it's a woman. Matthew seems to sag, give up whatever protest was trying to make.

'Fine, fine. Whatever. Bye.'

He cuts off the call and stares out of the window a moment. Outside, it's an unseasonably sunny day. There's no breeze or bad weather; I can't hear any muffled movement in the rest of the apartments below. The silence feels oppressive. I feel like my words could burst it, like a pin in a balloon, but they seem to dry up on my tongue.

Then, with the curious sixth sense we all have when someone is behind us, Matthew turns and flashes me a wide smile. 'You're awake.'

'Was that Ana?' I join him at the window.

He loops one of his big arms around me and the duvet, as we stare down into the car park below.

Matthew seems distracted. 'No: Lou. Pain in my arse.'

I recognise the name, but a face doesn't come to me. Then I see her: the redhead at Elemental, shooting me suspicious daggers as she fills glasses from the optics at the bar.

I lean my head against Matthew's broad shoulder. He smells of sleep, warm and fusty. I want to ask him about Ana, how she'd been at home the night India died. Matthew knows his twin better than anyone; he can put my mind at rest.

Instead, I lean forward, to place a kiss on Matthew's lips. Matthew's mouth opens as our lips touch. He pulls me to him, holding me by the elbows, as if I might run away. But as my eyes close, the dream of Tim flashes through my mind. I want to believe the worst

Tim is guilty of is a terrible accident, but even that is too much. Matthew must sense my hesitation, because he turns his face away.

'It's OK.' My fingertips find his waist.

His dark-brown eyes search my face, like he's looking for something. *Permission?* I smile, letting the duvet drop. I stand naked in front of him.

'I got myself into this,' I remind him.

But Matthew's expression is still earnest. 'I'm not playing.'

'Nor am I.'

He stares at me, his gaze flitting to my lips, my chin, the curve of my neck. The moment passes and he smiles at last. He pulls me into his embrace, his chin resting on the top of my skull.

'You need to brush your teeth.'

I laugh. We lie down together on the sofa instead, our bodies pressed close. My back to him, he puts his big hands around my waist. I can feel the rise of his chest; I feel safe. I close my eyes.

'I love you.'

He doesn't say it back. He doesn't need to. I can feel his usual inscrutable expression shift into a smile behind me.

Fifty-two

The Wolf

You always missed a spot. That day I could see the usual tiny patch of hair. I told you I would get rid of it for you.

'Do you trust me?' A razor, shining in the light.

You shrugged, prone in the chair. 'Sure.'

I stood over you. I massaged your temples, placed the warm cloth over your scalp. As I applied the foam, I saw you close your eyes, stretch out your legs, feline.

You were in my power then. I could have done anything. I could have drawn that blade across your throat. Maybe I should have.

Then she would have been free.

But instead I scraped away that small cluster of hairs. I didn't even nick the skin. You laughed and said I had missed my vocation. Maybe I should open a barber's, you said. Maybe, I replied.

Who are you?

You are the key. You could stop all of this.

What are you?

Protector. Jailer. You know which.

Time for the delusion to stop. Actions speak louder than words.

Time to stop falling into line.

India

POSTED BY **@1NDIAsummer**, <u>6 December 2016</u>

11,543 insights ⏎ **SHARE THIS**

⏎ *__Milliecat_456__* likes this

⏎ *__Blithefancy__* comments: *RU OK? IM ME xxxx*

⏎ *__lilybelle9__* likes this

⏎ *__markotron__* likes this

⏎ *__Alfie98__* likes this and comments: creepy

⏎ *__writerchic88__* comments: *YIKES* ®

Fifty-three

I wake again to the sound of the shower running in the tiny bathroom. I sit up and grab one of Matthew's t-shirts from the floor, pulling it on. The hot, musty smell of him envelops me. I smile.

My body tingles, feels heavy, as if Matthew has sucked all my strength from me. Maybe he has, like some kind of emotional vampire? Perhaps that's why I can't seem to help myself around him now. I didn't return to the Coach House; I stayed with Matthew for the rest of the day and night. We watched movies and moved from the living room back to the bedroom, exploring each other's bodies.

My mobile sits on top of a neat pile of my clothes on the floor. Matthew's been tidying again. I check the LCD of the digital clock on the nightstand and see it's coming up for ten o'clock in the morning. The beautiful, sunny skies of the day before are gone. Rain lashes down onto the skylight above us.

I want to check on Mum, so I lean down to the floor and grab my phone to call the hospital. But the battery is gone again. I clamber out of bed and pick up a charger from on top of the chest of drawers. But the connector doesn't fit. *Damn it.*

I search for Matthew's phone. He won't mind if I use his. His clothes lie on the floor next to mine. His jeans pockets bulge. I pull out his keys; a flyer folded over in his efficient, pedantic way; some chewing gum; a pebble from the beach, its surface smoothed and rounded by the tide. One of the back pockets of his jeans holds his wallet. I put it all back.

Finally, I find his phone in the breast pocket of his shirt. It's the latest model – *obviously* – but locked. I cast my mind back. I remember the old PIN he used for everything, back when we were together.

I would tell him it was too easy to guess, but he would reply I was paranoid.

Sure enough, the screen opens, allowing me access to his apps and user history. With clumsy fingers I try to press the phone icon, but instead tap the email one next to it. The app expands.

I take in the words in front of me, disbelief unfurling in my brain as I fail to fully comprehend the word in front of me.

I drop the phone and lurch backwards as if I've been punched. More bright spots spring up in my eyes.

A million thoughts, denials, questions all clamour in my brain, but I can't focus on any of them. The impact is total: I gulp for air in shallow gasps, which makes my head reel even more.

Matthew's username is *Wolfman404*.

PART THREE

The Perfective Aspect

/has/, /have/ or /had/

Fifty-four

'You OK?'

Matthew's arms reach out behind me and pull me to him. He's wet, smelling of tea tree shower gel. His skin feels cold against my neck. At any other time, I would welcome his attentions, but now I stiffen with alarm, fighting the urge to scream as he cups my breasts with his big hands.

'I … have to go.'

I untangle myself from his embrace. He gives me a lazy smile. Droplets of water cling to his dark skin; a towel is around his waist. He looks just like he always does, no hint of any potential danger. But I can still feel the grip of his fingers around my throat. *Had the same hands closed around my sister's?*

I give Matthew the fakest smile I can muster. He watches me pull my clothes on, thoughtful. Despite the passage of four (*nearly five*) years, Matthew knows me too well.

'What's wrong?'

I bite back the accusation that threatens to shoot from my mouth: *Did you kill my sister?* I think back to Ana and her odd proclamations. Perhaps this had nothing to do with Jayden, or her. Maybe Ana has been covering for her twin all along. I feel sick.

But I can't just blurt all this out. If he didn't kill India, that would be bad. But if he did? Even worse. We're alone. No one knows where I am.

Anything could happen.

'Nothing.' My voice is bright and breezy, false. 'I've just got to get back, get some clothes…'

'Why don't we buy you some new stuff? Come into work with

me, get some lunch at the club. Then we can go shopping. Let me treat you.'

That lazy, almost arrogant smirk is back on Matthew's face. He reaches out and grabs me as I'm pulling on my jeans, wrapping his arms around my waist as I struggle in his grasp, like I'm a little girl.

Panic surges through my veins, but I tamp it down.

This is Matthew; he wouldn't hurt me.

Would he?

'Come into work with me,' Matthew murmurs, placing his lips on mine.

The kiss is momentary, but it seems to last much longer, the betrayal of my sister made flesh. I laugh as I disentangle myself.

'Matthew! I've got stuff to do.'

Matthew pulls away. Shrugs in a *You missed your chance* kind of way. He swats me on the backside as he grabs his own clothes.

'Whatever, I'll call you.' He grins.

Relief floods through me. 'Right. See you.'

I walk out, trying to look calmer than I feel. The door closed, I break away and rush down the stairs, out of the building, across its car park and down the leafy street beyond. I only stop, gasping, about two streets away, adrenaline making me feel light-headed. This only serves to remind me of sleeping with Matthew just hours earlier. I'd lain down with him so willingly. I feel sick all over again.

Matthew is a liar.

Fifty-five

I return to the Coach House and sit under the shower for a full half-hour, staring at the water swirling down the plughole until it goes cold. Forced to get out, I curse; I've forgotten to bring a towel into the bathroom.

I skip naked across the landing to my room, leaving a trail of water behind me. I already checked for Tim on my return, but my stepfather was nowhere to be seen. I looked to see whether any of his things were missing, but in my parents' wrecked room, it was too hard to tell, so I gave up.

I towel myself dry roughly: across my chest, under my arms, between my legs. I pull on a t-shirt and some leggings, lace up my boots over bare feet. I drag a brush through my wet hair, pulling it into an unruly knot, then yank India's red hoody over my head as I amble down the stairs to the kitchen.

The house is deathly quiet. The winter light is fading, evening just half an hour away. Perhaps I notice something in my peripheral vision; a shadow moving idly across the wall. Or maybe I hear a sharp intake of breath.

Someone is in the house with me, in the living room.

Perhaps it's paranoia after discovering Matthew's lies, but something stops me calling out. Still looking ahead, I grasp for something, *anything*. The kitchen is in disarray, dirt masked by cheap floral air freshener. In the sink, dirty dishes; cigarette stubs float in the stagnant water. My nose wrinkles in distaste.

My fingers find a bread knife. It's on the chopping block where Tim left it the day before. I clench my fist around the knife's plastic handle. I hold it to my side, slightly in front of me like my self-defence instructor showed me years ago.

'Don't slash in a straight line,' he said, 'but an arc.'

But had he said that arc should be *inwards* or *outwards*? *Or both?* Butterflies of panic beat their wings in my chest and stomach. I don't remember. I push on. I'm at the living-room door; it's ajar.

I reach out and push it inwards, the knife still at my side.

'Jesus, you nearly gave me a heart attack!' I present the knife in my hand as evidence.

'Oh, darling…'

Adrenaline surges through me at the near miss; I burst into tears. *Mum.*

I let her throw her thin arms around me, folding me into her bony embrace. India is with me again, momentarily: 'Hugging Mum is like hugging an ironing board!' she would cackle. We'd all laugh, even Mum, because it was true.

Mum soothes me as I cry with abandon, my sobs reduced to awkward hiccups. Mum rubs me between my shoulder blades like she always has done, rocking me like a little girl. She smooths my wet hair back from my face.

'When did you get back?'

As these words leave my lips, I'm suddenly aware of my mother's distracted air. I realise she hasn't been waiting for me. I sniff, wiping my running nose on my sleeve.

I take her in: my mother looks frail, old. She's always taken pride in her appearance, but now she's in a shapeless t-shirt and jeans and a long cardigan that she's wrapped around herself, as if she's cold, but the central heating is on. She's not wearing make-up, and her dyed hair is greying at the roots.

'Where's Tim?' My voice cracks.

Her eyes are red from crying, tracks of tears on her cheeks. She sighs, closes her eyes. 'I don't know.'

My mind is running fast – too fast almost. After the revelation that Matthew is Wolfman404, aka 'The Wolf' from India's blog posts, I feel I must have jumped to ridiculous conclusions about Tim. He loved India. He can't have been the one at the station, or if he was, there is a rational explanation. I realise I've not been thinking straight at all.

Yet there's something else, I can sense it in Mum's manner.

'Mum, you're scaring me.'

She sits down on the sofa, patting the seat beside her. Obedient, I sink onto the overstuffed cushion next to her. I don't want to hear whatever she has to say. Yet I can't *not* hear what she wants to tell me, either.

Mum draws a shaky breath and looks back to the window. 'I'm so sorry. I never meant for it to be like this...'

'Like *what*?' I wait, willing her silently to hurry up.

Mum picks at a sofa cushion with her spindly fingers. 'In therapy, they made me realise I have to come clean. I came back ... to try and make amends.'

Confusion clouds my mind. Every time I think I have the thread of a revelation, it unravels on me again and pulls me even deeper into its tangled web.

I choose my words carefully. 'OK. What does that mean?'

Mum sighs. 'Tim knows ... India wasn't his daughter.'

I'm not sure what I expected, but it definitely wasn't this. I gape at her. 'What?'

So I was not the only cuckoo in the nest. But there is a key difference. Tim knew I wasn't his from the very start. I'd pre-dated Mum and Tim by some five years. India was born nearly fifteen months after they wed. So Mum must have become pregnant with my sister roughly six months *after* she and Tim had married.

More infidelity. The words lodge in my throat.

'You told him, today?' I managed to say.

'No.' Fresh tears spring from Mum's eyes. She wipes them away with the heel of her hand, an unnecessarily savage gesture. 'A couple of days ago.'

Another piece clicks into place: Tim's fury, the day before yesterday. His destruction of their bedroom, his packed suitcase that came flying down the stairs at me. His anguished yell, 'Bitch!'

So it *was* directed at Mum, just not for her abandonment, as I supposed.

But as I see this replay in my mind, something else flickers into being. Jenny, in the booth at the Prince Albert. She told me that India had needed to say something to her. Could this be it? But what would that have to do with Jenny?

'It's been a nightmare,' Mum's focus is on the window now. She can't look me in the eye. 'It was just a stupid mistake, one I've spent years trying to cover up. I just wanted my family together. And now…'

'How did India find out?'

I wonder if Mum knows about the blog – about Ana, Jayden and JoJo. Had my sister become some sort of moral vigilante? But this doesn't sit well with my vision of her. I recall her on the beach again, wheeling round and round, laughing. India had been a meddler, sure, but she'd been a free spirit, deep down. Live and let live.

Mum pinches the bridge of her nose between her finger and thumb. 'Apparently, she did some school project, found out everyone's blood type. Worked out she couldn't be related to Tim.'

I blink in confusion. This doesn't fit. 'But … India left school ages ago?'

Mum just shrugs, helpless. She doesn't know the answer.

'Who is India's father?' I'm amazed there is no tremor in my voice.

But Mum sighs. 'I need to speak to Tim again, first. I have to make it right.'

'Tell me who India's father is!'

Mum seems to shrink under the weight of my raised voice. I don't want to judge my mother. I know I could easily be in her place, having made so many poor choices about relationships in the past – and even now (*Matthew*). Back then, she'd have been younger than I am now, too. I am a hypocrite.

A strange weariness descends on me, like a giant hand is pressing down on me. My body feels heavy. Everything seems pointless. I've tracked India through the last weeks of her life … for this? *Surely not.* I'm still missing a large piece of the puzzle, I am sure of it.

Mum looks up, her expression defeated. 'Not until I've told Tim. I owe him.'

'You should have thought about what you owed him twenty-odd years ago.'

My hand flies to my mouth as soon as the words are out of it. I'm horrified at the condemnation in my tone, yet still a part of me believes my mother deserves it. Perhaps she thinks so too, because she does not flinch. She absorbs my vitriol.

'I never wanted it to be this way. You have to believe that.'

'I don't know what to believe anymore.'

Out of nowhere, that lethargy infecting my bones dissipates. My energy returns. I spring up from the sofa and stride towards the door. I have to get away from this house, the decades of secrets contained within it.

'Poppy, where are you going? *Poppy!*'

I don't look back at Mum, even though she calls after me. I run out of the Coach House, leaving the front door open. Night has fallen; clouds gather over the city, obliterating the stars. Rain starts to patter, lightly at first, then harder. The paving stones become slick with it, shining like mirrors under the streetlamps.

I race down our street towards the bus shelter at the end, knowing a night bus should be on its way within the next five minutes. I'm right. A big double-decker turns the corner just as I arrive. The doors open and let me inside.

I take my seat among some bleary-eyed shift workers and wired party-goers. Chatter echoes all around me. But I hear none of it. I just wait for the slow vehicle to take me to my destination.

Fifty-six

He blunders down the seafront. He's not wearing a coat. Hands in his pockets, arms drawn to his sides; but this offers little protection against the harsh winds coming off the beach. He's tired, irascible. After another fitful night's sleep, he ended up single-handed most of the afternoon. Tonight, he's going to relax. There's a box set, a pizza and a six-pack of beer with his name on. He doesn't normally eat junk food or drink heavily, but he needs it. Maybe if he's lucky, *she* will join him.

As he unlocks his car, the lights flash and the alarm chirrups. He slides in behind the wheel, shoving the box onto the passenger seat. But he doesn't move or turn the key in the ignition. He enjoys the silence for a moment.

He finally fires up the engine. He takes a deep breath, breathing it out slowly in time with the indicator, as if it were a metronome. A dull ache throbs in his left side, and there is a sharp pain in the crook of his elbow. Distracted, he rubs at them as he turns the wheel, reminding himself of their cause. Phantom pains: nothing more, nothing less.

All that is over now.

In his pocket, his mobile rings. Pulling it out with one hand, he baulks at seeing her name – *She Who Must Be Obeyed* – flashing on the smartphone's screen. It feels like he's under surveillance. Worse than that: *trapped*. Not for the first time, he wonders if he could get rid of his phone or change his number. But he needs it for work; it would be a hassle.

Besides, she would only present him with a new one, in the box, proclaiming she 'just wants to help'. She'd only sense his antagonism. The smile would fall from her lips. The guilt and shaming would follow, her endless recriminations. It would be his turn on the kitchen chair. He's not sat there for years, has sworn he never would again, vowing he would do everything he could to appease her, contain her, try and keep her at bay. If he were to sit in that chair, she would catalogue everything that has been done for him, listing each one on her bony fingers, the clank of her bracelets sounding like chain links. *No escape.*

'Who's been here, all along?' She would hiss, 'Who's always picked up the pieces?'

In return, that duplicitous part of him would grovel to her. He'd promise to be good, to fall back in line. And a part of him would mean it, wanting her to love him again. Anything to be back in favour, to not see the dark anger shining in her eyes.

He presses the hands-free button on his phone. 'What is it?'

Beyond the windscreen, darkness falls over Brighton. The pier's lights flash in the twilight as bunting flaps against the wind, which is picking up speed.

She takes his gruff tone in her stride. 'I've been calling you all day!'

'Been working.'

But for once, she does not launch into her usual repertoire of emotional blackmail. She sounds breathless, like she's been running. She's svelte for her age, but it's by luck, rather than design. She counts walking to the corner shop for a *Daily Mail* and up and down the stairs her workout for the day. Too late, he regrets answering; he realises from her tone that she is excited. He knows what this means. He can feel his early night disappearing from him, receding like the dark tides of the beach below the seafront.

'Guess who's got out?'

He can hear the wide smile in her voice. *She's always loved drama.*

His fists clench around the wheel. 'Again?'

'Don't be like that.' The unmistakable pitch of a pout at the end of the line. 'I'm doing my best here.'

He takes another a deep breath, composes himself before answering. 'Fine. I'll go. But I'm not coming all the way this time. Send one of the others to my place.'

'Of course. Thank you, darling,' she purrs, hanging up.

He chucks his mobile on the passenger seat, next to the box of folders. He catches sight of his weary, bloodshot eyes in the rearview mirror: he must be mad. Flicking the indicator switch back again, he turns the car around.

Back towards The Lanes.

Fifty-seven

The bus drops me a few streets away from the Prince Albert. My breath recovered, I break into a run again. It's a massive assumption that Jenny will be at the club, but I have no other means of getting in touch with her. I pray she's there, because who else can help me? Not Tim, not Mum. Definitely not Matthew. Not even Ana will give me a straight answer.

Jenny links all of this together *somehow*. But how?

As I round another street corner, I hear raised voices. I fancy one is Jenny's, though part of me is sure it's wishful thinking. As I draw closer to the Prince Albert, I see the female bouncer shouting, her big mate standing behind her. He's silent as ever, his big arms crossed, an intimidating figure.

A black car waits outside the club, pointed away from me. It's parked unevenly, two wheels mounting the pavement. A large man has his back to me; no jacket. Even though I am too far away, I know who it is.

Matthew.

He has someone with him: someone much smaller, slighter. A girl. It's difficult to see who she is – his bulk blocks my view.

I can see her struggling though, but he easily maintains his grasp on her arm. Matthew ignores the complaints of the female bouncer. He holds her off with his other arm, his own threat clear. The two bouncers could probably take him, but they give Matthew a wide berth, maybe because they fear their intervention will make the confrontation worse.

The girl Matthew is holding fights him now. She tries to twist her body away. She grabs and punches at his hand and arm ineffectually. But he manoeuvres her through the passenger door of his car. He slams it after her. And as he does I catch a glimpse of who it is.

Jenny.

'Wait!'

The wind snatches my words away. Up ahead, Matthew slides into the driver's seat, never looking in my direction. He guns the engine and hares off towards the seafront.

Another burst of adrenaline takes me towards the front of the pub. The female bouncer and her mate quit their gesticulations. They look to me, surprised, as I appear in front of them.

'What the hell was that?'

The female bouncer curls her lip at me. 'Don't criticise what you don't understand.'

I stand there, speechless and glowering. *Too right I don't understand.*

'Who is Matthew to Jenny? Tell me!'

The Korean bouncer seems surprised, but folds her arms. 'I don't know what you're talking about.'

I eyeball her back. 'You expect me to believe that?'

'I don't care what you believe.'

Irritated and confused, I shoulder past the two door people, intent on some answers.

It's not busy. The front bar is deserted; my heart sinks. But then I spot Adonis, carrying a tray of glasses through from the back kitchenette. He hasn't seen me. Humming along with a EuroPop version of Prince's 'When Doves Cry', he places the glasses upside down on the shelf by the till.

I stride towards him, taking no notice of the curious stares from the few customers at the pool table or draped in booths. I muscle my way in front of a young woman with a mullet who's been waiting for a drink. She rolls her eyes but says nothing.

'Oi.'

Adonis turns. He has a cloth over his shoulder. He does not look as pristine as he usually does. His shirt is rumpled, like it's on its second day of wearing. There's a shadow of stubble on his usually clean-shaven face, dark lines under his eyes. He has not been home. Seeing me, the barman's expression clouds. What is he trying to protect Jenny from? *Surely not me.*

'You again.' Adonis's hands are on his snake hips.

I get straight to the point. 'Why did Matthew take Jenny?'

'You know him?' Adonis averts his eyes, but not before I see the surprise in them. For the first time, I see uncertainty in his demeanour. But if he is going to tell me anything more, he stops himself.

'Who is she?'

'Who are *you?*' Adonis counters, a smirk on his lips.

I stand there, glowering. Adonis's loyalty to Jenny, the way he protects her, is infuriating me now. The woman with the mullet tuts impatiently, drawing his attention.

He rolls his eyes skywards. 'Look, Jenny's not in any direct danger, OK?' Adonis looks to the other woman at the bar and indicates he's seen her.

My eyes narrow. 'How do you know that for sure?'

Adonis stalls. He acts like he hasn't heard me. He draws some pale ale, places the pint glass on top of the bar. Foam spills over the lip of the glass, pooling underneath.

I can sense a revelation, just out of my reach. I stretch for it, but still it eludes me. I take a deep breath; bite my tongue. Adonis has information I need. It won't help to alienate him now.

'*Please.* Where is he taking her?'

Adonis's gaze meets mine. 'I think you probably know, if you really think about it.'

Insight crashes through me. I *do* know.

But I can't accept it, not yet.

I turn on my heel and race back out of the Prince Albert.

Fifty-eight

I don't have a plan.

A mixture of disbelief and dark fury transports me to Elemental in what feels like an instant. I find myself at the glass doors of the club on the beachfront. There are people gathered on the pebbles nearby: party-goers quaffing last-minute cans before going into the bars; lovers walking hand in hand.

But I blunder past them all, single-minded. I move towards the decking of the beer garden at the beachside bar. I am refusing to acknowledge the truth. I gulp in the cold night air. Adonis's words follow me all the way: *…you probably know … if you really think about it.*

I grab the smooth steel handrail of the steps. Below, I spot Matthew's black car, now parked sideways up the slip road by the beach. I duck behind a closed umbrella on one of the patio sets, staying out of sight.

The back door of Elemental opens.

I hear them before I see them. A low voice hisses through teeth: the unmistakable growl of someone trying to keep an argument under wraps: Matthew. Jenny's voice soars above his, semi-hysterical – angry and tearful.

'Get your hands off me!' Jenny bucks like a toddler, dragging her feet as Matthew guides her across the decking, 'I hate you!'

Matthew mutters something to Jenny that I don't hear. He scoops her up at the waist, yanking the skinny teen off the ground. He tucks her under one burly arm. She slumps, knowing when she's beaten. All fight leaves the girl.

Another car drifts down the slip road, parking next to Matthew's, at the back of Elemental. The passenger door opens.

Ana clambers out of the car, opening her arms to the teenager as if to try and usher her into a hug. But Jenny pushes past her, wrenching open the back door of the car. She slams it shut after her. Ana shakes her head at Matthew, her condemnation obvious. He shrugs as if to say, *What?*

The handover complete, Ana gets in the passenger side. Matthew seems to sag at the click of the door, still waiting by the slip road; the outsider. He watches the other car reverse away, then he turns around and moves back across the decking and into Elemental, the door closing after him.

I can't believe it. Betrayal pierces through me. All this time, Matthew has entertained my investigation, in order to try to take it in the opposite direction. Towards JoJo, even towards Tim!

Yet all this time, not only was Matthew talking to my sister online as Wolfman404, he must have known who Jenny really is. Ana, too.

The Temple twins are both liars.

Fifty-nine

A taxi deposits me outside Matthew's place in that big, white converted house. I watch the cab reverse back out of the small car park and go back the way he came before turning back to the tall block. A porch light comes on as I come into its range, setting a dog off somewhere.

Another bulb flashes on. A woman looks down at me, her face partially obscured by the curtain. Aware of her gaze on me, I jab a finger on all the buttons. A female voice swears at me – presumably the woman on the second floor – but there's a buzz of static, followed by the click of the outer door. I'm admitted inside, into the communal hallway.

I trudge up to the top flat, every fibre in my body resisting me. I sink down onto the landing, to wait.

About an hour later, Matthew appears at the top of the stairs. His eyes narrow at the sight of me, slumped by his door.

'Poppy?'

I feel something click inside me. *The dance has begun.*

'I wanted to see you.' I rise from the floor. My voice seems far away, like I'm outside my own body again. 'Get up to anything interesting tonight?'

That unnerving grin I'm unused to seeing appears on his face. 'Not really. Just work. Same-old, same-old.'

Another lie. Pain hits me square in the chest, but I don't give any outward sign of it. I recall Jenny's ineffectual, yet resigned struggle outside the Prince Albert. Ana's angry expression. Who could Jenny be to her?

I move closer. I can smell cigarettes on him. The Matthew I know doesn't smoke. But I'm beginning to realise that Matthew no longer exists, no matter how far back our history goes.

Perhaps this new guy – *Matt* – is all that's left?

He smiles and curls an arm around my waist, pulling me to him. I stiffen against him as he attempts to kiss me on the lips. A wanton recklessness works its way through my muscles, from my face into my shoulders. I feel it melting the ball of pain in my throat, blooming in my belly. A tingle works its way through my spine, down my arms to my fingertips. I meet Matthew's gaze, a seductive smile on my lip.

'I need you.' I drape my arms over his shoulders. Even though my nerve endings shriek, I push my body against him. His hands encircle my waist as I brush my lips against his.

Matthew will never tell me the whole truth. I realise that now. I don't know what he has invested in the deception, but it's something to do with Ana. And with whoever was driving the car that came to fetch the teenager. Maybe it was Jayden. Whoever it was, if I want to find out who Jenny really is, I need to get inside Matthew – *Matt's* – flat.

Tonight.

I can feel his body respond, stiffening against my thigh. I enjoy having the power back. This was how it used to be between us: I would lead and *he* would follow. He unlocks the door and I push in ahead of him. I pull India's red hoody over my head as I go. I let it fall to the floor in the hall. I kick off my boots as I wander into his bedroom. He's close behind me.

'Take me to bed.'

My gaze alights on the items in the impossibly neat room. I feel outside of my body again. I'm watching myself from above. Everything feels hyper-real, almost movie-like.

I turn towards him. 'I know you want me.'

Can I really do this? This could be the man who threw my sister from the bridge. But it's not like I've not done this with him before, since India's death. The only difference is that now I know *for sure* he's a liar.

Matthew regards me, apprehensive. 'Of course I want you, it's just…'

I pull my top off. I peel down my leggings. I stand before him in just my underwear. I unhook my bra myself and his gaze falls on my breasts. I almost enjoy the conflict that flickers across his face.

I lean towards him, whisper in his ear. 'Fuck me.'

I grab his crotch in my left hand, undoing his fly and slipping my hand inside. He's stiff against my palm. He groans softly. I press my lips to his.

He finally yields. He opens his mouth, letting me push in my tongue. As I undo his shirt buttons, I feel his hand on the back of my neck, the other on my breast. I feel the muscles in his big arms contract; his grip tightens.

He breaks the kiss, pushing me away. There's momentary fear as I fall backwards. I land on my elbows on the bed behind me, legs splayed.

I feel outmanoeuvred, but I don't betray this on my face. Instead I fix him with my best seductive smile as he looms over me. I reach up and grab his shirt, helping him shrug it off. I reach for his fly again, but this time he smacks my hand away, his expression impassive.

'Lie still.'

I do as I'm told. I'm surprised as he grabs both my ankles, pulling me towards him across the bed. He drops to his knees, still on the floor, as if praying. He presses his lips against my bare stomach. He rolls down my underwear.

Suddenly perturbed, I try to sit up.

A chuckle escapes him, hot breath between my thighs. 'Let me.'

I allow him to hold me down again, prise my knees apart. I stare at the ceiling as he puts his mouth to my cunt, his breath on my wet skin.

He teases with his fingertips and tongue. One of Matthew's hands moves up my belly, tracing the space between my breasts, circling one of my nipples.

My breath catches in the back of my throat as an involuntary moan pushes between my lips. I arch my back, bucking against his mouth's attentions.

He thrusts his tongue and fingers deeper inside me. As he massages and pricks at the skin, I feel teeth brush over my most vulnerable place.

I turn my head to one side. I can still see my sister's red hoody, lying on the floor out in the hallway. A momentary flash of India enters my head, but I banish it, bright spots jumping up in front of my eyes instead. A slow-burn orgasm starts to flower deep within me.

I am powerless to stop its assault. It works its way from the pit of my stomach, through my chest and arms and down through my body to my feet. Before I can recover, Matthew flips me onto my front. He grabs my hips, forcing me up on my knees. The street light outside casts our curious, joined shadow on the wall.

He pulls down his boxers and spears me hard on his cock, in one deft movement. I suck air in through my teeth, a gasp of both pain and pleasure, as I brace myself against the headboard. He thrusts into me five, six times before climaxing with a low grunt. He collapses onto his back on the bed, next to me.

He pulls me to him this time. I lay my head on his shoulder. He raises a hand to brush my hair from my face. His fingertips discover my silent tears in the darkness, tracking down my cheeks. He makes a soothing noise, brushing them away. He thinks it's the emotion of the past few days, or the release of sex that's brought them; or both.

But it's not.

Moments later Matthew is asleep. His chest rises and falls. As I drift off, too, my heart grieves. Looking at his peaceful, slack face, I realise: I've never known him at all. He's done everything he could to come between me and the truth, never wanting me to find out about Jenny. But why? Who is she?

Tomorrow, I will find out.

Whatever it takes.

Sixty

'You're sure you'll be OK?'

I smile and nod: *I'll be fine.*

I lie in bed and watch Matthew get dressed. He seems irritated. He mentions something about being late for a meeting with the brewery, which he can't get out of. I reiterate I'll be OK. He tells me we'll go out this afternoon, just the two of us, somewhere nice. *Take my mind off all this.*

Thin-lipped I absorb his words, ignoring my contrary urges. I let him take charge and fuss over me. Finally he smiles and kisses me on the mouth, before running out.

As soon as the front door slams, I drift into the bathroom, dropping onto the floor by the toilet. My body feels numb – not my own. I stare at my bare hands and feet as I contemplate what I've just done: the full Mata Hari. There are words for this, 'honeytrap' one of the nicer ones (*noun.* A seductive ambush. Related words: lies, deceit, corruption).

I force these thoughts out of my mind. I need to find out who Jenny really is, why Matthew and the rest of the Temples have tried to keep her a secret, plus what this could mean in relation to my sister's death. Jenny's words come back to me – that India had something to tell her the night she died.

Matthew's apartment is silent. Still wobbly, I stand up; my bare feet flinch from the cold floor tiles. There's just a linen basket and a mirrored wall cabinet in the cell-like bathroom. I open the cabinet door. Inside are a razor, shaving foam, toothpaste, deodorant. I pull the lid off the linen basket: a pair of dirty jeans, underwear, a couple of shirts.

I step back through to Matthew's bedroom. The window is open a crack, sunlight peeking through. The blind on the dormer stirs with a warm breeze. I can hear a lawnmower somewhere. It's just after eight in the morning, but I can tell already it's going to be an unseasonably warm day.

I turn out drawers in the room with reckless abandon, rifling through papers, socks, underwear. I open the wardrobe. I sort through the hanging clothes, turning out pockets. I check the shoes in the base of the wardrobe, the boxes lining the top. I heave up the mattress, turn the bed's baseboard over before letting it rock back on its castors.

What am I looking for, exactly? I'm not sure.

I go into the kitchen and living area. I open every cupboard and drawer in there, too. Just food, cleaning products, washing powder, plates and cups. All lined up, in Matthew's usual neat, anal way.

I push the sofa out the way; he's even vacuumed under there, too. A shelf in the corner holds half a dozen books and twice that number of DVDs. The place is so bare, it's easy to search; I'm done in twenty minutes.

Nothing.

My gaze falls on the bin, the only thing I haven't searched. I pull off the lid; there's hardly anything inside. *Figures, for a neat freak like Matthew.*

I know what I have to do next, but I want to delay it, so I go back in the bathroom. I make the water as hot as I can bear. I scrub at my skin, anxious to rid myself of Matthew. I thought sleeping with the faceless D before Christmas was a low point, but last night has plumbed new depths. Worse, because I can remember every moment this time. Plus my treacherous body *enjoyed* it. As I watch water churn down the plughole, I feel like my betrayal of India is absolute.

I have to make it right.

I finally exit the shower cubicle and dry myself off. As I squeeze moisture from my poker-straight hair, I recall Ana's corkscrews at my sister's funeral. Another flash of Ana's face ricochets back to me: her angry expression at her brother last night. *She seemed almost disappointed in Matthew.* Why?

I can't put it off any longer.

I have to go back to Coy Ponds.

Sixty-one

I take a bus to see her. I have to walk the last block, and as I go, I check the time on my phone: coming up for eleven o'clock in the morning. My mother has left several texts. She wonders where I am, entreats me to come home. I fire off a reply, telling her I'm safe and I just need time to think – none of which is strictly *un*true.

I sidle up the pavement. I watch Coy Ponds for some time, sheltered behind a large ornamental pine tree, next to that perfectly coiffured lawn with its ridiculous stone fairies and wishing wells.

I try to discern if anyone is home. There is no car on the drive. Alan has a beastly old Jaguar, so he must be out. Being the middle of the day, there are, of course, no overhead lights on, but I can see no movement inside the big house, nor any shining TV screens. It looks empty.

I feel eyes on me. I look around and see an elderly gentleman appear on his own immaculate lawn to pick up the newspaper. He forces a smile onto his face as if he wasn't thinking I look suspicious. But, of course, I do.

I nod in acknowledgement and look at my phone with an irritated expression, as if I'm waiting for someone. Then, knowing he's still watching me, I make a big show of walking off in the opposite direction, back towards the park.

At the end of the road, I wait five minutes. Then I skip back up towards Coy Ponds. The elderly gentleman is gone from his lawn. Just in case he's still watching from his own hallway, I race across Coy Ponds' lawn as fast as I can, until I'm out of sight.

I brace myself against the rendered white wall. I walk around the big house, picking my way through some rose bushes. I try to ensure I don't catch my skirt or tights on any thorns. I run my palm across the brickwork until my palm finds glass: the double patio windows of the extended, grandiose living room. I press my face against the pane. The room is as it was when I spoke to Ana last, seated on that massive, overstuffed three-piece suite: meticulously tidy, everything in its place, like every room in the big house.

I reach out and grasp the patio window handle. To my surprise, it is not locked. Carefully, I open it just enough to allow me access, squeezing through, into the room beyond. I leave it open, just in case, freezing where I am.

What the hell am I doing?

But then I remind myself.

There have been enough lies. We all need answers.

I move into the hallway beyond the living room. The other rooms downstairs are empty, so I move towards the large, wide staircase and the mezzanine above. One of the doors is ajar, light pooling on the hall floor. I push it open.

Inside is a riot of bedclothes, toys and trinkets. There's a double bed, unmade in the centre of the room. A cot in the corner. This must be Ana's room. I recognise my old friend's clothes scattered on the floor, her hair products left out, make-up on the bedside cabinet. Smaller clothes are stacked on top of a changing station, along with a pack of nappies and wipes, incongruously neat against the backdrop of havoc.

I move to the next door. No one is inside. It is a plain, boy's bedroom. It must be James's. It looks untouched. There is a dark-blue bedspread on a single bed; a cabinet; a wardrobe; a desk and chair. There are some books on a shelf, a vase of flowers. In comparison to Ana's, it is pathologically neat, like Matthew's place. There are no real personal touches: no posters on the wall, no cluttered belongings on display, no mess. A light film of dust has settled on top of the items in the room. Then I remember what Maggie said at India's funeral about her youngest child: 'He's away at school … He's *very* gifted.'

I move to the next door. The curtains are still closed in this room. A lamp has been left on, offering dim illumination. The décor is classically girly: pink and white; a gingham bedspread with matching curtains. There is a single bed, with matching white cupboard and ottoman. In comparison to the previous room, this one feels more lived in, though it is much tidier than Ana's.

So, this must be Jenny's room. But why would the Temples have this teenaged girl living with them? And how does no one else know?

I cross the threshold and slide open a drawer. Inside, a selection of toiletries and make-up. I open the wardrobe door. The clothes are wrapped in plastic. The smell of mothballs pricks my nostrils. I shift through the clothes: dresses, skirts, tops. Some of them I remember Ana wearing when we were teenagers.

I brush my hand against the bells fringing a skirt. They tinkle, loud in the silence. Another connection sparks in my mind: My sister was wearing this skirt, in her Facebook profile photo.

This prompts me to look closer, at the other clothes, the jumble at the bottom of the wardrobe. Something catches my eye. I reach for it, pulling it out.

I recognise it as Jenny's black gym bag, the one I saw stuffed in the kitchen at the Prince Albert. I unzip it. Sure enough, inside is that black, bell-sleeve top and long black skirt. And Jenny's red wig. I finger the strands: they feel fake, unreal – spun nylon.

I become aware of another presence behind me. I flinch, caught in the act. An automatic apology jumps to my lips, but it dies in my mouth as I take in who waits in the doorway.

The smell of cigarettes wafts in ahead of him. He has his hands in his pockets, just like his son often does, though this man is much shorter. And white. His pock-marked face is impassive, trying to work out what I'm doing.

Alan Temple.

Sixty-two

Alan blocks the doorway, just two or three good paces away. There is no doubt about the threat he presents. Something shifts between us: dark and ominous. It's a strain for Alan Temple to keep it in check.

And in that tiny fragment of time, everything finally fits together:
- My mother's screams reverberating around Elemental: 'It was you. It was always you';
- The Temples' consistent presence in our lives for twenty-five years;
- Maggie sitting on the stairs with me, the day India was born, commiserating;
- Frog King – pebbly skin – 'make froggy jump'!

India's biological father is Alan Temple. That's what India was going to tell Jenny that night. But maybe she'd decided she needed to tell Tim first. But I don't have time to puzzle all this, not now.

Though I've been in fights with men before, I don't fancy my chances with Alan. He's not a big man, but he's wiry and strong. I recall Matthew telling me his father had been a bare-knuckle fighter in his youth. Between *flight* and *fight*, I'm keen to avoid the latter. My gaze strays to the bedroom window. Could I jump out?

I take a step backwards, even though there is nowhere for me to go. 'Alan. I know about Jenny.'

Rage flickers across his face. His gaze falls on the red wig still in my hand. My panicked eyes skitter around me, looking for an escape route.

'It was you, driving last night. When Ana picked her up from Matthew at Elemental?'

Still Alan says nothing. Certainty coils around my gut again as the

Transport Police officer's words ricochet back to me: 'He was dark … Short. Nice face.' I meet Alan Temple's eye.

'And it was you, at the station the night India died!'

He does not react, his expression still maddeningly emotionless. The pressure in the room seems to intensify. I blot my palms on my leggings. My heart thuds in my chest as I try to breathe at a normal pace. I'm afraid hyperventilating might stop me evading him if he comes towards me. My mouth feels dry.

'What's going on?' I hear the words as a blur.

But it's not Alan speaking. It's a woman's voice. My heart lifts at the sight of Maggie Temple appearing behind her husband. But then, in that microsecond, just as I feel sure I am saved – that I can reveal Alan's involvement in India's death and that the danger he presents will be removed – I realise I am mistaken. My mind processes Maggie's words. And as I mentally unpack them, I appreciate their horror. She actually said: 'What if it was?'

She must know it was Alan at the station. And she doesn't care.

Yet, still I don't want it to be true. Even though every cell of my body tells me it's a bad idea, my treacherous mouth forms the words and I fire them at Alan:

'Then you know that India was your daughter?'

Finally, a reaction from the older man. A predatory smile flashes across his features. 'You always were a fantasist, Poppy Wade.'

Alan's mocking words are the fuel I need. My fear morphs into fury. The weakness in my limbs vanishes. My energy uncoils within me. The words rush out of my mouth, so I might convince Maggie. Get her on my side.

'India was Alan's daughter. My mother and Alan had an affair; one night, whatever. He killed her, to hide the fact my sister was your kids' sister, too!'

But Maggie sighs deeply. 'I know.'

Alan looks to his wife, bewildered. I am agog. If Alan hadn't known India was his daughter, and Matthew and Ana's sister, then what the hell was this all about? Those words of India's come back to me: 'make froggy jump'. Maggie was in charge of all of this. I can see it now. My stomach is in free-fall. Nausea paints the back of my throat.

'Your mum told me years ago.' Maggie shrugs at me, almost bored.

'And you didn't think to tell me?' Alan's tone is plaintive. He is forced to brace one hand against the door to steady himself. 'Jesus, Maggie. You had me—' He slams his hand on the doorpost. I watch as the horrifying realisation sinks in: *He's killed his own daughter.*

But Maggie's face is stony, remorseless, as she regards her husband. 'I won't let anyone take advantage of me. Not even *you.*'

I indicate the red wig in my hand and try again. 'But who is Jenny? Why is she living here? I know India was going to help Jenny get away from you all. Is that why you killed her? Is it?!'

Maggie and Alan's gazes lock as I shout this. Something shifts once more.

I feel my advantage slip away, though I'm not sure why. Maggie nods at her husband, casting her eyes downwards in resignation. Sorrow and trepidation move, fleeting, across Alan's features.

I hesitate, unable to believe what is happening. My legs lock with fear. Alan moves towards me with menacing purpose. I find my momentum, running for the window.

But I'm not fast enough.

I feel both Alan's hands on my shoulders. But rather than yanking me back towards him, Alan pushes me forwards as hard as he can. I'm propelled into the wall at speed. My forehead connects with plaster.

Stunned, I fall backwards onto the floor of the pink bedroom. I'm not knocked out, but when I try to get up, I can't. My senses have left me. I struggle to claw them back, raw instinct kicking in. Maggie yells some kind of encouragement, in case Alan loses his nerve, it seems. My breaths come in ragged bursts of panic as I attempt to crawl away.

Alan turns me over, kneeling on my chest, grasping my windpipe with both hands and squeezing. His face is desperate; I can see tears in his eyes. Pain builds in my chest and throat, a buzzing noise erupts in my ears. My arms feel heavy, almost jelly-like. I claw at his hands and wrists in vain.

I know what is happening. I know that I am ... I will pass out.

Sixty-three

There's nothing.

And then there's sunlight. An assault of colour, through a prism of glass. I blink. I can taste blood in my mouth. My throat feels bruised and sore.

My head bangs. Bewilderment becomes exhilaration that I am still alive. I force unconsciousness away, reclaiming my alertness. Just as quick, confusion returns. I am alone. I'm lying on my side on the carpet in the living room, facing the double patio doors.

For a moment, I think I am in the recovery position. Perhaps Alan and Maggie's attack was simply a particularly vivid, nasty nightmare brought on by mania. Then I realise: my hands and feet are tied.

What the fuck is going on?

I pull at the ropes securing my hands with my teeth, but stiffen as I hear Maggie's voice behind me.

'What do you want me to say?'

She's not in the room; the sounds echo like she's in the next one. *Which is that, the kitchen?* I can't think straight.

I move my hands towards my pocket, as surreptitiously as I can. I can't feel my phone in there. Maggie or Alan must have taken it. For a moment, hope dashes through me: Would Matthew come looking for me? *No, he's at Elemental. Mum probably thinks I'm with him. Shit!*

Alan sounds weary. 'How are we going to explain this to Matt?'

'We don't need to. That little bitch ran away from him before – abandoned him when he was sick; she can *run off* again.' Maggie's reply is cold, flat. 'She just needs to not be here anymore. Do you understand me, Alan?'

The two of them could be having a minor marital dispute over something banal, like putting the bins out. And then, with sickening clarity, I realise what Maggie is telling Alan to do. She's telling him to finish me off.

Panic surges through me; I renew my attempts to gnaw at my bonds. I can't equate the voices of the two people I hear next door with the family friends I've known practically my whole life. I have never seen Maggie behave in any way that is not openly affectionate and respectful towards Alan. Similarly, he's always acted in public as if he adores her. But now he sounds put-upon, hen-pecked.

'I'm just the one who's had to pick up the pieces all these years, remember?' Maggie's tone is venomous, full of deep resentment and scorn.

Alan relents. 'How many times do you want me to apologise? It was one time with Kirsten! I couldn't have known all this would happen! And how could you let me kill India, knowing…?' He can't finish.

Though Maggie stops short of laughter, the gloating edge in her reply is unmistakable:

'Two birds, one stone.'

For a moment it's as if her icy reach has spread into the room where I'm lying. I'm frozen by the easy practicality of her tone. But what is the other bird? The other reason why she wanted India dead?

I find my strength again. But the knots around my hands won't budge. My flesh is turning purple. There's a flash of denim by the patio doors. I flinch, dread seizing me. I'm certain either Maggie or Alan has left the house by the back door of the kitchen and has crossed the patio towards me, intent on dragging me out so they can take me somewhere I won't be coming back from. A terrified sob catches in my throat.

The moment passes. I realise I can still hear the Temples' debate in the other room. The figure outside crouches down. In one hand, a Stanley knife.

He opens the patio door, deliberate and slow, ensuring the sound of it sliding back is as quiet as possible. The figure squeezes through quickly and quietly, like I did before – how long ago it was, I don't know now.

He looms over me as he raises a finger to his lips. Eyes wide, my gaze flies from the sharp blade, to his face. He looks so much like Matthew did at the same age. But he's longer in the face, bonier, ganglier than his older brother was.

He raises the knife.

'James,' I whisper, my voice a rasp. 'Don't!'

Sixty-four

I'm sure James is going to stab me, or draw the blade across my throat as I lie prone and helpless on the living-room floor. I don't utter another sound. I'm utterly frozen with fear.

But James does not push the Stanley knife into my flesh. The teenager squats down and cuts the ropes around my hands, then my feet. The rope unspools. I am free. I stare at my saviour, still unable to comprehend what is happening.

'We've gotta go,' James murmurs.

I stand, shock making me vacant. But there's no time for further thought. James springs to attention as Maggie and Alan appear at the living-room door. Their eyes widen at the sight of me, untied.

'Stay back!' James points the blade at his parents then thrusts it forwards, forcing Alan and Maggie to back up. He stands in front of me, his other hand behind him, indicating I should stay where I am.

Agog, I do as he says. I watch James reach towards the rack hanging over a bureau in the corner of the room. The teen swears under his breath. 'Where are the car keys?'

'Sweetheart, don't do this.' Maggie's eyes flit from James to me and back again. Her demeanour betrays her panic, though her voice is calm.

'Listen to your mother, son,' Alan growls.

Maggie seems to wince at his choice of words.

James's voice is low and dangerous. 'I am not your son!'

Spittle flecks at the corner of James's mouth. I realise with a jolt the teenager is not scared. *He's absolutely furious.*

'This has gone far enough!' James points the blade at Maggie and Alan, his other hand ushering me back towards the patio windows.

The situation seems to have turned on its head again. It's like James is the dangerous one now.

Maggie edges forward slightly, hands in front of her. 'We're just trying to do the right thing…'

This seems to infuriate James more. The feral snarl I've seen on Ana's face so many times paints itself on his visage now. But Maggie, her face earnest, does not stop edging towards him, hands raised.

'Right thing?' James spits. 'For God's sake, will you listen to yourself? … I said get back!' He lurches forwards, slashing the knife through the air.

The blade connects with Maggie's right wrist. The skin splits open. Blood floods out.

She freezes.

The three of them take this in, for a second unable to compute what has happened.

Maggie's knees buckle. Alan grabs her. He follows her to the floor of the living room, clamping one hand over the wound. There's no time for recriminations. Alan unknots his tie. He wraps it around Maggie's forearm, a makeshift tourniquet.

The movement makes James refocus. 'Keys!'

Dazed, Alan rifles through his jacket pocket. He locates the car keys and throws them at the teenager.

James snatches them from the air and turns on his heel, guiding me towards the patio doors. I let him hurry me across the lawn, towards Alan's car, waiting next to the garage.

I feel movement behind us. Then Alan's rushed, pleading voice. 'We won't let you do this!'

James stops, turning back. Alan raises his hands, showing he has nothing in them. He beckons to the teen, asking for him to give him the Stanley knife.

But James does not relinquish the blade. Appalled, I watch the teenager hold it to his own neck. 'Come any closer … I'll finish it!'

He nicks his flesh. Bright red blood flowers at the base of his throat. Alan nods, hasty, casting his eyes downwards. He stays where he is on the lawn.

Satisfied, James dashes across the grass, pulling me with him. When we're out of reach, but not earshot, I hear Alan's voice:

'Hello, police?' He's on the phone.

As we draw level with the garage I can hear Alan's loud, artificially panicked voice, concocting some fantasy for the police dispatcher: A young woman has attacked his wife with a knife and has abducted his son.

'What is he … Why would he…?' My voice is hoarse.

James opens the passenger door and pushes me in. Then he clambers into the other side. James is not much of a driver. The car surges forward as the teen presses the wrong pedal. But then he remembers. He reverses the car down the drive and out onto the road.

James jerks the car through a three-point turn and we're on our way.

Sixty-five

'Where are you taking me?'

After Alan Temple's assault, it hurts to talk. I catch sight of my reflection in the car's side mirror. My eyes are bloodshot. There are long fingermarks around my neck. I shudder.

But James still does not answer. He stares at the road ahead. He has the Stanley knife clasped in one fist, the other hand on the wheel. He's muttering wordlessly, lost inside himself, replaying what just happened.

'Your mum said you were away at school.'

I gain his attention now. His jaw clicks, scorn entering into his voice. '*She's* not my mum.'

Dread seizes me a second time. I'm suddenly not so sure James intends to rescue me from Alan and Maggie, to take me to safety.

I force some authority into my tone. 'James. Where are we going? Tell me.'

'You'll see.'

I don't like the sound of this. I try and drag my thoughts together. But I find nothing. My mind insists on seeing James as the little boy who was always there, in the background, when we were kids. He'd drag a toy after him, thumb in his mouth. Now he's an angry young man.

'So tell me what I can do to help?' I try to come over friendly, motherly. But it's not me. It sounds wooden, false on my tongue.

'I'll show you.'

About ten minutes of excruciating silence later, James parks up on a deserted side road. He turns the engine off. My gaze follows his through the windscreen. Trepidation floods through me.

I'm not sure where we are. But I can see the railway embankment, an unmanned, automated signal box towering into the air. There's a level crossing above us, its red-and-white-striped barriers raised. Rubbish drifts in the breeze off the railway line and onto the road.

But it's not the railway that's drawing my attention. It's the small bridge further on, its struts filthy with pollution. There is a single, sad bouquet of wilting flowers strapped to one of them. I've not been here before; I've avoided it since I returned to Brighton at Christmas.

The bridge where India fell.

James gets out of the driver's side and comes around for me. The Stanley knife is still in his hand. My subconscious, animal side is petrified. Yet my more human, conscious mind insists on giving me a running commentary: *You always thought you would put up a fight, didn't you? You thought you would run. Yet now, here you are. Doing nothing.*

James wrenches open the passenger door. He grabs my arm and pulls me out, to my feet. He is wiry and strong, just like Alan. He holds the Stanley knife to my side, a reminder not to try anything.

I take in the quiet road and the chicanes on the one-way street. If I shout out, would anyone hear? Would someone get to me before I bleed out on the pavement? James was willing to raise a blade to Maggie, his own family. I am in no doubt that he'd do the same to me.

I'm desperate to stall. 'Are you taking me to Jenny?'

James shoots me an exasperated glance as he forces me along, up the embankment. 'You could say that.'

The teenager shoves me forwards. I stumble, putting out my hands, but I don't fall to my knees. I persist, determined to find out why I'm going to die.

'Why didn't they want anyone to know about Jenny?'

James regards me, slack-jawed. 'You really have no idea.'

I eyeball him back. 'So tell me.'

He indicates the bridge. 'It's easier if I show you.'

My chest rises with short gasps. I feel light-headed. 'So you can throw me off the bridge? No thanks.'

James's face clouds with hurt. 'I'm not going to kill you!'

I just stare, not believing him. I indicate the blade in his hand.

James looks at the Stanley knife curiously, like he's forgotten he was carrying it. He sighs and hands the blade to me. He opens his hands afterwards for emphasis: *Better?*

Feeling awkward, I pocket the knife. 'But you knew about India's blog, right?'

James shoots me another withering glance. 'Yes. C'mon.'

He walks past me. I flinch away, but James carries on, up the embankment and onto the railway. Then he walks over the level crossing without looking. I become aware of the sound of traffic beyond.

I follow, a few steps behind the teenager, just in case. I pick my way up the embankment then across the concrete-and-wooden rail sleepers, towards the small metal footbridge. As we climb higher, up the stairwell, I look down the line.

I can see Brighton station, a small rectangle down the track. Beyond it, the Brighton Wheel in the distance. It's a white circle floating above the buildings, bright sunlight glancing off the chrome and glass of the town centre. I reach the top of the steps. Suspicion still prickles through me. I stay where I am, one hand on the rail, just in case James tries anything.

The teen appears to take this in his stride. He kneels by the strut where the bouquet is strapped and plucks something from the wilted flowers.

He looks at it, as if uncertain about what he's going to do. Then he turns and presents it to me, pushing it into my hand. Defiance is written all over his face. I take it. It's a florist's card, handwritten with spidery letters: 'Sleep soundly, my twin soul. Jenny xxx'

A kaleidoscope of imagery, their colours bright and contrasting, yet every piece makes up a pattern. I've been looking at each one in isolation. To put them together – to truly understand them – I've had to return to the scene of my sister's death. And now, it's as if I'm standing back, taking in the entire picture, comprehending, at last, how each piece fits together.

The pink room and the blue room at Coy Ponds, the meticulous housekeeping in both. James's snarl: 'I'm not your son.' Jenny's irritation with me: 'You people.' Alan's desperate face, his hands round my throat, his shout after us: 'We won't let you do this!' Finally, from my sister's supposed suicide note: 'Real girls.'

I reach forward and grab James's forearm. He lets me. I roll his sleeve back, even though I know already what I will find there.

A tattoo.

A sugar skull.

Sixty-six

'You're Jenny?'

I struggle to connect the two: James and Jenny. The teenager in front of me looks so like Matthew had at the same age: squared-off jaw, brown eyes, rosebud lips.

My gaze falls on James's chest. The mounds under his shirt, the curve of his body. I realise: *It's not puppy fat, but breasts.*

'You've been transitioning in secret? How?'

A bitter, sad smile draws itself on the teen's face. 'It's amazing what drugs and hormones you can get on the Internet.'

I look for other differences. No pale make-up, of course. James's hair, short, yet still long in comparison to Matthew's smooth, shaven head. I recall Jenny removing her red wig at the Prince Albert; her long, poker-straight, black hair beneath. My heart fills with dismay. I reach forward, feeling his short locks beneath my palm.

'They cut your hair?' I mean Maggie and Alan.

The teenager flinches from my touch. 'They think no one will understand.'

'They're wrong. You know that, right?'

A flash of Adonis and the others at the Prince Albert enters my thoughts, their unapologetic stance: *We're here. We're queer.* But James shrugs, his face full of despair. It makes no difference. Jenny is trapped in James's body, his life.

So this was India's mission: to liberate Jenny from James – from the young man the Temples insisted Jenny be. I can appreciate, at last, what James (*Jenny*) has been put through. I feel out of my depth. Silence fills the chasm between us, there is only the sound of the traffic beyond the bridge.

My mind begins to work fast. I should take James to the police; but how do I stop him running away from me?

There is a squeal of brakes on the street below. The sound of a car door opening comes next, but the car owner does not slam it shut again. Instead he yells both of our names, ordering us both to stay where we are. I hear his footsteps running along the pavement. I see him scramble up the embankment, then stride towards the level crossing.

Matthew.

Alan is with him.

James freezes, his alarmed gaze meeting mine.

'I'm not going back with him. Not this time!' The teenager jumps up onto the bridge railing. He swings his legs over effortlessly; I have no time to rush forwards and grab him back.

But James does not jump right away. The teen sits on the rail, balanced precariously over the line below, his arms behind him. All he needs to do is push off. I resist the urge to grab both his wrists. I might startle him, make him fall.

Matthew and his father are now on the line below, on the level crossing. I watch them split up: Matthew runs towards the rail bridge's right-hand steps, the side closest to me. Alan is making his way up the left steps. A pincer movement. They have me and James trapped.

'Don't!' I warn, my gaze flitting from Matthew's face to James's perilous grip on the railing. I know Matthew is here to contain me, with Alan there to grab James back off the bridge. Inside my pocket, my hand closes around the Stanley knife.

'Poppy, what the hell are you doing?'

Matthew raises both hands, like his mother did in the living room at Coy Ponds – edging forwards, towards me. His suspicion stings, but I swallow my feelings down. I pull the Stanley knife from my pocket.

'No!' I shriek at Matthew and his father.

Then, as I speak, James's words return to me: '*She's* not my mum', he'd said of Maggie. Again, I see Ana, shaking her head at Matthew, the night he forcibly carried Jenny to the car.

I wield the blade at Alan. 'You might have been India's father, but you're not James's, are you?!'

Downwind, I can smell the older man's aftershave, the cigarettes on his breath. I breathe through the urge to lunge at Alan and plunge the blade into his pallid skin.

Colour drains from his face, but he doesn't try to deny my words. His nicotine-stained fingers find the bridge railing. His eyes are fixed on James, not me. 'I've loved him like he was mine. You can't say any different!'

James shakes his head, eyes fiery. 'Don't make me laugh. You never did anything to stop her!'

The truth hits Alan like a weight. He sighs, shoulders slumped. 'I'm sorry!'

'Too late.' James's gaze returns to the track. His knuckles are white from clinging on. He surely can't hold on much longer. But I know why James – *Jenny* – came to me.

'Ana's your mother,' I say to James.

Still seated perilously on the railing, James nods, his face a picture of relief.

I see it all now. There was no 'last baby' for Maggie and Alan. James was Ana's child, taken in and raised by the twins' parents.

I turn to face Matthew, and see he's barely reacted. He already knows this, I realise. He's always known.

He advances towards me, but I'm too fast. I turn on one foot, forcing him to jump back, away from the arc of the blade. I won't let him take me, suppress me, like he has Jenny all this time.

'Pops, are you OK? Who did that?' he indicates the marks around my throat, trying to deflect my attention.

'It was Alan!' James yells from the bridge. 'Maggie had him do it!'

'They killed India,' I say through gritted teeth.

Matthew is incredulous as he looks towards us.

'C'mon, they're being ridiculous!' Alan protests.

Disbelief spreads across Matthew's face. 'But you said…?'

He regards his father. His face is like a little boy's. I see horror, anger, resentment cross the features I know so well … and how he arrests it all, pulling the shutters down. His expression becomes impassive again, like marble.

He parrots his father. 'That's ridiculous, Poppy.'

'That's right,' says Alan carefully. 'We told you Poppy's not been well, Matt. Not since India died. She's gone crazy, with all these accusations … she's deluded.'

I twist around quickly, so I'm now pointing the knife at Alan. 'She's not crazy!'

We all jump – it's James who's said this. But the teenager is not looking at us, he's staring at the track.

'You're the ones who are deluded!' he screams. 'Saying it was just a phase I was going through…!'

'I thought you were gay,' Matthew mutters.

'I've never been gay!' James regards Matthew, his chest rising and falling with anxious gasps. 'Maggie said I was disgusting. A joke. Not a real woman! And you helped them both keep me a prisoner!'

I think I see a crack of recognition in Matthew's demeanour. The knife still pointed at Alan, I make my appeal.

'All of this … was your mum, Matthew. She took James off Ana. She had you keep Jenny a secret and your dad kill India, to stop her helping her leave! Maggie has had you all under her control!'

'I won't go back.' James's cheeks are streaked with tears. 'I'd sooner die!'

'No … no.' Matthew's face is taut. I can see tears in his eyes. I've never seen Matthew cry. 'I just wanted to keep you all safe. I was just trying to do the right thing!' The words fall from his lips like a mantra.

But James is unimpressed. 'Ana let me be myself!' he says. 'Those two would never have been able to control me if it hadn't been for *you*.'

James's jerky movements draw my attention back to him. He is hanging over the drop now, but I'm not convinced James would die by merely falling. He'd probably break his legs. My stomach lurches as a train appears in the distance; I see it with sickening clarity.

'They're done!' Matthew hollers, 'We'll make them pay for what they did. All of it! James, you don't have to go back. I promise! I won't stop you going out anymore. Ever … just come down!' He takes a stride forwards, his arms outstretched towards his nephew.

I wonder if the train driver can see James on the bridge and, if he can, whether he can apply the brakes in time. The train nears the bridge. In less than a minute, it will be upon us. I fancy I can hear a shriek of the train's brakes – wishful thinking…?

James fixes Matthew with a sad stare. 'I can't trust you.'

In my head, I can already see the teen do it. I visualise James leaping into the air, free for mere seconds, for the first time in his short life. Then his body connects with the punishing metal body-work of the train. Air is ripped from his lungs, his flesh pulverised as the train's shockwaves rocket through his bones. *The same as my sister.*

Matthew sees it, too. 'We don't have to do this! Come down, please James!'

The teenager twists his body to face Matthew now. But James does not come back over the right side of the bridge. I understand, perhaps too late, how pain makes people desperate.

The teen is defiant. 'My name is not James.'

His fingertips let go of the railing.

Sixty-seven

'No!'

I hear Matthew yell, helpless.

James pushes himself away from the edge of the bridge.

I drop the knife. I lunge forwards, thrusting my arms through the railings. My mind's rehearsals of James's fall allow me to pre-empt the teen's launch into the air by a sliver of a second. I manage to grab him as he lets himself drop, my hands catching him around the waist.

'Help me!' I scream.

James is lighter than I thought he would be, but still his dead weight crashes against my forearms. White-hot pain sears through as a bone in my wrist snaps, bringing nausea to the back of my throat. But my grip has already closed around James's chest. My elbows prop him up, holding him to the bridge as stars burst behind my eyes. I struggle not to loosen my grasp.

'I'm gonna drop him!'

Matthew leans over the balustrade, grabbing for James's shoulders. It's a precarious position: only Matthew's weight keeps him in place; his feet don't touch the ground. Alan stands to the side, eyes wide, hand clamped over his mouth in shock.

'Take my hand!' Matthew hollers.

Below, the train is slowing. The shriek of brakes I'd heard was not fantasy. But momentum still pushes the vehicle forward. James hangs in our grip, shocked by the sudden arrest of his fall. He looks up at Matthew's hand. I see a shimmer of something in the teenager's eye. I realise, with a jolt, what he's thinking:

If James grabs Matthew's hand and yanks, he could send him over the bridge, onto the train below.

'You're better than that, James!' I scream, my grip beginning to slacken.

James's sights move from his brother, then to me. I see his lips move, the words form. Though the wind snatches them away I still feel the words; nearly two decades of humiliation, abuse, invalidation courtesy of Maggie:

'I'm disgusting.'

Matthew hollers, 'Please, take my hand!'

But James just dangles. I can feel my hurt arm beginning to numb. I know I can't hold on much longer. Matthew won't be able to continue his purchase on the teen's shoulders with just his fingertips. James will drop.

I yell through the struts of the bridge. 'Jenny, don't let Maggie kill you. Take Matthew's hand!'

James's attention flickers away from the approaching train, back up at us for a microsecond. Matthew follows my lead.

'Jenny. Take my hand. Pull yourself up. Please, Jenny!'

Hearing Matthew's words, the teen reaches up at last. Matthew is able to grab him and haul him over the balustrade, back onto the bridge with us.

We collapse in a huddle together, our bodies unable to support our weight.

Below, I hear the hiss of the train engine coming to a standstill below.

A siren blares through the air; the police are here already. I can hear voices on the embankment; more footsteps on the steps will sound next. My mind reels, shock makes everything seem brighter.

'Oh, thank Christ.' Alan runs across the bridge. He leans down and attempts to hug both his son and grandson, but Matthew pushes his father away.

'That's it; you're done. It's *over*.'

Hurt, Alan backs off, but he does not try to run. He is resigned; there is no point. He almost seems relieved.

I hear a burst of static and then there are men and women in black uniforms milling about on the bridge, making demands and barking orders. There's a rustle of foil blankets, the sound of an ambulance backing up near the level crossing below.

Matthew pulls both of us to him, his arms around us. Though his voice is calm, I can feel his heart beat erratically in his chest. I slump, hardly able to hold my own head up. I place an arm around Jenny's shoulders, though she simply stares ahead, almost catatonic.

'We'll get through this,' Matthew murmurs.

But I know we can't.

Sixty-eight

'There you go.'

The nurse stands back to admire his handiwork. He's a tall, large guy with chiselled features, who'd look more at home in his uniform if he was stripping out of it, than actually performing medical procedures.

I raise my wrist and inspect the quick-drying cast. 'Thanks.'

The nurse takes a squirt of antibacterial hand gel and rubs it over his large palms. 'It was a clean break. You were lucky.'

I give him a wan smile, matching his cliché with one of my own. 'I don't feel very lucky.'

The nurse notes something down. I sign below and then I'm on my way.

I know exactly where I want to go now. I drag my knackered body down the corridor and into the lift. Exhausted, I get out near a locked ward. There's a deathly hush here, the weight of the silence is oppressive. I stalk towards the intercom and press the button.

A crisp, starchy voice crackles on the speaker. 'Hello. Are you a carer or relative?'

'Relative.' I am not lying. *Technically, I am.*

The door buzzes and I push my way in. The ward is all but deserted. A sister sits at the nurses' station. She sorts through paperwork as a receptionist with a headset taps at the keys of his computer. I can smell the sharp tang of disinfectant more than usual. The floor is just-been-mopped shiny, yellow triangles propped up in warning. A woman with lank grey hair, dressed in a pink dressing gown, shuffles towards me, her thoughts elsewhere.

I'm about to enquire at reception when someone I recognise appears from a side room, her shoulders hunched, her expression twisted in agony.

Ana.

She looks up at me. Black tears from her mascara streak down her otherwise perfectly made-up face, though her cheeks are dry now. I wait for the inevitable sneer of Ana's top lip. I brace myself, in case she comes for me with those talons of hers.

But she doesn't. My old friend looks small, lost. She regards me with a resigned expression. 'So, *your* mum and *my* dad?'

'That's not the strangest revelation today.' My voice is soft. 'Can I say congratulations … on the baby?'

'You'd be the first.' Ana smiles, rueful. 'She said I was a disgusting, common little chav.'

She sits down on a padded bench in the corridor, her body unable to hold her.

'Maggie, you mean?' I sit down as well, my hands folded on my lap.

Disgusting. The same word Maggie used to describe Jenny. I'm lost. Teenagers get pregnant every day, up and down the country. It doesn't have to be a big deal, especially in a family with unlimited resources like the Temples. Ana could have been a mother and still been anything she wanted, with the *right* support from her family.

'Why did she make you hide it?'

Ana sighs. 'A fifteen-year-old daughter up the duff didn't fit her vision of her supposedly perfect family.'

I recall hearing the ugly truth of Maggie and Alan's marriage, back at Coy Ponds. I've already seen what the secrets and lies have done to this family, how all of them would rather oppress James's true self than let the truth get out.

'How did you hide it – the pregnancy?'

'Wasn't difficult. He was a neat little bump.' Ana's wan smile becomes genuine as she remembers. 'When Mum found out, she took over, like I knew she would. I got bigger, so I stayed with relatives for a bit. Remember when I said I'd had a bad reaction to some hair-relaxing product and couldn't come to school? That was my third trimester. I was away from Brighton that whole time. Mum's idea, of course. She drilled us constantly. She even told people *she* was pregnant, had Dad pretend to drive her to the hospital and everything. She didn't leave anything to chance. Mum had it all worked out.'

'Who was the father?'

Ana snorts. 'A guy at school. Remember Tom Fox, from Art? The one with braces who was always ragging on me, dipping my ponytail in the blue poster paint? Turns out he fancied me. And me, him. For about two minutes.'

I do remember. I chuckle as the ridiculous, paradoxical nature of teenage dating comes back to me. *He's being horrible to you? Then he must like you.* Then I think of Matthew, how he's been punishing me since I came back. Maybe I haven't grown up quite as much since those days as I would like.

My thoughts return to James. 'Didn't you want to keep him?'

'Of course I did.' Ana's tone is harsher now.

'So why didn't you?'

Ana closes her eyes. 'You don't understand what it's like, being in a family like mine. If you step out of line, there is only drama. And it never ends. The only thing you can do is what you are told, or life isn't worth living. Everything is controlled; you're trapped. You hate it, but you hate being out of favour, more. *She* saw to that.'

With Matthew as her enforcer, I want to add.

I've always known Matthew is a little staid, unquestioning. But this? I can't believe Matthew ensured they all stayed in line for so long, or that I could have missed this dysfunctional dynamic in the Temple family so spectacularly. Moments of our lives ricochet back to me, with new meaning attached: the moments I'd seen the twins in a corner at family meals, their heads together like co-conspirators. I'd thought it was just them being close. But had Matthew been threatening Ana? And all those times Matthew had 'popped out' of our flat and been habitually late back – had he been keeping Ana and then Jenny in line? He must have been.

But there's one more thing I *do* have to know.

'Ana, where were you really, the night India died?'

Sixty-nine

'Jenny, where are you? Jenny!'

Ana pulled her long cardigan around herself, against the bitter December air. She knew it was pointless; the teenager wasn't lurking in the garden, yet Ana couldn't just sit in the house, waiting. As soon as she'd seen the television news – the BBC red ticker tape on the bottom: 'YOUNG WOMAN FALLS ON BRIGHTON RAIL TRACKS' – a cold stone of dread had settled inside her belly. *Please be OK*, she thought.

The night was clear, no cloud protection. The pale eye of a full moon illuminated her breath as it plumed out of her in short, anxious gasps. Ana became aware she was holding her folded arms tight to her chest, like she was holding a baby. This was worse than the day when James had been born; when her family had united to steal the tiny child from her, her mother taking his crib into her room. 'He's mine now,' Maggie had said. 'It's for the best.' Ana had never known pain like it, but at least she'd known her child was alive. Not like now…

A black car took shape in the shadows, its headlights momentarily blinding her as she stumbled out onto the concrete drive in her haste to meet it. Her twin slammed on the brakes, just as she knew he would.

'Matt! You got her?'

She moved towards the driver's door as Matthew clambered out. He shook his head, staring at his shoes. She could see he wasn't able to bring himself to meet her gaze. It was easier to circle his burly arms around her, pulling her into his rough embrace. She made no move to return it, her arms still clenched by her sides.

'I saw him, down by the marina. I'm sure it's not him … on the…'

He couldn't finish the sentence. She knew that, for him, as much as her, the thought of the boy taking his own life, pulverised by tons of steel as the train hit him, was just too much.

But then a fire lit under Ana – a sudden realisation. 'If it's *her*, it's your fault!' She wrenched herself away from her brother's grasp and turned her back on him. She heard the gravel crunch as he followed her towards the house.

The door on the latch, she stalked into the hallway of Coy Ponds, keeping an ear out for Ivy as she did. Silence. The little girl was still asleep. Behind her, she heard Matthew close the big oak door. The lock snapped back like a miniature gunshot, and they made their way into the living room.

His voice was low, barely audible. 'I'm sorry.'

'Not sorry enough.' Ana felt her lip curling up. 'What would it take, Matt? To stand up to *Mummy dearest*?'

This time, Matthew did meet her gaze. Defiance shone in his eyes. 'The boy needs help. We're just trying to do the right thing for him. For all of us.'

Those same old words. They made Ana stand to attention, no longer sagging with fear. Her anger like a steel rod through her body.

'Her. Name. Is. Jenny!' She flew across the room at him, raining a handful of blows on his chest as she spat out each word, saliva flicking on his cheek.

Matthew grabbed her wrists to stop her. Ana could still feel rage pulse through her veins. She yanked her arms from his and he ducked away, out of her range. Thwarted again, she turned and kicked the armchair instead. It rocked back on its castors, taking out a floor lamp. There was a satisfying tinkle as its glass shade broke. Neither of them made any attempt to pick it up.

'None of this would be happening if it weren't for you – helping keep her a prisoner!' Ana grabbed a crystal decanter off the bar and poured a large slug of their father's best Scotch. She'd feel it in the morning, but at this precise moment she didn't care. She just wanted some escape – from the anxiety, from this living nightmare.

Matthew dug his hands in his pockets. 'He's not a prisoner. James can go out whenever he wants.'

'But *Jenny* can't!' Ana knocked back the Scotch with determination. 'You just don't get it, do you? Jenny needs to get the fuck away from here. We all do.'

Matthew's face was infuriatingly impassive. He sat in the armchair opposite, legs spread, elbows rested on his knees. Taking up as much space as possible. Manly. No crossed legs for him, like a sissy or a poofter. It was what their mother had drilled into him since he was a child. Ana had watched her do it. She'd even felt sorry for her twin … until Maggie's indoctrination had finally worked, and she had brought him permanently onto her side: first to take James from Ana; then to ensure Jenny was kept in line. Now all her brother was, was their mother's secret weapon. The one that kept them all under Maggie's cruel thumb.

'Remember, boy: a man ain't worth much,' Maggie had said every week, straightening his tie for church. Ana would witness Maggie brush imaginary fluff from his collar, then lick her thumb and rub it across his cheek, shining him up like prize silver. 'But a son? Now, that's *somebody*.'

Ana watched Matthew's gaze stray to the clock now. Almost midnight.

'Where are Mum and Dad?' he asked.

Ana drained a second glassful, poured a refill. 'They've been out since six.'

'Doing what?'

'What they always do: arguing.'

Ana gulped back the liquor, grimaced. Their whole childhood, their parents' marriage had been a never-ending battlefield. Yet to the outside world, the Temples' was the perfect partnership. It made her sick to her stomach. She'd spent so many hours listening to their mother berate their father. *She Who Must Obeyed* had been Ana's name for Maggie. And once upon a time, it had been Ana and Matt against her. But now Matthew was a foot soldier, one of Maggie's underlings. Willing to do whatever their mother said. He would never choose his sister, not anymore, no matter how much Ana begged. He couldn't. He was too desperate for Maggie's approval.

Ana turned, and the room swam as the alcohol took effect. She wobbled, felt like she was all knees and elbows, like a day-old calf. She sat heavily on the armrest next to Matthew then leant her forehead against his, putting one hand to his face.

But while they were physically as close as they could get, she could still feel the distance that now existed between them. It was their mother's doing; the moment, all those years ago, she'd instructed Matthew to tear the newborn James from his sister's grasp and to give him over to her, she had severed their bond. Pain bloomed in Ana's chest at the memory: the nasty ball of betrayal and hatred, of all-encompassing loss.

'Let's go, Ana,' Matthew murmured. 'Get Ivy. Let's just get out of here. Never come back.' He rested his head on her shoulder.

She squeezed his cheek. 'What about…?'

He took a deep breath. 'We can take James, too.'

Ana moved her face from his. 'You just can't accept her, can you?' She affected a bitter laugh; but there was no humour in it. 'You're the most fucked-up of all of us!'

Ana felt, rather than saw, the dark fury that bristled through her twin, then. His face still curiously impassive, he grabbed her arms. His fingers pinched her skin. Shocked, she dropped her glass. It didn't break on the carpet, but she heard the whisky slosh onto their mother's £2000 hearth rug.

Just as quickly, Matthew let go of her. 'I'm sorry.'

'Fuck you, Matt.' Ana staggered from the armrest of the chair and turned, stopping dead where she was.

Maggie Temple stood in the doorway.

'Kids.' Their mother's voice was breathy, almost excited. But her face was pinched, drawn, her pupils dilated. She crossed briskly to the bar as if to make a drink but she fiddled with the glasses instead.

Her back was to the twins, but Ana still saw that her movements were oddly skittish. Not like her mother at all. 'Something's happened…'

'I knew it!' Ana erupted. The pressure inside her burst out in an uncharacteristic sob. 'It was Jenny who fell on the railway. Wasn't it?'

Maggie turned now, eyes wide. Her expression was slack for a moment as genuine surprise crossed her features. She recovered quickly. 'No. God, no. Don't worry about that, darling…!'

Maggie stepped forwards and tried to take Ana in her arms, but even scared out of her wits, Ana was repelled by her mother's touch. She pushed her away roughly, uninterested in comfort from this woman.

'Then where is she?' Ana cried, backing away still. 'Has Dad found her?'

Maggie glanced across to Matthew now, taking in his calm demeanour. 'You didn't find … *Jenny* … either? All night?'

Maggie's words hung heavy in the air; Ana could sense expectation in them. A suspicion lodged itself in her mind. Ana sent a demanding glance of her own at her twin, but he was as unreadable as ever.

'No,' Matthew confirmed.

A ghost of a smile appeared on their mother's red lips for an instant. But then it was gone, replaced by that faux concern she was so good at projecting. Maggie sat on the sofa, beckoning both twins over, attempting to gather them close to her.

Matthew went to her, unquestioning as always. Desperate not to be in the dark any longer, Ana perched next to Maggie, allowing her mother's hand to rest on her shoulder. If Ana had to fake affection in order to get information, so be it.

'India Rutledge is dead,' said Maggie.

Surprise made Ana sit up straight. 'That was her – on the telly?'

Maggie affected a sad expression: wistful downturned lips, and somehow even her eyes looked watery. Ana marvelled momentarily at what her mother was able to do with her face.

'Yes, it was India who fell,' said Maggie, her voice soft, yet steely. 'You know she and … Jenny … would meet at the station, sometimes? We don't know what happened; perhaps they argued…'

The inference swelled into the space between the three of them.

'No. No, there must be a mistake.' Ana shook her head with vigour, as if that might dispel the thought. 'Jenny wouldn't have hurt India. She couldn't have!'

Maggie took Ana in her arms. Weakened with the news, Ana let her this time.

'I know, darling,' said her mother. 'But it's even more important now … for us to keep her safe. We have to make sure no one suspects. Don't you agree, Matt?'

Her tone was flat. Ana saw Matthew nod, automatic. Maggie smiled gently, beckoning him closer to her. He shuffled closer to the two women, placing his arms around their bodies, the protector. The role he'd been groomed for.

Ana inhaled, taking in their mother's cloying vanilla perfume. Maggie wore her usual expensive clothes: a red jumper dress, dark maroon boots. Her newly relaxed and lacquered hair was coming undone, a length of it trailing where she'd tucked it behind her right ear.

Ana frowned a little at the dishevelment. Not like her mother at all. And now she noted that the pashmina around Maggie's shoulders did not match her dress. As with everything else in her life, Maggie was fastidious about accessorising. But this time, it was as if she'd grabbed the first thing that came to hand as she'd rushed out of the house. Ana had never known her mother do such a thing. Over a lifetime, Maggie Temple had kept the lot of them waiting, sometimes for hours. Ana recalled loitering irritated in the hall, trying to leave as Maggie had swapped scarves and hats and pashminas and earrings that 'didn't quite go'.

'Blue and green, should never be seen!' she'd recite, her voice light and singsong. Then, adding her own embellishment: 'Orange and red, you're better off dead!'

Ana took a sharp breath.

Dead.

Seventy

I become aware of the crashing of trolleys, a buzzer going somewhere. 'Why did you tell me and Jayden you were alone if you were with Matthew?'

But as I voice the question, I put two and two together. A vision of the playboy back on the bandstand the night of the spring ball, shrieking 'Jenny who?' springs into my mind's eye.

'Jayden doesn't know, does he?'

Ana shakes her head. I whistle through my teeth. I can't believe they've managed to keep Jenny under wraps for so long. I take the plunge with the next piece of the puzzle. Though my old friend would never admit it, she must have wondered where Jenny got to that night. To have stayed quiet, she must have thought it possible the teenager did really push India, like Maggie had insinuated.

'You knew – about my sister and Jenny hanging out, didn't you?'

Ana averts her gaze from mine. 'I was glad … she had a friend. I thought she had her best chance with her. India was always so brave.' She flashes me a watery smile. 'She sent me home, didn't she? That's why she did the whole JoJo thing – to split me and Jayden up. She wanted me back home at Coy Ponds, so I could help get Jenny out of there. But I didn't do enough. I tried, but Matt was always one step ahead. The best I could do was help smuggle Jenny out, so she could go to the Prince Albert once in a while. Meet India. Have some kind of a life.'

But I'm not angry with my old friend anymore. 'You didn't know what your parents were truly capable of. None of us did.' As I link my hand with hers, something occurs to me: 'You wouldn't tell me you were with Matt the night India died … because you wanted to be sure he would go down instead of Jenny. I'm right, aren't I? If it came to it – if the police tried to arrest Jenny, saying she'd killed India – you would have sacrificed Matt, wouldn't you?'

Ana hesitates, then sighs. 'Yes.'

Just as quickly, the shame is replaced by steely determination as she meets my eye. I can't deny Ana's logic. It seems almost appropriate, that Matt, Jenny's jailer, should take the fall. He owes the teenager. On cue, the double doors open and Matthew appears, coffees in hand. He falters as he sees me and his sister together. Stricken, he just stands there, his gaze locked with mine.

'Poppy. I'm so sorry…' He stares, downcast, at his shoes.

He seems small, diminished somehow. Little-boy-like. Perhaps he's always been this way, I just didn't see it. Pain spears my chest. I want to scream at him, *Why did you tell Maggie that India knew about Jenny? You signed her death warrant!*

But I hold up a hand. He wants clemency, but that is beyond me. I accept he can't have known how far his parents would go, but even so, he had a part in my sister's murder. I can't forget – *or forgive* – that.

Matthew nods and retreats back through the doors, giving us some space. I turn my attentions back to Ana, squeeze her shoulder.

'You get to be Mum, now. No interference. Jenny's yours, at last.'

As I say the words, Ana's demeanour brightens, as if she's needed someone to confirm this. She will be lost for a while, trying to make sense of her new freedom. But I know, deep down, she can handle it.

'Can I?' I indicate the side room we're sitting near, seeking her permission – her first act as Jenny's real mother.

Ana rubs a hand across her face, then nods. Before she can change her mind, I make my way into the room.

Seventy-one

The teenager lies sideways on the bed, still fully clothed, shoes on, curled on the mattress like a fallen baby bird. I make my way round the side of the bed. I seat myself in the chair by the scratched Formica bedside cabinet.

'Hello, Jenny.'

There's a plastic jug of water on top of the cabinet, a selection of buttons and cables on the wall. The blinds are pulled halfway down the window, the waning sunlight behind us.

'Stupid question, but how are you feeling?'

Jenny shrugs. She blinks, yawning in an exaggerated fashion. I can relate: her eyelids will feel heavy, a combination of shock and meds.

I reach forwards for her hand and she lets me take it. I expect her skin to feel like Matthew's, calloused and scratchy. But I couldn't be more wrong. Jenny's fingers are tapered and skinny, her nails perfectly manicured. *Of course.*

'I'm so sorry.' I blurt the words out. It's a fruitless quest to make myself feel better.

But she neither blames me nor condones me. Jenny simply shrugs: *Whatever.* 'It is what it is.'

I process Jenny's resigned anger. Every one of us is culpable. We all failed India and Jenny. We weren't there for them. Instead we shut them down, kept them apart, denied their realities. That's for us to live with.

Only India tried to show Jenny she was there for her. She broke down the Temples' secrets and lies, piece by piece. India didn't even hesitate when she realised the tangled web included our family as well. Maggie talked about 'The Right Thing', but that's too often a misnomer for people's own rigid thought patterns, supposed moralities and self-interest. India pursued the truth and didn't waver, even when it took her places she can't have wanted to go – like betraying JoJo in order to split Ana and Jayden up.

Now I have to do the same. I can accept it now. It *was* my choice to leave. I should have stayed. After the cancer, it's clear Matthew retreated into himself. Maybe I could have helped India and Jenny. Instead I ran away.

A deep yearning rises in me. *If only Mum told Tim or even Alan, not Maggie.* Would India be alive, now? Possibly. Probably, even. Mum told only Maggie about India, trusting the other woman to inform Alan. There's no way Alan would have killed India, another daughter, just to keep his grandson's secret.

Every one of us has unwittingly danced to Maggie's twisted tune. Maggie must have seen a way of protecting James in her own warped way *and* having revenge on Alan for his infidelity. Her gloating words: 'Two birds, one stone.' The logic, though perverse, is clear.

'I need to ask you something,' I say to Jenny, who regards me with her big brown eyes, so like the twins'. 'Did my mother know about you and India meeting up? Hanging out together?'

The teenager sighs. I dread her answer, but try not to betray it on my face. I need her to tell me the truth, not what I want to hear.

'No,' Jenny says.

Thank God.

Fresh air floods through my lungs. Jenny smiles, reassured, too. I can finally understand now my mother's guilt, her behaviour after my sister's death. She imploded inwards in her grief, unable to tell her husband the real reason why. Mum had been on the run from the truth for nearly twenty-five years, pretending her daughter was *theirs,* unable even to seek solace from India's real father. She must have thought she was the only one.

Poor Mum.

Poor Tim too, having to pick up all the slack. I hope they can make it back to each other. They have to. So much has been lost already.

I lean forward and put my arms around Jenny. She does not respond at first, just stays limp. Then she hugs me back, her arms around my neck. As I squeeze my eyes shut, India appears in my mind, a teen again, those black kohl eyes, that flippant smirk.

But my sister is gone forever. I can't undo that, or make up for what I didn't do for my own flesh and blood. As I move back from the embrace, I see Jenny has drifted off again. I place her arms back in the bed, plump the pillow behind her head. Devoid of make-up, without the trappings of her goth get-up, she looks like a child.

I smooth a hand across Jenny's forehead, almost maternal. I kiss the top of her head. She does not stir.

For a second, I see my sister in Jenny's place. Her hair falling in soft waves around her porcelain skin, she looks peaceful; at rest.

I am not Sleeping Beauty now; India is, that perfect princess.

'You're free now,' I whisper.

Epilogue

So, tonight I saw you. The REAL you.

I can't believe you've had to keep Jenny hidden so long; I think I always knew she was there … just waiting. James was the caterpillar, waiting to turn into Jenny, the beautiful butterfly. I'm sorry you've had to do that. Your family is the one with the problem. NOT you. You don't need anyone's permission to live the life you need to. Unlike your home-life, YOU set the rules now.

I will admit, there *were* times over the years I had questions. But I kept quiet, believing you would tell me when you were ready. And you did – and for that, I am so grateful. Thank you for trusting me. I love you.

People might say biology is everything, but don't listen to them. If that were true, then people with cancer genes would kill themselves … They'd say there is no point in waiting for your body to flick the switch at some random point in the future. Just get it over with!! But they don't. Instead, they do whatever it takes to avoid getting ill and get on living the life they have, because what is the alternative?

Jenny's got some stuff to learn yet: that first blouse did not suit her! I can't remember having laughed so much over pussy bows with someone. But hey, that's fashion – experimenting. I didn't expect her to be goth, or punky, but that's cool, why not??

She can do whatever you want when she's with me. I think black looks awesome on you. Jenny can keep her stuff at my house, so SHE doesn't confiscate or destroy it. *She Who Must Be Obe*yed can't take anything more from you now, not on my watch!

(I know you said we should get a baby-naming book – but I think your first choice, Jenny, was the best! A shiny new life calls for a shining name.)

It'll be alright now, I promise.

India xx

POSTED BY @**1NDIAsummer**, 13 November 2016

46,778 insights ⏎ **SHARE THIS**

⏎ ***Blithefancy*** likes this and reblogged it from ***1NDIAsummer,*** adding ***love you too*** *xxx*

⏎ ***warriorwasp*** likes this

⏎ ***Emz2011_UK*** likes this

⏎ ***lilyrose06*** likes this

⏎ ***gothprince78*** likes this

⏎ ***Alfie98*** likes this

Acknowledgements

I'm so lucky to have gone on this journey in writing and publishing *The Other Twin,* so I'll try and keep this brief and not descend into complete ickiness!

Thank you so much to my fabulous agent, Hattie Grunewald, who saw something in this story back in 2015 and gave it the benefit of her formidable expertise and talent; thanks also to everyone at Blake Friedmann, but especially Julian Friedmann, Isobel Dixon and the wonderful, late Carole Blake, who championed it as well. My gratitude also goes to Karen Sullivan and West Camel at Orenda Books, whose enthusiasm, flair and sharp eyes have elevated this book to the next level. You are awesome!

Special thanks go to Jenny Day, whose outlook and story captivated me. Kudos to everyone else in the LGBT community for trusting me and sharing their stories directly with me – you know who you are. You are brave and beautiful and deserve every happiness.

Thanks also to LGBT activists for making sure everyone online knows who you are and that you're not going anywhere! You rock. Thank you also to my BAME friends, both offline and online (especially via Black Twitter), who were able to advise this very pale writer on the complexities and politics of hair relaxants, interracial families and queer black youth.

A shout-out to Charlie Haynes at Urban Writers' Retreat; your brilliant meals, cakes and wine fuelled much of this book, written in mad, intense binges at Stickwick Manor, Devon. Same to Deb and Bob at Retreats For You, Sheepwash, Devon; your legacy will continue.

Thanks to the Bang2writers for keeping me accountable, plus the wonderful book bloggers, book groups and crime authors who have welcomed me into their community. A fist bump to my fabulous beta readers, especially JK Amalou who read EVERY SINGLE DRAFT, right from the offset, even when *The Other Twin* was at its most screwy!

Thanks also to Joanna Penn, Amy Corzine and Paula Daly, whose insightful feedback gave me the impetus to keep going. Special thanks to Elinor Perry-Smith and Jenny Kane, whose rational and calm outlook always kept my feet on the ground, even when I wanted to delete the damn thing!

Lastly, many thanks to my family, especially my parents Ian and Jan, who instilled a love of reading in me at a very young age, making this book possible. Also, to my three long-suffering kids: Emmeline, Mummy's sorry for always being busy when you wanted to play. Lilirose, you're not allowed to read this book so DON'T try. Alf, I'm sorry I am so embarrassing – I'll try not to include any sex in the next one, but no promises!